RED-HEADED WOMAN

Katharina Brush

KATHARINE BRUSH

Red-Headed Woman

eglantyne books

Published by Eglantyne Books ltd,

The Club Room, Conway Hall, 25 Red Lion Square, London WC1R 4RL.

www.eglantynebooks.com

All rights reserved

©2021 Eglantyne Books

ISBN 978-1-913378-08-0

Printed in the UK by Imprint Academic Ltd;

Seychelles Farm, Upton Pyne, Exeter, Devon EX5 5HY, ImprintDigital.com

A CIP record for this title is available from the British Library.

Book layout and design by Eric Wright

Production team: Robert and Olivia Temple, Michael Lee, and Eric Wright

CHAPTER ONE

The second Mrs. William H. Legendre was red-haired, and rather beautiful. Her husband said that she was much more beautiful, twice as beautiful - good Lord, ten times as beautiful! - as Irene, his first wife, ever could be. He said, "Why, of course you are, honey!" He said, "Why sure I think so!" He said it often. He was often asked.

The second Mrs. Legendre was twenty-one years old. Her name was Lillian. She had been Lillian Andrews, daughter of old Tim Andrews, the watchman at the rail road crossing out by Renwood Falls. Her parents had called her Lily, and other people had called her Lil; but now that she was Mrs. Legendre she was Lillian. Nowadays, when anyone on the street said, "Hello, Lil," she did not look around. It wasn't anyone. It was just somebody or other she used to know.

She liked her new name. Lillian Legendre — you couldn't beat that. You couldn't think up a better name if you tried. It had it all over Irene Legendre. She liked the monogram too. With one of the L's linked under the other, she had it embroidered on nightgowns, and on chemises, and on pockets, and on the corners of big fluttering pastel chiffon handkerchiefs. She had had a die made of it, for her scented Nile-green notepaper; and a little marcasite pin to pin on hats. Almost the very first thing she had asked Bill to do for her was to put "L.L.," in thin, sharp black, on the doors of his cream-colored roadster,

"I want to show them," she had said. "I want to show them all."

She meant the town. She lived in town now, right in the heart of Renwood. It had been one of her ambitions always. A house on Harding Avenue had been a corollary. She had a house on Harding Avenue. Though it took time, the former Lillian Andrews got what she wanted - almost always. Irene Legendre's husband had been another case in point.

Harding Avenue, Renwood, is a little piece of the Lincoln Highway. From the passing tourist's standpoint, it is a stretch of new brick paving, beginning at a ball park on the outskirts of a town, leading onto a bridge at the other end. Houses line it all the way, small ones at first, set near together — then larger ones with lawns and sun porches and rear garages. It is a nice street, obviously. Prosperous and pleasant. It might well be the nicest residential street in the town.

As a matter of fact, it is not quite that. Hilldale Avenue, near the Country Club, comes first of all. It was strange that Lillian had not aspired to Hilldale Avenue, or even considered it; but this was strange in only one way. Hilldale Avenue was fashionable — but it was country. It had trees and birds and grass galore. It lay two miles from Market Square, and you could hear the crickets chirping. It was too much like Renwood Falls for Lillian Legendre.

Her house on Harding Avenue was at the corner of State Street. That is to say, it was just three blocks from the Square. It was also, less happily, only a very few blocks from the Garden Apartments, where Irene Legendre, the divorcée, lived alone. On the subject of this proximity, which was Irene's fault, Lillian was rabid.

"Wouldn't you know?" she demanded furiously and often of Bill. "Wouldn't you know she'd wait till we bought a house — and then move just as near us as she could?"

Bill might have answered. He might have pointed out that the Garden Apartments was the only decent apartment house in Renwood, that it only happened to be near, and that Irene's father's house, the one alternative for her, was really only two blocks farther off. Bill thought these things, but did not say them. He had been married to Lillian for three months, and he had acquired wisdom. Anything that might be interpreted as a defense of Irene was better unsaid.

"Maybe she thinks she's going to get you back again," Lillian sneered, "if she sticks around. Maybe that's the big idea!"

"Don't be silly," Bill said merely, wearily.

The Harding Avenue house had belonged to a Mr. and Mrs. Elmer Blynn, whose wealthy New York son had built it for them. It was a fairly new house, only eight years old. Mr. and Mrs. Blynn were moving to California, where, they explained, it was always sunny. Mr. and Mrs. Blynn were seventy-two and sixty-eight years old respectively.

Mrs. Blynn at first had been more than a little hesitant about selling the Renwood house to a divorced young man and his red-headed former stenographer, of whom he had only recently, tardily, made an honest woman. Mrs. Blynn had feared that Mrs. Horace Coulter, who lived next door, and the Misses Ella and Julia Sayre, who lived in back on State Street, might object.

Mr. Blynn, however, had had no neighborly compunctions. He had been firm. He had said, "Let them." He had pointed out that buyers for forty-thousand-dollar houses did not grow on every bush and tree in Renwood. He had gone so far as to add that the Misses Sayre and Mrs. Coulter could yelp their blooming heads off. Mr. Blynn chuckled. He would not, he said, be there.

The house was large and low — a spreading, squat two story oblong of dark red brick, with a snug brown roof. It had a porch at the side, glass-enclosed, and another at the back; and there were nine large rooms, two baths, two upstairs sleeping-porches. The interior was Lillian's pride. It was her handiwork. Bill had thought they might have a decorator down from Cleveland, but she had spurned the suggestion. She had even rather resented it. She did not need a decorator, she informed him coldly. She might not know all about art, but she knew what she liked.

She bought it. She bought a great deal of it. The rooms were crowded to the doors with what Lillian liked. Brocaded satin chairs. Brocaded satin divans. Wrought iron Spanish benches with red cushions and gold fringe. Fern stands, shoulder high, with English ivy trailing from them. Standing lamps with rosy fringed-silk shades.

Lillian liked scenic wall papers, or floral ones, and she liked bric-à-brac and statuettes and portières. She liked framed reproductions of Maxfield Parrish pictures. She liked taffeta sofa cushions adorned with satin flowers. Her taste in wooden furniture inclined to carved mahogany, but she was also fond of lacquered pieces, red or black, with Chinese scenes and figures embossed on them in dull gold. Her piano, a desk, a smoking-stand and two or three small tables were lacquered.

The piano, to heighten the effect, was draped with two Mandarin skirts — Lillian had felt that one looked skimpy on such a big piano — and the skirts were held in place by an enormous pottery lamp, green and blue, with scarlet dragons on it. Under the lamp there was a bowl of shell flowers, and an incense burner, and a Buddha. There were also photographs of Lillian, and a photograph of Bill, in leather frames with bits of jade embedded in the leather. The whole arrangement, as Lillian said, was really awfully Chinese. It was indeed.

She had enjoyed buying things for the house. She enjoyed buying any sort of thing. She had bought so little in her life, and coveted so much. During the second month of her marriage, she furnished her house with the whirlwind spendthrift speed with which, during the preceding month, she had purchased her trousseau. Five or six dresses and three or four hats a day had been easy for Lillian. Everything for a bedroom, down to the powder puff container and the telephone doll and the tasseled cords to hang the pictures from — this was the work of an afternoon, with time for a chocolate milk shake at Deems ' and a manicure at Sally's Shoppe left over.

When the house was done, when nothing more could be crammed into it ("without spoiling it," Bill added hastily, for the remark was his) Lillian forgot about it. Complete, it interested her no longer. It was a place to sleep and eat and dress. Sometimes it was a place through which to show exclaiming people; but this was not often. Almost nobody came to see the second Mrs. Legendre.

Nobody she particularly wanted to be friends with — none of Bill's old crowd — came at all.

Her days were idle. She had a "helper," Mrs. Hoxie, who did everything. Mrs. Hoxie insisted upon being addressed as Mrs. Hoxie, and she insisted upon being referred to as a helper. Had Lillian ever called her her maid in Mrs. Hoxie's hearing, as she did elsewhere, there is no telling what Mrs. Hoxie would have called Lillian. She had little or no use for this employer anyway.

"I don't take any orders from her," she told the town, "believe me! Him I do, but her I don't. Some are my betters — and some ain't."

Fortunately Lillian gave no orders to Mrs. Hoxie. She ventured suggestions now and then, and if they were vetoed — and they invariably were — she nodded swift assent. "Yes, I guess you're right. Never mind, then." She was almost sure that Mrs. Hoxie was always right. Mrs. Hoxie had "helped" in the very best families. She was middle-aged, and her eyes were cold and her lips thin. Lillian was afraid of her. She was afraid of making mistakes before Mrs. Hoxie. She was afraid Mrs. Hoxie would tell somebody who would tell Irene.

In the mornings, Bill had his breakfast alone, and left before nine for the office. Lillian usually appeared about ten o'clock. She breakfasted in the dining-room, in mules and a negligée, with her red hair mussed from the pillow and her face still greasy-pale. On Sunday mornings, she performed ablutions before breakfast, nearly always. But on other days there was no use. Bill wasn't there.

She would have liked breakfast in bed, on a tray, like a lady in a movie. She had even bought the proper tray a glass-topped wicker one with feet, and with wicker pockets for the morning paper and for letters, if any. Mrs. Hoxie kept the tray on the top shelf of an upstairs closet. She had said when she beheld it first that if some one was sick, it would come in handy; and doubtless if someone was sick, it would.

All morning Lillian did not dress. She gloried in the luxury, the laziness of not dressing in the morning. She thought of the girls in offices. They had been dressed since seven, in their business clothes. And here, at noon, was Lillian Andrews Legendre in her nightgown - a lace and satin nightgown, and a metal-cloth negligée.

She had converted one of the sleeping-porches into an upstairs sitting-room; it had windows, and was enough in winter. There was a chaise-longue there where she reclined, propped up with cushions, reading the latest movie and fashion and fiction magazines. She liked stories about New York, about young millionaires named Perry or Barry and demimondaines with sleeves of diamond bracelets up their arms. She liked the smallish magazines with the grayish pages and the damsels in chemises donning their stockings on the covers. Often these magazines contained little quarter-page poems that pleased her, and she tore them out. Poems on the "live-for-the-moment," "I-only-regret-what-I-did-not-do" theme. Mrs. Hoxie found them all over the porch.

Sometimes Lillian read novels also. Her favorites were those that were published anonymously, for reasons plain from Page 1 on. She often thought that she ought to sit down and write her own life story and publish it anonymously. She thought with pride, "It would make some of these look tame." She smoked while she read, and unless it was almost lunch-time, she ate candy. She was particularly fond of certain little chocolate cubes that came wrapped individually in silver paper. She would unwrap these automatically, not interrupting her reading, and while she munched one, make a pellet of the silver paper with her fingers. Poems and pellets the indignant Mrs. Hoxie found all over the porch. She was going to leave, if this kept up.

CHAPTER TWO

BIll was twenty-five. He was a large young man, high and broad and long-legged, with crisp light hair taped tight through the center by a part, and an unremarkable nice young American face with blue eyes in it. He had a straight nose, and a perpetual tan, and very white teeth. Irene had thought him gorgeous. Perhaps she still did.

Lillian thought him fairly good-looking. "So-so,"she would have said. When it came to looks, she preferred dark vivid men with little mustaches, like Ronald Colman in the movies, or like that salesman for the Broadway Custom Shirts she used to know.

Bill was indigenous. He had been born in Renwood, where his parents had been born; he had attended the Central Grammar School and the Renwood High School and, like his father, he had gone then to the State University, where he had learned a fraternity ritual and a number of football signals, and other things of vast if transient value. Graduating with difficulty, but graduating, he had come home — to take his ordained place in the Legendre Coal Company; to marry his girl; to buy a plot with trees on Hilldale Avenue, and to build a little red-roofed stucco house, and to dwell in it.

This was his biography, until a year ago. You would have said that there would not, if he lived to ninety, be much more.

The little red-roofed stucco house was still there. It stood empty now, and Bill Legendre, when he passed it in his car on the way to the Club to play golf, or on the way home again, never looked at it. But Lillian did. She always looked at the house and thought that it wasn't much of a house. She thought of it in the past tense always.

"It wasn't anywhere near as nice as mine is," she thought. And she hoped that Irene Legendre, passing her house, realized that.

Lillian could remember when Irene and Bill were married. She remembered reading about it in the Renwood Herald. It was on the front page.

"POPULAR YOUNG COUPLE WED AT EPISCOPAL CHURCH. WILLIAM H. LEGENDRE, SON OF BYRON LEGENDRE, MARRIES IRENE BRICKLEY."

It had been a big wedding, for Renwood. The description of it, with a picture of Irene set in, had run all the way down the column and over onto Page 6, the society page, where there were further paragraphs.

"Immediately after the reception the bride and groom departed by motor for Atlantic City, N. J., for New York City and the White Mountains." ... "Upon their return, on or about July 15, the young couple will reside temporarily with the groom's father, Mr. Byron Legendre, pending the completion of their beautiful new home on Hilldale Avenue, which will be ready sometime in September."

Lillian had read every word. She did not then know Bill Legendre and Irene Brickley, except by sight. She didn't know any people like that — society people, rich people. Of course Irene's father, Brickley the druggist, probably wasn't terribly rich. But young Legendre's father was.

He was said to be worth a million. The daughter of old Tim Andrews of the railroad crossing gazed long and hard at the printed photograph of the bride of the heir.

"Pretty soft for you," she thought. "Pretty soft."

That had been almost four years ago. Lillian was seventeen then; and the Renwood Business College, which is two flights up, over Schrifftgisser's Hardware Store and the Painless Dental Parlors, was trying to make a stenographer of her. This was difficult. Though she left Renwood Falls on the eight-thirty car every week-day morning, she only appeared at school once in a while. She explained to the principal and faculty, a Mr. Degan, that she was obliged to stay at home and help her sick and feeble mother. Mr. Degan was sympathetic. He had never seen

Mrs. Tim Andrews, who weighed one hundred and seventy-seven pounds, most of it muscle, and who had the constitution of a plow-horse.

When Lillian came to class, she learned quickly —I mpatiently fast. She was what Mr. Degan called a very smartbrightclevergirl; and despite the fact that her absences outnumbered her attendances by approximately four to one, she was nevertheless able to finish the six months ' course in only a little over a year. Mr. Degan, who advertised that he placed all his stenographers, placed Lillian with the M. C. Plummer Cooperage Company, in the private office of Mr. M. C. Plummer. She remained a week, and was discharged at the behest of Mrs. M. C. Plummer, who was going to the mountains for two months and did not wish to have to worry.

Her jobs in the ensuing year or year and a half were several, and they are unimportant to her story. Her diversions and her associations matter more. She had one close feminine friend, Sally (born Sarah) Holtz, who had lately opened Sally's Beauty Shoppe on Market Street. Sally was red-headed also, but Lillian could forgive her that, for Sally's hair was a hennaed imitation, obviously and admittedly. She wore it cut in a straight bob with a bang, and with points curving up toward her temples. It was a style that suited her. She was small and plump, and she had a droll little nose. Men said Sally was cute. She was a cute kid. But they said her friend Lil Andrews would knock your eye out.

"Boy!" they said.

There were many men. Sally knew a great many, and Lillian had met them through her, and had in turn presented all her male acquaintances. The sum total was gratifying. Sally and Lillian were always surrounded. Though they set forth alone after business hours, they were never long alone. You saw them on the corners of the downtown streets on summer evenings, vivacious and flirtatious in the midst of a group of loud and frisky swains.

They were always escorted when, in their vague phrase, they "went places." The phrase was vague, but the places were definite. They went to the movies. They went to Jake's on Water Street, where there was a nickel piano and you could get beefsteak sandwiches and all the liquor you wanted. They went to the Log Cabin, four miles out of town, and stayed till dawn.

On Wednesday and Saturday nights in the winter, they went to the Cloverleaf Ballroom - five cents a dance, six tickets for a quarter. In summer they danced on board the excursion steamer Playland, which sailed down the moonlit river and anchored for hours and then sailed back. They danced in the dance hall at Avalon Park, which is in Renwood Heights, and they rode on the roller coaster and on the Ferris wheel; and on Sundays they swam in the outdoor swimming-pool at Avalon. When there was a circus in Renwood, or a street carnival, or when a musical comedy— "Direct from the Gotham Theater, New York, N. Y. "-played a one-night stand at the Bijou in Market Square, you saw them there.

They really, as Sally said, got around a lot.

They went riding sometimes. They were not particular about their vehicle — they drew the line at trucks, but at nothing else that moved on wheels. They rode in flivvers, in rattling sedans that were taxis in the daytime, in huge high touring-cars, broken-down aristocrats of the road. Occasionally they rode grandly in brand-new shining sport cars and roadsters and even limousines. Their friend Joe Gratz, who was a bootlegger, had a fine new car; and their friend Tuffy Lascari, who worked in the Maple Street Garage, had his choice, when his boss was away, of any car in it.

There were Joe and Tuffy, and there was Chuck Hansen, the caddie master at the Country Club, and Harry Hoffman, the day clerk at the Harding Hotel, and Lefty McCarty, who pitched for the Renwood baseball team and owned a share in his cousin Patrick's pool room. There was a curly-haired young barber named George Beauvais, and there was Bones Jones, who drove his own taxi, Manny Lippman, proprietor of a stall in the Central Market, where he sold butter, eggs, milk, cream and cheese. There were various clerks and mechanics, there was an undertaker's assistant, there was Fred Kelly, motorcycle policeman on the Turnpike, and Gus Vidabeck, who managed Avalon Park. There were salesmen from out of town, of course, upon occasion; and there were several young men who seemed to do nothing, but seemed to have spending-money.

These were the friends and companions of Lillian and Sally, and Sally was content. But Lillian was not. Though she accepted their attentions and, in one or two cases, their affections, she was at heart indifferent to and scornful of them all. She said to Sally that they were all right, she supposed, but that they didn't mean anything.

"They won't get you anywhere," she said.

"Won't, eh?" said Sally, and sniffed. "Where you trying to go?" she demanded.

Lillian didn't know exactly. She had only formless, dim ambitions in those days. She smiled, however, as if she knew very well.

"You'd be surprised," she said.

It was Lillian who always directed Tuffy or Joe or who ever was driving them, to drive out by the Country Club 6 - and on out that way." It was the longer route to any of their destinations, but Lillian always said that it was prettier. In case they should guess what she really meant, she also said that it was a smoother road. She didn't want them making fun of her.

When they neared the Club, she exhibited no interest in it. Almost always she appeared not to notice it at all. The road ran past the clubhouse, past the tennis courts and the swimming pool, around a bend, and along beside the golf course. In winter there was not much to see, and Lillian's indifference was easier for her. In summer, on Sundays or in the evenings or late in the long hot afternoons, there was so much to see that she wished the driver would slow down - irritably she wished he would, though she never asked him to.

She caught fleet, vivid pictures from the tail of her eye, that enchanted her. Pictures of luxury, pictures of leisure and gaiety and sport. The clubhouse porch with the basket chairs and the flutters of flowered chiffon in them. The flying white figures on the slate-gray tennis courts. The golf links with the little numbered red flags here and there, and the golfers in their light clothes on the emerald velvet grass. Rich people. Society people.

She loved the swimming-pool they had. It was a white stone pool, painted turquoise blue on the inside, so that the water was a heavenly color. Lillian knew that the color was paint, because Chuck Hansen had told her. Once she had thought that it must be some kind of expensive dye they put in. The pool was small — the one at Avalon Park was several times larger; still, there was more room to swim than there was at Avalon, where you could hardly see the water for the bathers on hot Sundays. The Country Club pool was never crowded. There were never more than ten or twelve young people, and a fat old gentleman or two. The young people were brown with sun, and they wore snug bright suits. At Avalon you wore a dark gray suit that didn't fit, with "Avalon" across your chest in red letters.

Around the bend, the road ran close to the golf course for a little way — so close that it was possible to recognize the players. They were familiar; they were people you saw downtown almost every day. But they seemed different. They had a very particular glamour here. Down town, in the stores, at the bank, you could rub elbows with them. Here they were aloof. You could only look.

Lillian to this day remembered riding beside the fairway once and seeing Irene Legendre, with a pickaninny caddy, hunting a ball in the underbrush at the edge of the road. It was one of those incidents you forgot at the time, and then recalled much later, when events had given them significance. Irene wore a yellow sports dress and a little yellow hat, and a perforated glove without finger tips on her right hand, and she held a stick with which she beat the grass. Just as Joe Gratz's car swept by her, she glanced up — there was a sudden flash of blue eyes, turquoise blue, like the water in the painted swimming-pool.

Lillian remembered. She remembered Sally's saying, "In all this heat! I wouldn't be her, believe me," Lillian thought sardonically.

CHAPTER THREE

She was twenty when she lost her job at the Renwood Chamber of Commerce, which she had held for six or seven months. The secretary, Mr. Herbert L. Mason, had just learned that her reputation around town was, as he said, "—er — well—"

"Bad," Lillian supplied for him calmly. "I suppose so. Some cats in this town can't stand it to see a girl have any fun."

Mr. Mason was genuinely sorry. Lillian was a good stenographer. He wrote a note to that effect to whom it might concern, and he paid her two weeks' extra salary. Lillian spent the money on a weekend in Detroit. Her railroad fares and her hotel expenses cost her nothing; still, she spent every penny. It was only thirty-six dollars. It bought a facial massage and a negligée and a bottle of perfume, and one or two bits of black chiffon underwear.

When she returned and left the negligée and the underwear at Sally's, Sally said, "Well, and what are you going to do now?"

"Now I'm going out home," said Lillian, shutting her suitcase again, "and tell 'em all about my trip."

She laughed, and Sally laughed.

"No, what I mean is," Sally said then, "what're you going to do about a job?"

"Oh, I'll get one."

"They want somebody down at Legendre's," Sally told her. "There was an ad in the paper today— Wait, I saved it."

She found it, after some search. "'Wanted:" she read aloud. "Experienced stenographer, neat appearance. References required. Apply in person. Legendre Coal Company."

Lillian nodded. "That's me," she said.

The mines of the Legendre Coal Company were in the hills, but the business offices were on River Street, Renwood. There was a two-story building of buff-colored brick, with sheds behind it and freight-cars full of coal on tracks at the side. Mr. Byron Legendre's spacious lair was on the second floor. His sons William and Byron, Junior, and his son-in-law, Frank Reynolds, had cubbyholes downstairs, connecting with the central office.

In the central office were clerks and bookkeepers, and four stenographers, including Lillian. "Miss — ah - Andrews," she was to Bill at first. Sometimes she was "Miss-ah-Anderson." Bill was not very good at remembering names.

Finally he decided for his convenience to call her "Red"; and did. "Hey, Red, take a letter, will you?"

He was an informal and a jovial young man, very popular with the employes. "The help," he called them, and made them like it. He joked with them in passing, and grinned impersonally and expansively. It was hard, and yet somehow easy, to remember that he was the boss's son.

He had tremendous energy, an over-accumulation, and he strove to work it off daily, with the office as his gymnasium. This was the secret of what appeared to be great business zeal. People said that that young Bill Legendre was a hustler. It was not altogether true. He was an athlete cooped up.

Bareheaded — he never wore a hat - he arrived of mornings in his roadster, in a small but violent temporary tornado of pebbles and dust. He never stopped to open the roadster's door, but flung himself over the side. He rushed into the office, and rushed all day. When he left his swivel chair, which he did every two or three minutes, he left it in such haste that it overturned more times than not. When he mounted the stairs to his father's office he mounted them three at a time. You heard him crashing down again, whistling as he came. Except for the whistling, if someone had thrown him it would have sounded the same way.

Byron Legendre, Junior, was two years older than Bill, and he was several decades more sedate. Their brother in-law, Frank Reynolds, was thirty-five, already bald; nervous, humorless, and rather haughty. It was young Mr. W. H.'s desk buzzer that Lillian jumped to answer. The other three stenographers also jumped to answer it; but Lillian, who wasn't doing anything just then, was quicker.

There was quite a little hard feeling about it.

Bill wore custom-made monogrammed shirts, and he worked in his shirtsleeves. He smoked cigarettes or sucked at a short chubby pipe. It was almost impossible for him to dictate sitting down. Indeed, it was almost impossible for him to dictate. Stalk the floor as he would, head lowered, thumbs tucked into his belt, to the door and turn, to the window and turn, to the water-cooler and drink, his letters were not masterpieces.

"Oh, hell," he would say eventually. "You finish it, Red. You know what I want to tell ' em, don't you?"

Lillian did. She made it her business to know. It had seemed to her since her first week at the Legendre Coal Company that young Mr. W. H. should have his own stenographer. Not just one of the girls, but a special one. Lillian, for example.

She managed this, in due time. It was one of the several things she managed. Though Bill for politic reasons did not officially promote her, he rang for her when he rang. She handled all his affairs. She was better informed about them than the other girls in the office, though they had been there so much longer. To his brother and brother-in-law Bill said that Red was the smartest girl of the lot. Byron Junior and Frank, who found her lazy, slow and careless, couldn't understand it.

"If you mean the best-looking", Byron suggested dryly.

"Well, sure," said Bill. "She's that, too."

She was. She would have been the best-looking stenographer at a convention of considerable size. There was her hair, which was thick and long and the color of tea in a crimson cup. She had worn it in a rigid marcel wave by Sally Holtz, until just lately. Now she wore it straight, and divided in two and slicked against her scalp, to the ears, where it was pinned in braided wheels. Though Bill did not recognize the coiffure, the girls in the office did. Mrs. Bill Legendre appeared there sometimes with no hat on.

Lillian had lovely skin, of the delicate translucent white that freckles in the sun, so that she had to be careful of it. She had hazel eyes and a bright, soft mouth. She complained that her figure was old-fashioned because it was not boyish, but she secretly approved of it. Her dresses were tight and thin. Her skirts were knee-length. This was the summer of 1929. She viewed with alarm the longer skirts in the fashion news from the cities, though she thought the normal waistlines would be nice.

She affected exotic perfume and noisy bracelets, and her working costumes were alluring first of all. Nothing tailored, nothing stiff. Nothing high in the neck. She took her movies and her "confession" magazines to heart; she knew what a young girl trying to get along should wear.

She knew how one should act. She acted that way. Usually Bill did not seem to notice, but once or twice he did. It was irritating that when he did, he laughed at her.

"Not trying to vamp me, are you, Red?" he asked her once.

His grin was wide, and he cocked one eyebrow in a way he had. Lillian saw that he thought it was a joke. It was not a joke to her. Financially, socially, in every way that mattered, this was the grandest young man with whom she had ever come into contact. It might profit her nothing, but she would do all she could about it.

She had never seen a coal mine. She told Bill so, over and over, and with a touching wistfulness, in the tone in which one might say, "I have never really had a good time." Bill promised to take her, and one June afternoon he kept his promise, upon being reminded of it just as he was setting out. "You said you'd take me next time," Lillian pouted. "Aren't you going to? I finished those files. I haven't got a thing to do this afternoon."

Bill was in his usual rush. "All right, come on," he said.

They left the office together, and drove to the Legendres' mine at Gray's Ferry, fifteen miles away. From there they drove to the one at Cold Spring Hill — another twelve miles. They visited three mines in all, and Bill vanished into each. Lillian, in a white dress and sunburn hose and high-heeled white kid pumps, waited in the roadster.

"A lot you're finding out about what a mine looks like!" Bill jeered amiably. "All you wanted was an afternoon off."

"It's your fault," Lillian said. "You didn't tell me there was no use going in these clothes."

"I didn't see what you had on."

They were late getting back. Some of the roads in the vicinity of the mines were bad, and there was a long and confusing detour with a dearth of signposts on it, so that Bill had twice taken wrong turns. It was almost seven o'clock when they rode into Renwood. Everybody was on the downtown streets, bound for the movies. The roadster's top was folded back. Everybody saw them.

"Scandal," Bill said, and smiled. Lillian also smiled. That would be fine.

Her luck was amazing in the weeks that followed. Afterward, in retrospect, she was to perceive that it had been - that she had had what were called the breaks, all through that summer. There was the street-car strike in July and August. No trolleys ran to Renwood Falls, or anywhere else for that matter; and the busses at five and five-thirty could not accommodate all the commuters. Lillian remarked to Bill at the office that often she didn't get home until seven; and Bill, in the naïve belief that this was a hardship, took to running her out to the Falls after work in the roadster. Having deposited her on her door step, he cut across country, via a little back road, to the golf course, where he usually played nine holes, or eighteen, before dark.

He did not seem to realize, and Lillian did not tell him, what Renwood had to say about these daily departures from town. As one worthy lady whose home was en route expressed it to other ladies, "Every night about five o'clock they start out, as bold as brass — and heaven only knows when they come back!" This point was much discussed. No one ever saw Bill's car returning, though people on their porches watched for it for hours and hours. The theory was that it stole by at dawn or thereabouts.

Bill should have realized. He had lived in Renwood always. No doubt he would have been more careful, had his conscience been less clear. As it was, he was insanely indiscreet — Renwood being Renwood. Thrice he was seen buying Lillian a soda at the drug store near the office. Several times on the way to the Falls he let her practice driving his car. In July he was laid up for a few days with a bad sinus, and on the third day he had Lillian come to his house to take dictation. This was in the morning. Irene was playing golf. Mrs. Walter Jameson, the Legendres' neighbor on the right, said that Lillian stayed an hour and a half. Mrs. Henry Ives, of the house on the left, begged to differ with Mrs. Jameson. It was, insisted Mrs. Ives, two hours if it was a minute.

By the first of August, Bill Legendre's affair with Lillian Andrews was the talk of the town. Everybody, apparently, knew about it, except Bill and the members of his immediate family. Lillian heard all the gossip through Sally. "Tell me everything you hear," was her standing order, and Sally, who in her beauty shop heard everything there was, readily complied. Sally was proud of Lillian, though somewhat envious of her. "You're in the big leagues now, all right," she sighed. "I've got to hand it to you."

Lillian was well aware that when Bill's father heard the rumors, there would be trouble. He might even discharge her. She visualized a scene in his office, herself teary-eyed and appealing. "But Mr. Legendre, that isn't fair! How can I help what people say?" It was a relief when the first of August came, and Byron Legendre, accompanied by Byron, Junior, departed on their annual fishing trip to Canada. They wouldn't hear anything for another month, anyway.

Bill's wife had not heard anything — not yet. Lillian was sure of that. There was not the slightest change in her bearing when she came into the office. She still smiled sweetly. "Hello, Miss Andrews! How're you today?" If Lillian knew wives ("—and I ought to," Lillian said to Sally), this continued cordiality indicated ignorance. Nobody had told Irene the news.

She proved it additionally, conclusively in Lillian's mind, by going away blithely for ten days.

This was in mid-August. "Mrs. William H. Legendre," said the Renwood Herald, "of Hilldale Avenue, leaves today for Cincinnati to visit friends. Mrs. Legendre will be matron of honor at the wedding on August 21 of Miss Barbara Blair of Cincinnati to Mr. Jackson Hastings of the same city. Miss Blair was a classmate of Mrs. Legendre the former Irene Brickley, at the Breckenridge School for Girls in Cleveland."

Lillian had known beforehand that Irene was going. She had telephoned the station for her ticket and parlor car chair. She had arranged about her trunk. On the day of Irene's departure she had gone to the bank for Bill, and cashed his check for a hundred and fifty dollars, pocket money. Irene on her way to the train had stopped in at the office for it, and Lillian had had it ready: a sheaf of brand-new ten and twenty dollar bills, clipped together

"I hope you'll have a lovely trip, Mrs. Legendre. "Thanks a lot," Irene smiled. "Good-bye!" "Good-bye, Mrs. Legendre."

Lillian remembered well. It had been their last conversation, ever.

Bill gave a poker party that night at his house, and another the next night. And another the next. This was the custom. When any young Renwood wife went away, the temporary bachelor quarters thus established became the scene of as many stag poker parties in succession as the forsaken wives who remained in town would stand for. Since the games often lasted till morning, since very much liquor was consumed, and since the stakes from time immemorial had been high beyond all reason, the number of such parties that were stood for was not many. Having played host and banker on Friday and Saturday and Sunday nights, Bill found himself on Monday night alone.

In the afternoon, in the office, Lillian heard him at the telephone, trying vainly to get up another game. She heard him laughing over some of the replies. "Oh, Lord," he moaned, "I certainly am in wrong! They'll be telegraphing Rene a petition to come back home! Well. Tonight's out, then. We'll put it off. Maybe Wednesday or Thursday night. Okay?"

He drove Lillian to Renwood Falls after work as usual.

"Aren't you lonesome," Lilian said, en route, "with Mrs. Legendre away?"

He nodded, his eyes on the road. "You bet I am."

"But I suppose you have lots of things to do in the evenings."

"Oh, I kill the time all right," Bill said. Lillian waited, but he said nothing about this evening.

"Well, you're lucky," she sighed, after a moment. "I wish I could say as much. I get so bored sometimes evenings, I think I'll go crazy."

He turned his head then. "Oh, no, I don't believe that," he decided aloud. "You've probably got fifty boy-friends. I can't see you sitting at home."

"Oh, I go to the movies" Lillian's voice was scornful—"and over to Avalon, and those cheap places." She made a little face, and shrugged. "It's hell to be poor."

"But I like Avalon," Bill protested. "I think it's great. We were over there just the other night, a whole crowd of us—"

—"Slumming!" Lillian said. Again he looked at her. "Why, not at all. We—"

"You wouldn't like it if you didn't have better places to go, I'll tell you!" Lillian cried passionately. "You'd hate it, just like I do! The only reason you like it is because it's so different from what you're used to. That's why you go there. I haven't got any choice!"

Bill frowned a little. From under her lashes, Lillian saw that he was surprised at her bitterness, and troubled. He was ever a sympathetic young man.

"Well, but listen, Red," he said, "I'm not used to much. You talk as if Renwood was New York or something. Nobody has such a hell of a gay time around here, that I know of. And there aren't many places. Where do I go that you don't go, after all?"

"The Country Club."

"Oh, yeah. The Club. That's a hot spot!" Bill scoffed. "Except for the golf, and occasional dances with bum orchestras, it's as dead as your great-great-grandfather."

Lillian did not argue. The Country Club was beside the point just now. "And you go places out of town,"she continued. "Grand places. Like last week — remember you told me to call up the Summer Palace on the Cleveland road and reserve a table for eight for that night? You go places like that, all the time."

"Oh, for heaven's sake," Bill said, half laughing,"_the Summer Palace isn't anything, Red! It isn't grand at all. It's just a roadhouse. I'll take you there some night," he added involuntarily, "and you can see for yourse —"

"Oh, take me tonight!" interrupted Lillian ecstatically.

She was reproachful the next minute, eying him with hurt gray eyes. Biting her lip. "I see, she said. "You didn't mean it. I'm sorry."

"Why, sure I meant it," said Bill.

"Sure I did," he repeated with more conviction, as Lillian continued to look wounded to the quick.

She shook her head. "I'm sorry," she apologized stifly again. "After all, I work for you. I forgot my place, I guess."

"Boloney!" Bill snorted.

He all but stopped the car. They had been flying. They barely moved now. "Look here," he said. "I've got a golf match on, but I'll be through by seven-thirty. I'll pick you up about eight o'clock-how's that? And we'll go to the Summer Palace. And," concluded Bill, "that's a date. No more of your nonsense, young lady."

He picked her up at Sally's at a little after eight. Lillian had said, "I'll be at my friend's, in town," and she had given him the address. Sally lived in the Iroquois Flats on Maple Street, over the Maple Street Garage. "Just blow your horn," Lillian had instructed Bill, "or ring the bell marked 'Holtz,' and I'll come right down."

She herself had reached Sally's at quarter of seven, after an hour and a half of dressing at home. She wanted Sally's little lavender hat that curved off the forehead to wear with her pink-blue-and-lavender flowered chiffon. She wanted Sally's handbag made of small pearl beads, and she wanted Sally's butterfly-shaped rhinestone shoe buckles. The fact that the buckles were firmly sewed onto slippers of Sally's made no difference. "I'll take 'em to Marek's tomorrow morning," Lillian promised, hacking with fingernail scissors, "and have 'em sewed back on as good as new."

It had begun to rain.

"It's raining," said Sally at the window. "Maybe he won't want to go."

Lillian merely smiled. She thought, "And wouldn't you be tickled!"

"It's coming down in buckets," Sally presently reported. "You'll ruin your clothes, in that open roadster."

"His wife's got a coupé," Lillian said. "He can borrow that.... Say, Sal."

"What?"

"I've got three quarters of an hour yet. Be a sport and give me a facial, will you?"

"Oh, my Gawd!" groaned Sally. "Don't I give enough facials all day long. I'm sick of giving facials! I should slave for you for nothing!"

She was already languidly going for cream and towels, "I'll pay you," Lillian said, "—some day." "Some day is right!" Lillian laughed. "Well, I might. You can't tell. ""

The facial took half an hour. Lillian and Sally together powdered and painted Lillian again, and touched her ear-lobes with red and her eyelids with blue and her curved bronze lashes with black. In her artistic fervor Sally forgot her little jealousy. "You look swell," she said. "You look like a million dollars. Let's see your nails," she added professionally.

Lillian presented them.

"Nice nicotine-stains you've got there," said Sally. "Where's my Remover?" She rummaged in a drawer and produced cotton and a bottle. "Here, sit down here. Gimme your paw."

It was still raining when Bill rang the doorbell, and Sally made a sudden maddening last-minute fuss about her hat. It was, she insisted, her best hat. She had paid eight dollars for it. She wasn't going to have it worn in a pouring rain like this. Lillian could wear her own hat.

"Or else take my umbrella," Sally said finally, relenting somewhat.

Lillian, in a frenzy to be gone, seized the umbrella. She could have struck Sally with it. "All right, all right!" she cried angrily. "You just want to be mean and you know it!"

"Oh, go to hell," Sally said. They often parted on that note.

Lillian left the umbrella outside in the hall, propped against the plaster. It wasn't raining very hard now anyway.

Bill was waiting at the foot of the long steep tunnel of the stairs, beside the six bells and the six brass mail boxes. There was a fly-specked light bulb burning in the wall beside him, and Lillian descending could see that he was bareheaded as usual, freshly combed and slicked, and immaculate in a brown double-breasted coat and tan flannel trousers. He seemed altogether too big, and too well dressed, for the tiny, dingy place.

"Say, it's raining," he said. "Haven't you got an umbrella?"

"No, I haven't." "You'll get wet between here and the curb." "I don't care."

"I'll put my coat over you," Bill said, taking it off, "and we'll run for it…. There, now. All set?"

… "Um-hmm."

They opened the door and scurried together across the gleaming sidewalk, Bill in his waistcoat and shirtsleeves, Lillian's head and shoulders hooded. She hoped that Sally was watching from the window, and then, in a flash, hoped she wasn't. It would be like Sally to put her head out and scream, "Where's my umbrella? Well, you bring back that hat this minute! You know what I said!"

"It's letting up," Bill remarked of the rain, when they were in the car. Parenthetically: "Thanks," he muttered, for Lillian was helping him on with his coat. The monosyllable was gruff, and at once she knew that one shouldn't help. Her hand dropped away as if she had burned it.

"I think it'll stop before long," Bill continued. "Hope so, anyway. Say, but didn't it come down when we were playing the fifth! On the second round, that was. We were drowned by the time we made the clubhouse."

"You didn't catch cold?"

Bill was kicking at the starter. "No," he said, and laughed. "We took care of that, all right. We were afraid of that, so we killed a quart of Scotch between us. He sat back abruptly in his seat. "Oh, good-night!"

"What's the matter?"

"I forgot the liquor. I had a flask all filled to bring along, and like a dope I left it at the house."

Lillian whimpered appropriately.

"Well—" said Bill. He sat up again, and again kicked at the starter. "Guess we'll have to go back. You don't mind, do you? The stuff they sell at the Summer Palace isn't fit to drink."

"I don't mind a bit."

"If I can ever get this buggy started," Bill said. "It's Irene's, and it has the pip. Got to get her a new one."

This was the first time he had spoken of his wife by her first name to Lillian, but Lillian failed to mark this. She was preoccupied with the realization, which she found not displeasing, that Legendre's share of the quart of Scotch in the locker room had been generous. "He's a little tight," she thought, watching him. She was not surprised. It was her understanding, derived from downtown hearsay, that all members of the uptown crowd drank hard on all occasions, and the men especially hard when their wives were away.

The starter worked at last and they wheeled from the curb and turned around, directly in front of the yawning door of the Maple Street Garage. Several youths were lounging just inside, out of the rain, and among these Lillian looked for, and discovered, Tuffy Lascari, dark in his business grease and overalls. She saw him recognize first the car, then Bill, and then herself. She had an inclination not to speak to him, but the urge to acknowledge his recognition, and so confirm it beyond question, was, under the circumstances, stronger. Unseen by Bill she fluttered a white hand briefly at the window. She was smiling to herself when they drove on.

"I feel grand," she said to Bill. "So do I. Never better!" They started up the gradual two-mile hill.

"Did you phone the Summer Palace?" Lillian asked. "I mean to make a reservation? Or did you want me to? I thought of it, but I didn't know."

Bill shook his head. "There'll be tables, all right. They won't have much of a crowd on a Monday night and rainy at that."

She was a little disappointed. She wished he had made a reservation. "A table for two, for Mr. William Legendre" —and for Lillian Andrews. She would have liked to think of it as all arranged.

Bill's house was set back from the avenue, at the head of a terraced lawn. Around the lawn there was a low, vine-clad stone wall, and the foot of the driveway was marked by square stone posts, not quite so low, that supported twin globes of pale white light. Bill turned in between these with the safe but shocking swerve of three years ' practice, and the coupé fled up the driveway, flinging gravel behind its wheels. They passed the side door of the house, visible under a wrought-iron lantern, and continued to the back, where the driveway made a loop around. Bill achieved the loop and returned to the side door, where he stopped. The whole entrance had not taken thirty seconds.

He opened the door on his side. "I'll only be a minute."

"Look," said Lillian quickly, " do you mind if I come in with you? I mean — I'd love a little drink before we start on that long drive."

"There's no bad idea!" Bill said. "We'll both have one. Sure, come on in."

Lillian hesitated now. "But maybe your servants, what will they think?

He was amused. "'They' is 'she'," he said. "Our one and only. Oh, she's gone home hours ago. And it wouldn't matter anyway."

"Come on, hop out," he added.

He helped her out and then leaned into the car and shut off the motor. He forgot the headlights, but Lillian reminded him, and he turned back to extinguish them. She waited in the shelter of the little gable that jutted over the side door, while Bill slapped his pockets to locate his keys. She said to herself, "Glad I thought of this."

There was no light inside when the door was open, and Lillian, entering first and stepping sideways, tripped over something that slid with a crash to the floor.

"Goodness! What was that?"

Bill found the wall switch.

"Irene's golf clubs," he said. "I'm sorry. I didn't know they were there."

He stood the clubs up again, in a corner this time. The initials "I. B. L. ", in black, looked at Lillian from the bag, and Lillian looked stonily back at them.

There were open doors on both sides of this little hall. Through the door on the right a billiard table was discernible in the shadows. Bill led the way through the door on the left, and found another switch. This was the big living-room, that extended across the front of the house. Lillian had seen this room before. The front door opened into it, and she had passed through it, bearing Bill's mail and her notebook and two or three newly-sharpened pencils, a month before.

It was different now. She was a guest this time, and catering to her pleasurable awareness of the fact, she dropped at once into the biggest chair and took her hat off. She tossed the hat to another chair nearby. She leaned her head back, and crossed her knees, and let her arms lie along the arms of the chair. She said to Bill. "Is there a cigarette around somewhere?" and almost dared to call him "Bill," but did not quite.

He supplied cigarettes and a lighter, having first put a record on the phonograph — a thing Bill always did, had Lillian known it, the minute he entered this room. To the beat of Am I Blue?, the song of the summer, he disappeared in the direction of the kitchen to mix highballs. "Gin and ginger ale," he had inquired, "or Scotch and soda?" and Lillian had said, "Scotch and soda" because it had a society sound. Left alone, she rose and began to ramble about, examining pictures, fingering materials, picking things up and putting them down. She thought the room was not as beautiful as it should have been. It was too plain. She thought, "Say! If I had her money!"

She wandered into the dining-room and out again, and crossed to the threshold of the billiard room and stood there a minute. She decided that a little later, before they left, she would go upstairs and look around. She had seen only the upstairs hall and a sort of study, that other time. She thought she would like to see Irene's room. She remembered a glimpse as she passed it. A big, cool room, all green and lavender, with twin beds in it.

She thought how Irene would hate it if she knew that Lillian Andrews was here in her house, roaming all around, making herself at home; and the thought entertained her. She wished there was some way to make it certain that Irene would know, and know by finding out and not by hearing it from Bill. Lightly she said to herself, "I might leave something of mine in her room! My handkerchief, or some bronze hairpins or something." Her lips smiled over this whimsy. But her eyes narrowed, weighing the pros and cons.

They drank their highballs leisurely, with the phonograph playing all the while. Bill never for a moment let it stop. During a record he did not seem to listen, for he talked of everything else, but automatically, toward the end of the piece, he lounged to his feet and crossed to the instrument, carrying his tall glass with him and still talking. He set the drink down sometimes on the polished wood, sometimes on a pewter coaster which somebody - doubtless Irene — had hopefully placed there. He played both sides of every record, always glancing at the labels but apparently merely from habit, for he never discarded one.

It was plain that at home Bill lived, conversed, played cards and read and ate his meals to this jazz accompaniment, and that peace and calm were disquieting to him.

"Don't you have a radio?" Lillian asked.

"Yeah, but it's in the billiard room. I don't like it so well anyway," said Bill. "I'm old-fashioned or something."

He was slurring his words a little. Since their arrival, he had had two drinks to Lillian's one.

"Let's have one more highball," Lillian suggested. "And then we'll go."

They had two more highballs each, and Bill brought a bottle from the kitchen and set it on a stand where he could reach it easily. He also presently produced some potato chips and some olives, and the remains of a roast duck on a platter. "Mus' have a little something to eat," he said. "Can't drive thirty or forty or how many miles on an empty stomach. I haven't had anything to eat since noon, 've you, Red? And it mus' be - What time is it?"

It was ten-thirty by Lillian's little white-gold wrist watch. She looked, then put the ticking thing to her ear.

"Stopped," she said. "I guess it's about nine o'clock, but I don't know."

"Who cares anyway?" Bill cried genially. "Have a potato chip, Red." He surveyed her with sudden fondness.

"Good little Red," he said. "I like you!" Lillian softly smiled. "Do you really Bill?" "I cert'n'y do. I think you're swell." The phonograph was playing I'd Rather Be Lonely.

With her smiling eyes still on Bill's eyes, Lillian hummed it low in her throat. She stood up suddenly, setting her drink down on a little table.

"Dance with me!"

Her voice had a new exultant undercurrent. "Why do we bother about the Summer Palace anyway, Bill," she said, "when we've got music and food and liquor and everything here?"

CHAPTER FOUR

R. Byron Legendre, Senior, was awaiting his evening meal. He lived alone, and he sat alone now on a small side porch of his stately house. He was a widower, and his sons and his daughter had married and left him; he was, however, reasonably cheerful. He liked solitude. He was glad when his children dropped in, and not displeased when they departed. Bill was his favorite son, because Bill was like him, Bill was himself again; and he adored his daughter-in-law Irene. The fact remained that quite the most awful month he could remember in recent years was the month Irene and Bill had spent under his roof when they were first married, when their bridal trip was over and their house was not yet done. He thought about it often, and sometimes spoke of it. "The phonograph! Ah!" he murmured, and closed his eyes.

He was a stout man, heavy and slow-moving. People said, "He gets there, though." In stature he was short to be the father of two such tall sons as Bill and Byron Junior, who were both over six feet. Mr. Legendre was five feet five and a half. He had white hair which he brushed in his bedroom and ruffled on the way downstairs, and he had white eyebrows thatching sharp blue eyes. His face was especially red now, being burned with sun and wind. He had been back not quite a week from Canada.

He was attired in a white duck suit, for the September day was hot - hotter now than it had been at noon. It was six o'clock. In the great gloomy dining-room inside, the massive table, suitable for well-attended family Thanksgiving dinners, was set with one oblong of linen, one plate, one butter-plate, one glass. Mr. Legendre's cook-butler-valet-chauffeur-gardener, named Ephraim whom he had had for years, sang in the kitchen. Ephraim always sang. He always let the kitchen screen door slam when he sought the refrigerator, which was outside on the back porch. Mr. Legendre from the porch at the side could hear these sounds. He did not mind them. He read his Cleveland paper and sipped a dry Martini cocktail. He was cool and he was comfortable. Peace was upon him.

He finished the cocktail, and was removing the silver cap from the nozzle of the shaker, preparatory to pouring himself a second cocktail — he always drank two at this hour - when his ears apprized him of the approach of a motor on the driveway. The next instant Bill in his roadster passed the corner of the house and stopped, using all brakes, at the porch steps. He shut off his engine. Legendre, Senior, from his chair surveyed him mildly.

"Hullo, son." "Hullo."

Bill had a suitcase in the seat beside him. It was an immense and dilapidated old one, his father noticed, with part of a college sticker still fast to its side. It had evidently been hastily closed and inadequately fastened, for as Bill climbed out and yanked it by its handle it flew open. Wadded clothing of all kinds spilled over the seat and the running-board, and a pair of socks bounced off into the driveway.

"Bless my soul!" said Mr. Legendre. "What's all that? Laundry?"

Bill did not answer for a grim interval, during which he collected and crammed everything back in again. He mounted the steps with the suitcase under his arm, and laid it down on the porch.

"No, it isn't laundry," he said. He straightened, presenting a carefully impassive face to his father's gaze. "It's moving day or something. Rene and I have had a row."

Legendre, Senior, said, "So? I'm sorry to hear that." And waited.

"After which," said Bill, "two of us in the house was one too many. Or she thought so, anyway. So I got out."

"I see," said his father. "Well." He cleared his throat. "Sit down. Have a cocktail."

Bill sat down.

"Ephraim!" Mr. Legendre bellowed toward the back porch.

"Yes sir! Coming!!!"

When more cocktails had been shaken up, and another glass provided, and when Ephraim had gone to set an extra place at the table, Mr. Legendre said, "This isn't any thing serious, surely?"

"I don't know," said Bill. "Maybe it is." "Want to tell me about it?"

Evidently Bill did not, at the moment. He was mute, turning his glass by its stem on the wooden arm of his wicker chair, watching it narrowly.

"It's my fault," he finally said. That was all he said. He scarcely spoke at dinner. He mumbled monosyllables.

His longest sentence was, "Is that a fact?" Mr. Legendre talked about business, golf, forest fires in Canada, the eyes of the deer in the woods at night when you trained a flashlight on them, the proposed new bridge across the river at Gray's Ferry — business again. He knew that Bill paid scant attention, and he saw that he ate very little, for Bill. Mr. Legendre became more alarmed.

He wanted to stop making conversation, to say abruptly, "All of which is neither here nor there. What's on your mind, son? What was the row about?" He wanted to say, "Was it about that red-headed girl in the office, by any chance?" Only today Josh Hammond, his good friend and legal advisor, had hinted to him that there was talk around town about Bill and that girl.

Urged to be precise, Hammond had said that the town was saying that Lillian Andrews had been seen on Hilldale Avenue, just starting for home, at half past six one morning when Irene was in Cincinnati. Mrs. Henry Ives, who lived next door on the avenue, was supposed to have seen her. Mrs. Ives was quoted as having offered to swear it on a stack of Bibles.

Byron Legendre's irate comment had been, "Stuff and nonsense!" He had roared it. He had cursed the town and Mrs. Ives. In Renwood there was very often smoke without fire, and Mrs. Ives was among those most often responsible. "I know Bill better than that," Legendre, Senior, had said stoutly. But now he wondered. ... True or untrue, he thought, the story would distress Irene. It was the cause of the quarrel undoubtedly.

He wanted to say to Bill, "Why is it your fault? What did you mean by that?" Would Bill have said that, if the gossip had been false? His father wanted to ask. Blunt questions came to the tip of his tongue. But he did not voice them. Better to wait. He thought, "In the mood he's in, he'd deny it anyway."

He said, "Finished? Some more cake? Coffee?" Bill shook his head.

"Cooler on the porch," his father said, pushing back his chair.

They went outside again." If you're sure you're staying," Mr. Legendre remarked, "better put your car up, out of the way."

"Somebody coming?" "Jane said she might stop by." Jane was Bill's sister, Mrs. Reynolds. "I think I'll take a ride," Bill decided after reflection.

He did not immediately start, but stood at the railing with his back to his father, looking down at the roadster or over into the garden, or off into space. His father eyed his blond head, his wide solid shoulders. Bill's hands were in his pockets. One of them was rattling change.

He turned. "Well."

"Going anywhere in particular?" his father inquired lightly. He had to make sure. "Or just going to ride?"

"Just ride." Legendre, Senior, nodded. "I'll have Ephraim fix up your room."

"I won't be late," Bill said. "I'll be back before Jane goes." But he wouldn't, he told himself. He didn't want to see anybody.

His father's house was on Spruce Street. It had been built in the days when there was no Renwood Country Club, when Hilldale Avenue was a footpath curving through thickets up a hill. Emerging in the roadster from the driveway, turning from Spruce Street into East High, Bill was glad that his father lived downtown. He was glad not to have to go through Hilldale Avenue, past his own house. He would steer clear of that section. He would turn again at Monument Street and get onto Harding Avenue, and follow it to the bridge and across the river. There he would find some country road, and he could take it easy. He could jog along and think things out.

There was a road along the bluff above the river on the other side; and he chose that. It was an old brick road, narrow and full of holes, and only cars that meant to park and not to drive were wont to use it. It was too early for the parking cars, being not yet dark. He saw no one at all for several miles. He drove slowly, sitting low and slightly sideways, with his elbow outside the roadster's door. His fingers on the wheel curled around it when the going was rough. Otherwise they merely rested on it.

He drove by instinct. He was unaware of the turns he took, the bumps he avoided. In his preoccupied mind he was miserable, and his face betrayed this. The eyes held suffering. The jaw was set so hard that the cheeks seemed thin.

He came to a place where the stone wall that bordered the road bulged out, forming a sort of balcony high over the river. He had not planned to stop, but he stopped here, drawing his car aside into the curve. He lit a cigarette. Below him the trees went steeply down to the water's edge, a hundred yards or more. The river was quiet, silken smooth. He was well beyond Renwood. On the opposite shore there were woods and fields and occasional farmhouses. There was the railroad, and a long freight moving on it. He thought dully, "I'd like to catch on that and start for somewhere." No matter where. He wondered what Irene was thinking now; how she was feeling. She had been so white and cold and queerly quiet when he left. She had been someone he didn't know, and he hadn't been able to think what to say to her, or what to try to say. He had said finally, "I'll be at Dad's. If you should — I mean — if you change your mind, or—"

She had cut him off. "I won't change my mind, Bill," she had stated simply. "I mean it. You've made your choice — and that's all there is to that."

He thought, "It is, too. It's finished. She's absolutely through with me." Now he knew it. Her curious quiet had made him realize. In the height of the quarrel, when she was hysterical with grief and anger, and with wounded pride, because the whole town knew what she had not known, it had seemed to him that when she was calmer he might reason with her, she might come to understand even to forgive him, after a while. Now he saw how mistaken that hope had been. She would never forgive him. She would never understand as long as she lived.

She would never believe what he said. She believed the town. She believed that his affair had been going on all summer long — ever since Red first came to work at the office. Whoever had told her the truth had told her that astounding lie as well, and though he vowed his innocence there, protested it violently, she would not listen. "Oh, hush," she had said at last. "What difference "does it make? The other part is true, isn't it? You admit that."

That was enough.

For the hundredth time in the past two hours he wondered who had told her. He supposed it didn't matter really, but he wished he knew. He devoted a scowling interval to trying to guess.... Well, anyway, he concluded wearily: somebody. Some kind friend. If he had told her himself, as he almost had when she got home, would it have been better? Maybe. Maybe not. No use speculating about that, at this late date. He hadn't told her.

She believed that he was in love with Red. She thought he must be. "You've made your choice" She had said that several times. To her young simplicity no other explanation of his conduct was comprehensible. He had been untrue to her. He did not love her any more. He was in love with Lillian Andrews. He had chosen.

Thus Irene, in the deadly calm that had followed the storm of her grief. It was very clear to her. She was very sure. To Bill, who was sure of nothing, who had been bewildered in secret for days, her conviction was impossible to shake. It was a wall around her, firm and hard, against which his frenzied defenses and denials destroyed themselves, before his eyes.

It was so absolute a conviction that, in spite of him, it swayed him. It was stronger than his weakening belief that she was wrong. She might be right, after all. Maybe he was crazy about Red, subconsciously. Maybe that accounted for everything. There was no accounting otherwise.

This was an unprepared, an inexperienced young man. He had married the first and only girl of his life. He had fallen in love with Irene when they were in high school. When they were in grammar school even. Neither of them had ever gone around with anyone else. They had monopolized each other always;

and the town had helped them. Young people pair early in such communities. From adolescence on, Irene Brickley had been Bill Legendre's girl. This was understood. Potential rivals understood it and kept their distance.

When he went to college, and Irene to finishing school, it was the same. All those four years he had not given another girl a thought. His letters had been to Irene, Irene had attended all proms and parties with him; his fraternity pin had been something nice for Irene to wear. Irene's had been the only photographs belonging to him in a room like a gallery of his roommate's loves. Through college there had been nothing important in the world save Irene and football. He had graduated: football had been supplanted, albeit inadequately, by business. There was still Irene. There was Irene in a mist of tulle as white as the quivering flowers she carried. "Dearly beloved, we are gathered together here in the sight of God, and in the face of this company ..."

That had been three years and two months ago.

There would always be Irene. He had never dreamed of doubting that. Nothing had suggested a doubt in the three years — nothing whatever. They had taken their marriage very seriously, both of them. They had not been modern and post-war about it. Neither had indulged in the little extra-marital flirtations common to the wives and husbands of the younger crowd. No minor trial had tested them, or taught them.

Now there was Lillian Andrews. Looking back now, Bill perceived quite suddenly that she had been a factor from the first. He perceived that all this summer she had interested him more than any girl save Irene ever had, His memory proved it. Belatedly, in the light of the outcome, he recognized the significance of the daily rides to Renwood Falls, the sociable sodas at Jackman's, the laughing conversations that had interrupted work.

These had been attentions paid to Red because she attracted him; he saw that now. He had thought he was just being kind to an employee. "Yeah!" he jeered in his mind. "Kidding myself along. "... He had bought no sodas for Ellen Schwartz, the drab little book keeper. That Mary Okie with the glasses lived farther away from town than Lillian did, but he had never once driven her home.

He had never taken any girls driving in his life, except Irene and friends of hers who needed transportation. He had never noticed anything that women wore — even Irene's new clothes had to be announced as new, to make him look. Yet he could remember noticing certain dresses of Red's, in particular a filmy black one; he remembered fish net stockings, one knee mounted on the other, and a swinging high-arched foot in a shiny patent-leather shoe. He remembered bracelets strung with little silver coins. He remembered single straps of narrow pink ribbon across pale shoulders under black chiffon.

As far back as June or early July there had been a Saturday afternoon when he and Red were working alone at the office. He remembered that. There had been some letters to get off, and Red was busy typing them; he himself was killing time, waiting to sign them. He remembered standing behind Red, looking over her shoulder. Then he had found himself looking down at her. She had the whitest neck. Between red hair and a sea-blue dress, her skin was startlingly white and beautiful. It held his eyes. It looked so cool, on this hot day. It would be cool and soft to touch. He could touch it. He could bend his head and touch it with his lips.

He had not done so. Now he thought, or rather sensed in a vague and wordless way, that it would have been better if he had. Obedience to his impulse would have made him aware of the impulse. If he had kissed Red that day, he would have known that he found her desirable. If he had even acknowledged to himself that he wanted to kiss her, he would have known. He would have been warned, before it was too late.

He saw it all now. She had appealed to him subtly from the very first — irresistibly finally. His capitulation had not been the inexplicable thing it had seemed. Irene was right. He was in love with Red. "I'm in love with her," he said experimentally in a low voice. It did not sound quite true — it still didn't. It was, though. And you couldn't be in love with two people, could you?

He thought not. He accepted Irene's sophistry, adopted her conclusion: there had been a choice, and he had chosen Red. This wretchedness that he felt now, this utter desolation, was for roots torn up, for a life-long habit broken. This aching in his heart was sentiment, and nothing more. He would get over it. A little while, and it would pass. He would be all right soon.

CHAPTER FIVE

The divorce suit of Legendre vs. Legendre was filed in October, in the Common Pleas Court of Humboldt County, Ohio. Irene Brickley Legendre was the plaintiff. She charged gross cruelty. She had said to Bill in the presence of their lawyers that there was no need of making the thing more unpleasant than it must be. The technical grounds would do well enough.

She asked one hundred dollars a month alimony. Bill wanted her to have more, to have twice as much at the very least; but she would not hear of it. She maintained that alimony was a kind of charity — or so it had always seemed to her. She said, "I wish I didn't have to ask for any at all."

Lillian, to whom this was quoted, ridiculed it roundly. "That's a good line! That's a laugh if I ever heard one! As if old man Brickley couldn't take care of her! He did before, didn't he?" But it was to Sally, not to Bill, that Lillian made these observations. She was being careful what she said to Bill these days. As she expressed it, he was very touchy.

The divorce was tried on a Monday morning in January. Since it was uncontested, Bill was not present in the courtroom. Lillian was not there either, though she wished it were possible for her to be an invisible spectator. She had thought of going heavily veiled, and slipping into a back seat; but it would not do. She was sure to be recognized. Bill's lawyer had told Bill that they meant to arrive at the courthouse early, in the hope that the case would come up before the spectators' benches filled. No disguise she could think of would avail in that event. Even if the courtroom were crowded to the doors, the veiled lady could only be Lillian Andrews. She had abandoned the idea regretfully, well in advance.

But the morbid fascination that Irene's trial had for her would not be gainsaid. It kept her awake most of that Sunday night, and in the morning she rose at half past six and dressed, and took an interurban trolley to the town of Forsyte, the county seat, twelve miles away. Once there, she had some breakfast, for there was time enough; and at the railroad station she procured a taxi cab. This was to sit in. The morning was very cold.

"Drive to the courthouse," she directed the bundled chauffeur," and park across the street. There's a square there, isn't there? Well, get right opposite the court house-opposite the door if you can."

"I've got to watch for somebody," she added in explanation.

Around the courthouse square, all cars were parked fender to fender, their backs to the street, their noses to the curb. It was through a little oval window, not very clean, that Lillian watched. She sat sideways in her seat. Obliquely through the glass she could see the blackened stone facade of the courthouse - a little of it. Enough of it. She could see the doors that flapped in and out, and the long stone steps spreading down from the doors. She could see, and she could not be seen.

Bill's lawyer arrived first; Mr. Joshua Hammond. He was the attorney for the Legendre Company, and Lillian knew him well. He drove past the courthouse and around to the side in his familiar car, and reappeared on foot a minute later. He carried a briefcase, and he tucked it under his arm and stripped the driving gloves from his hands as he trotted up the long steps. "Attaboy!" thought Lillian, smiling a little. He looked so very purposeful and brisk.

She did not know Irene's lawyer, Mr. Graham Clement, though she knew his name. He might have been any one of the several gentlemen who now appeared and ascended the steps and disappeared through the doors. Lillian rather thought that the youngish one in the bear-skin coat, who carried no briefcase but had a plump brown envelope in his hand, was Clement. She was sufficiently sure of it to be concerned at his clumsiness when, on the way up the steps, he dropped the envelope and had to stoop for it.

"Hey, hang onto those papers," she adjured him, under her breath.

There was rather a long lull. Five minutes, ten minutes, fifteen.... Lillian became uneasy. What if the little fool had changed her mind? What if——

Then she saw the car coming. She could tell it across the square. It was Mrs. Johnny Bartlett's big closed car, with Mrs. Bartlett's chauffeur driving. As it drew nearer and rounded the corner, its passengers could be identified. They were Irene and her three witnesses, her three best friends— Louise Bartlett, Peggy Stone and Miriam Mason.

They might have been just out for a ride, or on their way to a party. Those four were often together in this big closed car, and they looked the way they always looked, exactly. This was Lillian's swift first thought, her second being, "Well, how else could they look, after all?" But it was for some reason a little surprising.

They were all in the rear seat of the car. Irene, in a tight brown hat and her leopard-skin coat with the beaver collar, sat in the middle, between Louise Bartlett and Miriam Mason. Mrs. Stone occupied one of the side seats. Their unanimous interest in the courthouse as they approached it was visible to Lillian, and she saw that the others smiled at Irene and said things to her. She could not see what Irene did.

The car slid out of sight behind hers, and Lillian dropped back in her seat, in a flash transferring her gaze from the side window to the rear one. They were stopping now, at the curb at the foot of the long stone steps. They were getting out. One of them slammed the door, and Mrs. Bartlett spoke to her chauffeur, and the chauffeur nodded and drove the car on out of Lillian's way. She could see Irene now, plainly. She could see the brown silk hem of Irene's dress, and her tan hose, and her snakeskin pumps, all lofty heel and little toe. Irene had a cigarette in her fingers, and she paused there on the sidewalk and took a single quick deep final inhalation from it. When she threw the cigarette away she threw it toward the street, turning her head.

Again, as on a sultry day a long time before, Lillian caught the sudden strange and vivid blue of Irene's eyes.

The halt was of an instant only. Irene started for the steps. She mounted them steadily, and rather rapidly than slowly, with her chin up and her leopard coat held trim and tight around her. There was a glimpse of her gloved hand pushing the glass of one of the swinging doors. Then she was gone, and the others were gone, and the doors were settling back again.

Lillian collapsed into her corner. Her eyes were sparkling, and her white teeth bit her lower lip to keep the laughter in. "It won't be long now!" her mind sang.

She pushed her left coat-sleeve up a trifle, and peeled her glove down, and consulted the tiny rectangular watch on her wrist. This was not the white-gold watch she had once worn. This was platinum and diamonds, with two slits of emeralds in it. It had been Bill's Christmas present. "I don't know what to get you," Bill had said. "Why don't you go yourself and pick out something?"

The wrist watch told her it was nine-fifteen. She consulted it again from time to time during the wait that. followed. She remembered afterward that the last time she looked, it was nine-forty-three. It could not have been more than a minute or two later when Irene came out. To Lillian the interval had seemed interminable, but when it was over, when she saw the quartet emerge with Irene leading and the lawyer in the bear-skin coat, with the brown envelope, holding open the doors, she was panicky, thinking, "Already?" Thinking that something must have gone wrong. Surely you couldn't get divorced as fast as all that? You couldn't break up a marriage forever in practically no time at all?

Crouching low and close to the oval window, Lillian scarcely breathed. She watched Irene and the lawyer descend the steps together, talking. Talking gravely. The lawyer explaining something, Irene nodding her head. On the sidewalk they still talked, while the others stood aside a little, and Louise Bartlett teetered on the icy curbstone, scanning the street for her car. Lillian ducked lower. She didn't dare not to.

When she looked again the Bartlett car was drawing up, and Irene and the lawyer were shaking hands. Irene was smiling. She was pale — Lillian felt quite sure that Irene was deathly pale. But she knew she smiled. She could see that. She saw another thing: when they were in the car, and seated, and the chauffeur was tucking them in with robes, Mrs. Bartlett hugged Irene enthusiastically, and kissed her. The spirit of the gesture was quite unmistakable.

"She got it!" Lillian almost cried aloud. "Oh God, she got it!"

She could have screamed in her relief and joy.

She telephoned Bill. As soon as the other car was safely off, she commanded her driver to take her somewhere where there was a pay station. "Anywhere! The nearest one! That drug store over there."

Bill was not at the office. Well, he wouldn't be, today. She tried his father's house. As always when she called him there, she was prepared to say, "Is this the grocery?" in a voice not her own if Legendre, Senior, answered. Legendre, Senior, knew now that Bill was in love with this former employee. He knew it, but he was not reconciled.

Bill answered the telephone himself. It had rung only once; he could not have been more than one swift stride away. His "Hullo" was impatient, harsh.

"Congratulations!" Lillian carolled.

She waited, listening, laughing to herself. Bill didn't speak, and in a minute Lillian laughed aloud. "Are you asleep, or what? I tell you she got it, Bill! We can get married this afternoon if we want to!"

"Look here," said Bill in a queer way, "how do you know she got it? How do you know? Hammond hasn't called me."

Even when she explained how she knew, he did not seem to understand. "You're in Forsyte?" he repeated incredulously. "You mean you were there? In the court room?" "No, no, no!" Lillian laughed. "Why don't you listen to me? Of course I wasn't in the courtroom— am I crazy, do you think? I said I was sitting outside in a taxi cab."

"But what for?" She hesitated then. She mustn't strike the wrong note. "Oh, I don't know," she said, lightly. "Just for fun."

CHAPTER SIX

They were married eight days later. It was not a big wedding, and there were no headlines in the Renwood Herald. There was a paragraph among other paragraphs on the society page. "Married," it said at the top in modest type. Underneath it said:

"William H. Legendre, son of Byron Legendre of Spruce Street, and Miss Lillian Andrews, of Renwood Falls, were united in marriage yesterday at Cartersville by Justice of the Peace John Bemis. After a brief honeymoon in the East, Mr. and Mrs. Legendre will reside at 858 Harding Avenue, Renwood, in the house formerly owned by Mr. and Mrs. Elmer Blynn."

That was all. Nothing was said about the fur-trimmed velvet frock worn by the bride, the hat from Paris via New York via Cleveland, the matching accessories. No mention was made of the corsage of white orchids with purple centers that Nickerson the florist had imported from somewhere or other. There was no picture of Lillian, though she had had a photograph ready to give the Herald when they should ask for it. It was all extremely disappointing. It was Bill's fault, moreover. The society editor of the Herald had telephoned repeatedly, but Bill had had Ephraim say that he was not there.

When Lillian learned this, days too late, from a casual remark of Bill's, she was aggravated almost beyond bearing. He might have consulted her, she cried out. It was as much her marriage as his. How did he think it made her feel to have only a little tiny bit of a piece like that in the paper about it — when there had been columns and columns, and a picture and all, when he married Irene?

"Anybody would think you were ashamed of marrying me!" she concluded bitterly. "Wanting to keep it out of the paper. Maybe you are! If you are just say so."

Bill said, "Of course I'm not." He said, "Don't be like that, honey. Please don't." He said, "We're not going to fight on our honeymoon, are we?" He said, "Look, Red: can't you see my point about the thing? Here I'd hardly been divorced a week, and there'd been all that scandal — I just thought the less said, the better."

"The better for who? Irene?" Thus Lillian, still angry — too angry to be either logical or grammatical. She sulked for several hours. Then Bill, who had rushed out in desperation, reappeared with peace offerings from the hotel lobby - flowers, candy, theater tickets. "And listen," he said, "the fellow who sold me the flowers thinks you're an actress - he saw you in there with me yesterday."

It worked like magic. Their first quarrel ended with Lillian saying, "Oh, he was kidding you. I don't really look like one, do you think?" in a flattered voice; and Bill saying, "Sure you do. I've always thought so." He said also that he did not think Irene looked like an actress. "Not a bit," he said when Lillian asked him.

They were in New York. The brief honeymoon in the East predicted by the Renwood Herald consisted of ten days in New York and a weekend in Atlantic City. This was Lillian's itinerary. Bill had suggested going South instead of East. South, or West. What about Chicago? Chicago was a good town. Lots of people preferred it to New York. Well, what about a resort, then? French Lick? Pinehurst? Or what about Florida for a few days? She would like Florida, Bill assured her. She had never been South.

"I'd like New York," Lillian said flatly. "I've never been there either."

She wanted to shop in New York, and she wanted to see Atlantic City. She did not mention her ulterior motive — perhaps she only half knew that she had one. Whether she knew it or not, hers was the exact antithesis of Bill's obvious feeling about the trip. Bill had wished to go anywhere except to the cities where he and Irene had gone on that other bridal tour, three and a half years ago. Lillian wanted to go nowhere else. She would have included the White Mountains, had it not been winter. Bill had taken Irene to the White Mountains.

It was a perverse desire, but it was strong within her. She had envied Irene Legendre so long, she had believed for so many years that Irene had the best there was in life. She would have it now herself. She would have everything that Irene had had, and everything like Irene's; and this applied to her honeymoon, as it did to the new fur coat she bought — a leopard-skin with not only a beaver collar, but beaver cuffs and a band of beaver wide around the hem.

Another kind of coat, even a more expensive kind, would not have meant the same thing at all.

This was a strange honeymoon. It was primarily a shopping orgy, with the bride gone from the hotel before nine-thirty every morning, not to return, save perhaps for a hasty lunch or a fortifying highball, or for more money, until the late afternoon. They were staying at the Ritz, because slang had advertised it to Lillian. They had taken a suite, at her behest. In the late afternoons they found a use for some of their useless space, when bell-boys in a queue delivered Lillian's day's loot.

Then the chairs and the divans in the parlor of the suite, the writing-desk in the alcove, the table and bench in the private hall, would be piled with elaborate boxes —silver ones, rose ones, orange-and-black ones, striped and checkered boxes; and the floors would be strewn with tissue paper and corrugated paper, with sales checks and price tags and C. O. D. stickers and string.

Lillian, bright-eyed, absorbed, would unpack and exhibit her purchases, item by item. A coq-feather fan. An evening bag of brilliants. A necklace and bracelets and earrings to match. A pair of snub-nosed French slippers of purple satin with rhinestone heels. Eight boxes of gossamer stockings of various hues, three pairs to a box. A velvet evening wrap with a white fox collar. Dresses and dresses. A make-up box from a beauty specialist's. A seventy-dollar hat with a Paris label in the crown. A thirty-dollar hat with a label that said "Reproduction of," over a Parisienne's name. Six pairs of assorted gloves with fancy cuffs and fancy stitchings. A tango jacket of flashing silver scales. ... These things she had found in New York for Irene and the women of Renwood to see. She displayed them to Bill absentmindedly, scarcely hearing his comments.

Once or twice she heard him say, in a puzzled but indulgent tone, that he didn't know when she was ever going to wear all those evening clothes.

"There won't be much chance at home, you know. Nobody dresses up except for the Christmas and New Year's dances, and those are all over with now till next year."

"But don't they dress at the other dances at the Country Club?"

Bill didn't think so. "The men don't, I know that," he said, and added gravely. "You can't get men to wear their Tux, unless it's something special — and even then they beef all evening."

"They don't in New York."

"Sure they do. You just don't hear them."

Lillian was dismayed that the Country Club dances of her imagination - resplendent gatherings of decolleté ladies and stiff-bosomed gentlemen — were in reality no more formal and imposing in aspect than the dances at the Elks' Club, or even at the Cloverleaf Ballroom. Fingering an evening gown of purple taffeta, bought that day, a gown with flowing yards of skirt and a few snug inches of bodice, she suffered acutely for a passing moment. Then she recovered herself. She would dress up anyway, she determined, even if "they" did not. She had been in New York City. She would show Renwood what was what.

She was learning a great many things in New York every day — that was quite true. She was learning with her eyes and with her ears. She was not afraid to ask questions. Upon her return to Renwood she planned to snub the persons who served her, the salesgirls in the stores who had known her always, who said, "Hi, Lil." She would even snub Sally a little, as befitted her new status. Mrs. William H. Legendre of Harding Avenue could not have Sally Holtz for a best friend.

But here in New York, with the New York saleswomen and hairdressers, who called her Madam or Madame obsequiously, she fraternized. She felt no superiority over them — rather the contrary. They were New Yorkers. They knew everything. She consulted them eagerly on many matters, and listened with respect and gratitude to their replies. Often, having addressed her as Madame at the beginning, they were calling her "my dear" when she bade them adieu.

"Thank you so much, Miss …" "Miss Stein." "Not at all, my dear. Glad to help you."

Over manicuring tables and in fitting rooms she learned where to go for hats, for shoes, for imported lingerie; for the most expensive coiffures in all New York, and for the best facial massages in the world. She learned where to dine of an evening and what to wear there. She memorized the names of night clubs and their hostesses, of musical revues and their producers and their stars. She inquired, and found out, what a penthouse was.

She learned about skirt-lengths, and about the proper pronunciation of "chic." She learned to call a dress a "little model." She discovered fish knives, and afternoon tea, and the difference between a fifteen-and-five and a twenty-and-ten cent taxi. She heard of Harlem; of the Village; of a midnight speakeasy with modernistic decorations, where you sat on silver cushions on the floor. She heard of champagne cocktails, and of clam-juice cocktails; of Turkish baths, of wrist-corsages, of broccoli, of pumice strings, of pocketbooks to match your shoes and fingernails painted to match your frock -- black fingernails with silver rims with a black evening dress. She tried these things. She tried the black nails with the silver rims, and for a moment scared Bill rather badly.

They went to the theater every evening, to a musical comedy or a revue. They saw one play, through some mistake about tickets; and they saw one vaudeville performance and two movies — not counting the movies attended by Bill alone during shopping hours The two to which Lillian accompanied him, and the vaudeville performance, were their Sunday afternoon and evening diversions respectively. They had only one Sunday in New York. Bill said, "I suppose we ought to see a museum, or the view from a skyscraper." But they decided not to bother.

Nightly after the theater they betook themselves to a night club, where they danced once, found the floor so crowded that Lillian's dress would be crushed, and thereafter sat side by side at their little table, not saying very much — Bill drinking highballs, Lillian sipping and smoking and looking and looking — until the night club closed at three A.M.

Then they roused themselves and paid their check and repaired to Harlem, or to one or another of the midtown cafés where the curfew was ignored. They almost never returned to the hotel much before dawn. Bill kept saying that it was a mystery to him how Lillian stood it. She was up at nine in the mornings. He slept till lunch-time every day, but at night he smothered yawns from midnight on. Once, in Texas Guinan's, while twelve cabaret girls were singing and stomping, Lillian became aware that Bill had not stirred or spoken for some little time; and she glanced at him sharply. He was asleep with his cheek upon his hand.

CHAPTER SEVEN

They loved New York, and she liked Atlantic City, though she found it, by comparison, "sort of slow." She was happy on her honeymoon. It was when they got back to Renwood again that she began not to be happy. Then things began to go wrong. Everything began to go wrong.

In the first place, their house was not ready, the painters and plumbers were still holding sway, and they were obliged to live at the Harding Hotel while the work was completed, and while Lillian bought enormous daily consignments of furnishings. The Harding Hotel was Renwood's best, but it wasn't the Ritz, and Lillian complained that the food and the service were the worst she had ever known. The fact that a meal at the Harding had once been a social event in her life had slipped her mind.

She had another objection about which she kept her own counsel, perforce. Harry Hoffman, the hotel's room clerk by day, was an old friend of hers. Mr. Hoffman did not forget this, and he did not allow her to forget it. He seemed to feel that her marriage was a joke on Bill which he — Mr. Hoffman — and Lillian shared. His, "Yes, Mrs. Legendre" was a burlesque of deference, Lillian knew. When Bill was not with her he said irreverently, "Why upstage? Be yourself, Lil!"

She would have had him fired, if she had dared.

Of course it was an outrage that they were at the Harding, anyway. As Lillian repeatedly remarked to Bill, with three Legendre houses in town, you really wouldn't think they'd have to stay at a hotel! Such a thing was unheard of in Renwood. Hotels were for tourists and drummers — not for members of local clans. Too well she knew that Renwood must be laughing in its sleeve, and that Irene was probably delighted; and the thought was a constant irritant to which nothing Bill said was counter.

His attempts to mitigate his family's slight, to explain it away, all failed. Vainly he mentioned the fact that his brother Byron's house was small, and that Jane, his sister, had that three-months' old baby. ...

Lillian said, "You don't need to try to think up excuses for them. I know. I'm not dumb. I know they hate me."

Her voice shook a little, and Bill was filled with pity and concern. "They don't hate you!" he assured her, and himself. "They don't at all! It's just — they just haven't got used to the idea yet, that's the whole thing."

He fumed in secret over the situation. He did not realize that it was not his family's affection but their sponsorship, however grudging, that Lillian missed and mourned. In the back of her mind all through her honeymoon there had been, for instance, the thought that Jane Legendre Reynolds might give a reception for her, for Bill's sake. Jane had given one for Irene, three years and a half ago. "To meet Mrs. William Legendre." How much more reason for giving a reception to meet the new Mrs. Legendre! Everybody at that other party had known Irene since childhood. Nobody knew Lillian. It would be a reception at the Country Club, with Mrs Reynolds receiving and Lillian beside her in the new black fish-net dress. No, in the blue lamé. The blue lamé would be better. ...

Well. It had been a nice pipe-dream while it lasted, she thought grimly now. And she thought of Mrs. Reynolds, who was chic and cool and sure of herself, who spoke a clear crisp English with an inflection not of Renwood; who had been to college and abroad. "She makes me sick anyway," Lillian said to herself. "They all do. Bunch of snobs — I don't care if they hate me! I hate them."

But she needed them. She needed them on their own terms, on any terms, at any price. This was the lowly ground to which high hope had fallen in a few days. If the Legendres but seemed to accept her, if for the sake of appearances only they invited her to their homes, she thought she would not care at all how they treated her. She would not mind a private snubbing, an angry family scene, if publicly it looked like a family party.

She remembered various movies in which plutocratic fathers had waited upon the luscious ladies with whom their sons were enamoured, to remonstrate with them, to call them names — finally to flourish fountain pens and checkbooks: "Well? How much?" It was too late now, of course, to expect Mr. Byron Legendre with checkbook. The weeks during which Bill's divorce was pending had been the time for that, and he had not come, she had not had to say, as she had planned to say, "But, Mr. Legendre, you don't understand. I love your son!" — with a tremulous emphasis on "love," with a quiet dignity.

Mr. Legendre had not, so far, run true to form at all. Perhaps he wasn't going to, and this would be a relief in one way, but not in another. Lillian assured herself that she was not afraid of him, she could talk right up to him if he came and tried to bawl her out; or, better still, by being as sweet and lady-like as she knew how, she might be able to win the old boy over. In any case, if he came to call on her, the town would know it, the town would think that he had relented and that every thing was rosy. Let him come, then! She wished he would.

She wished somebody — some Legendre — would do something. Anything would be preferable to this nothing they were doing, this obliviousness of her existence they were showing. She scolded Bill about it. What was the matter with him, she demanded, that he could sit by calmly and let his family snoot his wife this way? Why didn't he have it out with them? Why didn't he stand up on his hind legs and simply tell them? Simply say that they'd have to treat her at least half-way decently? You'd think, Lillian declared, that they would anyway, for his sake. "A lot of fine, loyal, loving brothers and sisters they turned out to be!"

Bill winced at that. "That's all right," he said gruffly. "I understand them all right."

"Oh, you do? And I suppose you think it's fine, the way they're acting? I suppose you think"

"No, I don't," Bill said. "I'm awfully sorry about it. But they'll snap out of it, Red. I know they will. You wait and see."

Lillian waited a fortnight. Bill might be right. Some thing might happen, some yielding invitation, or at the very least, some auspicious sign, might be forthcoming still. Every afternoon late, when she first saw Bill after his office day, she eyed him eagerly. He had been among the men of his family. She questioned him: had they said anything? Had his father said anything? Had Byron?

The answer was as invariable as the inquiry. It was a negative motion of Bill's head, and it had been nothing else since the first late-afternoon after their return. On his first day back, Bill's father and his brother and his brother-in-law had greeted him as if he had been away on a trip alone.... This Lillian had learned by sharp cross-examination:

"But how did they act?" "Just as usual." "But how? Tell me!"

"Well, they shook hands, and said hullo, how are you, how've you been

"Where was this?"

"Up in Dad's office. The three of them were there when I blew in."

"Waiting for you, or something?" "No. Having a conference." "Well, what else did they say?"

"Said they were glad to see me back, and how was New York? —and I said great. And that was that. We started talking business right away."

"And they didn't ask you anything else all day?"

Bill thought a minute. "Byron asked me where we were staying" "We? Did he say that?"

"'Well, he said 'you.' Naturally he meant us. He said 'I hear your house isn't ready yet, and I said, 'No, worse luck,' and he said, 'Where're you staying?' and I said, 'At the Harding.'"

Bill stopped abruptly. "And what?" from Lillian.

"Nothing. That was all," Bill said, after a scarcely perceptible hesitation.

"He didn't say anything more?" "No."

"He didn't say — nobody said a word about me, or mentioned me at all?"

Bill's forehead wrinkled slightly, and then cleared. "Two or three of the girls in the office."

"Oh, the hell with the girls in the office!" Lillian cried violently. "I don't mean them, and you know it!"

But when then Bill suddenly, altogether too belatedly, remembered aloud that his father had inquired after Lillian's health, she knew he was lying. She threw him a glance of contempt for his poor effort.

"Never mind," she said shortly. "I got you the first time."

A few days later, Lillian herself visited the office. She chose a day when her father-in-law was in Pittsburgh. To confront her brothers-in-law, not knowing quite what they would do, not feeling absolutely sure that they would not humiliate her before the watching office force, required courage enough. She went because she would have to go some day soon, and this was a good day, as good as any. Better. If Byron and Frank kept off their high horses, it would even be fun.

She had not been near the office since the hot September morning when Legendre, Senior, in a curt typewritten letter from upstairs, summarily and significantly dismissed her. After such an exit, a return in furs and diamonds as Mrs. Bill Legendre— Well, there was a comeback for you! There was sweet revenge, and the last laugh, and everything! Thinking of the other stenographers, who had been so pleased in September, so smug and so "I-told-you-so-it-serves-you-good-and-right," Lillian developed a lively zest for the present undertaking, that banished apprehension. She arrayed herself enthusiastically, twinkling at the mirror. She could hardly wait, she mused, to see their faces.

She drove to the office in the roadster. The slush of day before yesterday's snow lay over the ground around the building, and she passed the parking space at the side and drew up before the main entrance. She would not stay long; and if in the meantime her car was in somebody's way, what could they do about it? It was Mrs. Legendre's car. They could just keep their shirt on.

Thinking this, Mrs. Legendre stepped regally from the running-board to the threshold, leaving the roadster's door hanging open behind her. She halted an instant to arrange the tiny nose-veil which the wind had blown, and to fasten her coat at her hip with her hand, in the familiar manner. Then she went in.

Inside, she pushed the door shut, posing against it. The office looked just the same. There were the white bowls of light overhead, the clean green walls, the desks with the typewriters in them; the cashier's cage, and the three doors to the private offices. There were the same stenographers in the same, or practically the same dresses, cuffed as always with cornucopias of office letter-paper held with elastics. There was the clatter of typewriters and of an adding machine; there was a buzzer buzzing; and midway of the room there was Byron, Junior, sitting against a desk, hurling his long-distance voice into a telephone.

Everything was just as she had left it.

She smiled at Byron, and waved her hand to him. She did not know whether he saw her, or whether he realized that it was she; but to wave and smile looked sisterly. The others saw her, if he did not. In some electric way her presence spoke, so that faces tilted up and typing fingers faltered, and there was a sudden lull.

Only Byron's remarks to Jersey City, New Jersey, continued.

Bill was nowhere in sight. He was in his little office, more than probably; but Lillian decided to inquire. The Legendre ladies always inquired. Irene had always inquired in the bygone days.

At the right of the entrance, an office telephone switch board with its back turned concealed all but the sweatered shoulders and the rearing head, chiefly spectacles and ear-phones, of Miss Mary Okie. Miss Okie stared resentfully as Lillian approached. Only by her resentment did she admit her recognition of this grande dame in the nose veil and the copiously-furred cloth coat.... Miss Okie had never liked Miss Lillian Andrews. Mrs. William H. Legendre remembered. Mrs. Legendre also, at the moment, had in mind the fact that only yesterday, Mary had been rude to her over the telephone. Well, not rude exactly —— not openly, quotably rude; but somehow subtly short and disrespectful.

This must be attended to. "Good afternoon, Mary," Mrs. Legendre said.

Miss Okie ceased staring. Her fluttering eyelids showed behind her spectacles. She reddened, mumbling something unintelligible. Simultaneously she reached forth and yanked two plugs out of the switchboard. They snapped into place with sound and fury.

Mrs. Legendre said, "Is my husband in his office, do you know?"

She said it while the other end of Byron's wire was talking. It reverberated beautifully.

Mary Okie mumbled again. Lillian regarded her with a kindly smile for the room to see, but with cold eyes under lifted eyebrows. She waited for Byron's voice to cover hers.

"What's the matter, Mary?" her undertone asked then. "Cat got your tongue, or something?"

"I noticed the same thing yesterday on the phone," she went on suavely, as Mary drew an audible sharp breath. "And I was thinking — wouldn't it be too bad if you lost your job? You might, you know. You know that, don't you?"

Her eyes flashed, catching Mary's eyes. For the audience her profile still smiled slightly. "Think it over," she advised Mary through shut teeth.

With a little casual nod she turned away.

Now for the rest of them. She had their undivided attention. "All right," she said to them mentally. "Watch."

She chose Byron's aisle. Liltingly she advanced with out haste, without trace of trepidation or even of concern upon the agog and hostile room. Her self-assurance was extraordinary. It was made of precious perfume, of white kid gloves, of broadcloth with badger, of a consciousness of apricot-chiffon-and-binche-lace lingerie; but it was magnificent, supreme.

It was effective. It defeated the insolence which Lillian's former associates would have liked to have dared to display in their eyes and in their attitudes, leaving them merely impotently sulky, and even in spite of themselves a little awed. They nodded to Lillian when she nodded to them and murmured their names. Her manner was graciously condescending, and theirs, in their helplessness, took the cue. It might almost be said that they bowed when Lillian nodded.

Thus, with banners, she reached Byron. As she came, he swung himself erect and backed against the desk-edge that had supported him, to let her pass.

This he did automatically. He was still telephoning. Byron looked like Bill, being as big and as broad, and having the same fine head; but his hair was lighter than Bill's, and straighter, and his eyes were neither so blue nor so blithe, and he wore shell-rimmed glasses and a small full clump of blond mustache. He did not really look very much like Bill when you came closer, but nevertheless, what resemblance there was somehow aided Lillian now. It strengthened the note of equality, of intimacy, in her tone. "Hello, Byron," she said, dimpling at him.

"———on the seventeenth," Byron was informing Jersey City. "Hullo, how're you?" he interpolated, lowering the telephone an inch. He raised it again at once. "Yeah. January seventeenth. Our invoice number ..."

But Lillian exulted as she went. He had spoken to her.

Bill's office door was the left one of the three at the end of the room. She opened it without knocking. Bill was there. He was ambling about within the narrow confines of this accustomed cage, with his pipe in his teeth, his thumbs hooked into his belt, his forehead corduroy. Lillian did not need the additional presence of one Amelia Noyes, notebook on knee, to tell her that Bill was dictating.

He seemed surprised to see her. "Why, hullo," he said. "Hello, darling."

She kissed him. This was because of Amelia Noyes, sitting stricken and gaping. Amelia Noyes was a homely little thing. She was sandy and plump, with a very small crowded face, like a poodle's. She often had cold-sores, and she had one now.

In the intervals of toil she read books recommended to her as "spicy" by the jocund spinster who ran the circulating library. The heroines of these tales, had anyone suspected it, were always Amelia Noyes. The heroes were always Mr. Bill Legendre.

Amelia had once written Lillian Andrews an anonymous letter, in which the printed lines had announced that if Lillian didn't stop trying to steal a Certain Husband away from his Wife, something terrible would happen to her. She couldn't do it anyway, a second paragraph had taunted. She hadn't a chance. This Certain Party wouldn't look at her. ... The letter had been signed, "One Who Knows," and Lillian was never sure that Amelia Noyes had written it; but she believed she had. Amelia Noyes always spaced three times after periods in typewriting, and she always stuck the stamp well inside the corner.

"So get this," Lillian thought now, and she put her hands against Bill's face and kissed him on the lips possessively. "How's my boy?" she asked him.

"Oke," said Bill. He was embarrassed. "All right, Amelia — that's all for now."

"Oh, hello, Amelia," Lillian said. "I didn't see you."

Amelia managed a response, and fled. Lillian forgot her. She stood smiling up at Bill, and liking him, feeling pleased with him and fond of him, in her jubilation. She had a moment of rare tenderness, and she kissed him again, although no one was looking. With her fingertip she touched his chin lightly, once, like a woman in love.

She laughed then. "Say, you should have seen me coming through the outer office!"

"Why?" Bill wanted to know.

Lillian laughed again. She made no other answer, but requested a cigarette. She hoisted herself backward onto Bill's desk and sat there pulling off her gloves.

"I saw Byron," she said. "I passed right by him, and he was awfully nice. He was talking long distance, but he stopped and spoke and asked me how I was. I don't think he's the one that's high-hatting us, Bill," she added thoughtfully. "I think it's that wife of his. What's her name — Nina?"

"Nina, yes." "She's peculiar anyway, isn't she." "Why, I don't know," Bill demurred. "Nina-"

"They say she is. They say she hates people and parties and going places — all she likes to do is stick at home and read poetry and deep stuff, and play the piano. Or the violin, is it? The violin. She's queer-looking too," Lillian remembered additionally.

The white dramatic face of Mrs. Byron Legendre, Junior, with its lost dark eyes and its blue-black hair under a careless hat, floated for an instant in her mind.

"Dowdy," she concluded succinctly.

"She's interesting, though," Bill said. "She's different from anybody else."

"She's different, all right! She's a freak. That's what I say."

Bill gave it up. He was silent, sitting tilted back in his swivel chair, with his head against the smudge it had long since rubbed on the painted wall.

"No," Lillian mused aloud, after a little pause. "Jane's the one. Your sister

Jane," she elucidated, as Bill raised his eyes. "She's the one I want to be friends with. I don't care about the other one."

Bill's glance fell again. He said nothing.

"Where's Frank Reynolds, by the way?" Lillian wondered. "His door was open, but I didn't see him."

"He's around. He's due here any minute, as a matter of fact."

"In here?"

"Yeah. We're supposed to go over some stuff together."

Lillian dropped her cigarette to the floor beneath the swivel chair. "Step on that, will you." She opened her elaborate handbag and produced a pocket mirror and a powder puff sheathed in a handkerchief. The mirror was powdery and she cleared its surface with her palm and held it up, instinctively rearranging her features, assuming her best expression, before she looked. She invariably did this. She always would. Her face would never catch her unawares.

She needed neither powder nor rouge nor lipstick, but she added touches of each, to be quite sure. Idly Bill watched her. For a moment his attention focused upon the venerable plush powder puff that, alone of all Miss Lillian Andrews's personal effects, had survived the metamorphosis of its owner. The puff interested Bill. In New York he had introduced it as a conversational topic, and had heard its history — it had cost fifteen cents, and Lillian had had it since she was in school. She washed it every so often, of course, she said. "Why not blow yourself to a new one?" Bill had suggested. But it seemed that new ones were useless. You had to break them in. It took years to make a puff like this one.

Bill looked away. His gaze wandered over the office, paused at the window for a moment — returned inevitably to Lillian. Now he saw her wholly. She had put back her little veil. Her hat was cut to show her forehead, like a fabulous petal tipped with Titian red and then with black. Pearls clasped her throat. The black-and-white crepe frock she wore matched the lining of her coat, and the badger of the collar stood up high in starry points, thick and diffused, behind her head. These things Bill saw. He saw how decorative she was, and how expensive, and how spoiled.

His eyes were quizzical. "Take a letter, Red," he murmured unexpectedly.

This amused him, and he laughed. But Lillian was not amused. She lowered lipstick and mirror and stared a withering rebuke.

"I suppose you think that's funny?"

Bill did not have time to reply. The door sprang open at this juncture and Frank Reynolds, bearing papers, hurried in. As was his custom, Mr. Reynolds had begun to speak as he grasped the doorknob. He was well into a sentence when he beheld Lillian.

"Oh, beg pardon," he said. "I thought ..."

Mr. Reynolds was a brisk, impatient gentleman in spats. He stood stock-still in them now, looking uncertain. His hand with the papers drifted to his side. Mr. Reynolds was youngish, with a middle-aged bald head. He talked very rapidly, and never smiled during business hours. He never removed his coat in the office, as Bill and Byron did. He wore it, together with a buttoned and slightly rotund waistcoat, to the left-hand slope of which he still pinned a college fraternity pin.

Otherwise there was no nonsense about him.

"Well!" he said now, recovering himself immediately. "How do you do?" He took Lillian's outstretched hand, rings, sharp red nails and all. He took it and dropped it. "Nice to see you."

"It's nice to see you, too!" Lillian assured him warmly. "I was hoping I would. I saw Byron outside a minute ago, and I was just saying to Bill, ' I wonder where my other new brother-in-law is??" She smiled ingratiatingly and gaily. "And speaking of angels!"

"You're looking well," she added, sobering, as Mr. Reynolds continued never to smile during business hours.

He was very well, he thanked her. "And you?"

"Oh, I'm fine. Just fine. Busy, of course," Lillian chattered on, toward a goal she had in mind. "I'm rushed to death these days, getting the house fixed up, and all. It's quite a job, such a big house. Oh, of course, the house isn't very big really," she amended, lest Frank should fancy that nine rooms impressed her. "But it's quite cute inside. You haven't seen it, have you? You and Jane? You must come and see it-mustn't they, Bill?"

"Um-hmm," Bill said.

"Soon," Lillian stipulated. She nodded cordially at Frank. "Any time at all. You don't have to wait till we're in and settled, you know! We're over there almost every evening, working — and we'd adore to have you stop by."

"Thank you. That's very good of you."

"What are you doing this evening?" Lillian thought of saying. But perhaps she had said enough, for the initial invitation. She didn't want to seem to be rushing things.

"I must be going," she observed. She gathered her gloves and trinkets as she spoke, and slipped down off the desk. "You two've got work to do — and so have I. I'll say I have! I've got a list of errands as long as your arm!"

This was Frank's arm.

Going took her a moment or two. She had to stuff things back into her handbag, she had to force her gloves onto each finger, she had to fit her coat around her figure once again. She had to kiss Bill and adjure him to be good.

Smiling her prettiest, she had to point a snowy kid forefinger at Frank. "Now don't forget! We'll be looking for you at the house, you and Jane."

He bowed courteously. "That's a promise!" Lillian sang.

But it wasn't, evidently. Evenings came and went, a week of evenings came and went — and Mr. and Mrs. Reynolds failed to appear. It was not going to be so simple as all that, Lillian perceived. A mere offer of hospitality and a display of charm which she hoped and trusted had registered with Frank in a big way — these things of themselves would not do it. She must try something more. She must get at Jane directly, somehow. But how?

Bill was a stumbling-block. He who should have been such a help was nothing but a hindrance. Vouchsafing no ideas of his own, he opposed each and every one of hers. He would not take her to call on Jane. He would not hear of her going alone. He refused to permit her by telephone or by note to invite the Reynolds to the hotel or the Country Club for dinner.

"No," he said. "No. That wouldn't do." Whatever it was.

"Let's wait," he always said.

There was the episode of the baby jacket. This occurred some days after Lillian's visit to the office. At her command, Bill was opening various paper-wrapped parcels from the stores, one of which would contain a shower bath curtain to be hung. It was evening, and they were working at the house.

"I think that's it," Lillian said. "That underneath one."

"Not heavy enough."

"Well, it's a table-runner, then. It's something. Open it."

Bill tore the wrappings and fished from the tissue paper in the box inside an infinitesimal garment of white angora.

"Oh, that," Lillian said. "I forgot that."

She seemed disconcerted. She said nothing further and there was a short, strained pause. Bill was holding the tiny coat suspended between his hands. It might have been a mitten for one of them. Over it he looked at Lillian inquiringly, one eyebrow up. He was smiling a little. He was smiling, but his eyes were not.

He spoke lightly at last. "This isn't an announcement à la the movies — is it?"

"An-Oh!" said Lillian. She saw his eyes then. They were terrified. She gave a little boisterous laugh. "Lord no! Don't be a dope!"

"It's a present for somebody," she added guardedly. "A present," Bill said.

He examined the jacket again, and appeared to approve it. He grinned at its size. Gently he folded it and put it back in its box again.

"A present," he repeated, as if she had just spoken. "For whom?"

Lillian became defiant. "Well, you'll probably make an awful fuss, as usual! But I bought it to send to Jane for the baby!"

"Oh, no," Bill said instantly. "There you go!"

"I'm sorry. But you mustn't do that, Red. I mean I'd rather you wouldn't, really."

"I don't see why not. After all," Lillian said crossly, "I'm its aunt. I guess I can give it a present if I want to."

"Something's got to break the ice," she insisted, as Bill was silent. "If I send Jane's baby a jacket she'll have to thank me for it, won't she? What else can she do? You don't think she'd send it back?"

"I don't think anything," Bill said. "I just know you mustn't do it — or anything like it. You can't, Red! Don't you see you can't? Not now, anyway."

"Not even if it's a present from you, too?"

"It wouldn't be," Bill said. "No. Not even then."

Lillian argued no longer. But she did not so promptly abandon the little scheme. Bill had offered no reasons justifying his obstinacy about it, and she still felt that it might work out well. She would think it over some more, and perhaps she would send the jacket anyway. Perhaps she would add a cap and bootees to match —yes, she would, if she sent it. She would make it a set. Bill's wife was no cheap skate, Jane should see.

She took the jacket in its box to the hotel with her that night, saying to Bill that she would return it to the store. As it turned out, she did so. She returned it three days later, —the realization having been borne in upon her in the interim, most forcibly and finally, that Bill was right. It wouldn't work. It wouldn't do any good.

Nothing would work. Nothing would do any good.

She knew it on the next morning but one. She was at breakfast. During these weeks at the hotel she had her breakfasts in her room, two hours or more after Bill had tiptoed through his dressing and gone. For the solitary meal she was caparisoned in her best lace negligée, and her feet wore silver mules with wishbone straps to hold the heels. Before coffee her face was washed and painted and her hair was combed and pinned. It was a bother, but the waiter was a man.

She sat in a hard hotel armchair somewhat too low for the portable table over her knees, so that she had to sit bolt upright when she ate. She ate quickly and drank coffee and fell back, swallowing. She read the Renwood Morning Herald. It was her custom to turn at once to the society page, but this morning a murder on Page 1, continued on Page 6, detained her long. It was a New York murder, of her favorite kind. There was a love nest. There was a show girl.

She had finished her second cup of coffee and poured her third before she was ready to return to Renwood and the doings of its élite. She folded the paper inside out at the proper page. "Society," it was simply and snippily headed. Lillian leaned back, carrying her coffee cup along with her. She took a tentative sip, and read: "Delightful Luncheon Given at Country Club. Mrs. Frank Reynolds Hostess to 40———"

It was the first news on the page. There was nearly a column of it, in Miss Carolyn Baynes's best style. Society had flocked to the Country Club yesterday at 1:30 p.m., when Mrs. Frank Robert Reynolds of Hilldale Avenue entertained at luncheon in honor of her sister-in-law, Miss Elizabeth Reynolds of Lexington, Ky., who was visiting her. Forty ladies had sat down to a delectable six-course repast served in the commodious clubhouse dining-room, which was tastefully decorated with beautiful hothouse flowers, ferns and candles. The candles had been pink, as had the nut-baskets, and the centerpieces had been pink roses, maidenhair fern and baby's breath. Candle-shades of pink had cast a lovely glow over the gay and brilliant gathering.

Following luncheon, auction bridge had been enjoyed by the guests. At the conclusion of play, attractive prizes had been awarded to Miss Kathleen Powell and Mrs. Irene Legendre, who held the highest scores. A special prize had been given the guest-of-honor. Among those present ...

Lillian telephoned Bill. She said that what she had to say could not be said over the phone: Bill must come at once to the hotel. Yes, now. This minute. Mindful of Mary Okie even at such a time, she controlled her voice heroically. There was only a little quaking, a little shiver of the breath, to hint that tears of fury blinded her.

Bill came. He looked unhappy and hurt and very sorry, and when he had shut the door he crossed to Lillian and would have put his arms around her; but she prevented him.

"Get away from me! I hate you! You knew about this ——you knew all about it beforehand, didn't you? Didn't you? And you didn't do anything! You let her go ahead and insult me and make me the joke of this whole town! Inviting your divorced wife instead of me to her damn luncheon — she might as well have slapped my face in Market Square in broad daylight——"

"Please, Red," Bill said. "Don't. You don't have to—— I mean, I feel as badly about it as you do. Worse." "Yes! I guess so! You let her, didn't you? You knew about it, but you didn't do anything——"

"I couldn't do anything."

"You didn't try!" He had tried. The flicker of his eyelids said so.

"Did you?" Lillian demanded.

He would not tell her. "Jane does as she pleases," he said instead. "She's independent as hell. She was always awfully fond of Irene—— and she still is, that's all."

"She must be! She must be fonder of Irene than she is of her own brother, by her actions!"

Bill, immobile, said, "That may be."

Lillian seethed for days. She would never get over it, she knew. She would never live it down. She was ruined socially before ever she had been socially made. She could die, she thought hysterically, thinking how the town was gloating. She could kill somebody. She could kill Irene,

Somehow it seemed that Irene had done this to her.

CHAPTER EIGHT

Eventually her rage subsided into a kind of virulent calm, deadly with bitterness and with resolution. She would show them. She had Bill, at least. Through Bill she would meet the right people, and she would give parties to which the right people would come——such parties as Renwood had never seen she would give in her house, one after another, while Irene and Jane sat twiddling their thumbs at home. Society would flock to her gay and brilliant gatherings, and Jane would be sorry, Jane would see what a frightful mistake she had made. As for Irene well, one could imagine how Irene would feel. One enjoyed imagining her frenzy.

The thing was, to get the house finished and to meet the people. The rest was easy. The rest was a matter of sparing no expense——or so Lillian conceived it. Such parties as Renwood had never seen would be parties with orchids instead of pink rosebuds, delectable nine- or ten- course repasts instead of five-course ones, and gifts for all the guests instead of prizes for the few. Evening parties at 858 Harding Avenue would be real ones, with jazz bands to dance to and bonded liquor to drink. To the younger married set, whose soirées at home were understood to be simple, even crude, affairs of phonograph fox trots and bathtub gin, Lillian's entertainments would be irresistible. No one invited would miss them for anything.

The house was almost ready now. It would be completely ready in another week or two—in a month at most she could throw a housewarming. Meanwhile she must make the necessary acquaintances, she must meet the Bartletts, the Stones, the Masons: all the young aristocracy. Bill must manage it for her, she thought, frowning suddenly.

Her frown was retrospective. In the past two weeks, certain tentative experiments of her own along this line had been discouraging. The aristocracy had proved elusive. Very.

It was not the open season for them. Things would have been different, she felt, if this had been summer, with young and old convening at the Country Club, where she could get at them. But this was February. The golf course was covered with two feet of snow and the club house was deserted when, on their second afternoon back in town, Bill had driven her out to inspect it. The sensational toilette she had made for the occasion, the new manicure and the hand-massage and the mud-pack facial she had had were squandered upon a beardless boy in a hastily-donned white apron, who made them milk-shakes at the soda fountain. Except for him there was not a soul around.

Bill said that people dined at the club occasionally in winter, and especially on Thursdays, maids' days out. Accordingly the Legendres dined at the club on that first Thursday evening. They made a late entrance. Six o'clock is the dinner hour in Renwood for those who dine, whereas less pretentious folk had their supper at five-thirty. Bill and Lillian arrived at the club at quarter after six. In the long, low dining room with the open fire in the stone fireplace and the yellow-and-orange-and-black linen curtains at the many windows, four of the tables were occupied by people to whom Bill nodded and spoke—the Matthewsons, the Kruegers, a Mr. Lamson from Forsyte, Dr. Charlie Coe and his wife, and his wife's mother and sister.

All these people watched their entrance while pretending not to. All listened with electric interest to the sudden squeaking of one of Bill's shoes, out of step with the small explosions of Lillian's heels on the bare hardwood floor. All of them nodded and spoke to Bill save Mrs. Matthewson, who was, among other high and mighty things, Bill's father's first cousin. Mrs. Matthewson, with a noiseless but perceptible sniff, cut him dead.

This was deplorable enough; and it was an affront endured for nothing, since the club members present were not, by a generation or more, the right ones. Lillian should have stayed at the hotel.... This she was thinking when a worse moment followed the bad, with demoniacal dispatch. The steward of the club, one Maddox, approached and stood beside their table. Leading a somewhat sequestered life in the culinary department, Maddox had evidently not heard any drawing-room news for some time.

Furthermore he was near-sighted.

"Good evening, Mr. Legendre," he said. "Good evening, Mrs. Legendre." Then, as Lillian said, "Good evening," Maddox started and peered at her. In the enduring quiet of the dining room his anxious retraction rang. "Oh, beg pardon, Miss! I thought you were Mrs. Legendre."

"I am," proclaimed Lillian, frigidly and flatly. But later, in the roadster rolling down to the hotel, she wept and swore. It was too awful, she told Bill. It was the worst break in the world. "It'll be all over town by tomorrow," she predicted passionately, "—and they'll love it!" She was right. It was. They did.

The Country Club, in fine, had failed her wholly. It had been a washout, she thought now. So far, it had been. Nor were the prospects better for the wintry weeks to come. There were no dances scheduled, save perhaps private ones. A Washington's Birthday dance, such as any sensible club would have held, had been announced and subsequently cancelled "for lack of subscriptions" though not for lack of the William H. Legendres' prompt subscription, with Mrs. Legendre's personal check enclosed.

Fate was against her, that was certain. Fate was making things as difficult as things could be. Denied the opportunity that she primarily needed of mingling — just once — with the Four Hundred all assembled, she must track them down and catch them one by one. If she wanted to know Bill's friends before they came to her housewarming, so as to avoid all stiffness and strangeness on that gala night, she must encounter them individually, here and there on the street, at the soda fountain at Deems'—and Bill must be along to introduce her. It was a combination of circumstances only remotely likely in these days of evenings devoted to the house.

She glimpsed her prey often enough about town in the daytime, when she was alone.

Other proofs of Fate's malevolence followed hard upon, and overshadowed, the cancellation of the official dance and unofficial début. At this time, of all calamitous times, the matter of money obtruded. No sooner had Lillian made up her mind to buy her way with parties than it appeared that there was a limit to Bill's capital. Not only that: it appeared that the limit had very nearly been reached, and that Lillian, far from sparing no expense, must economize.

"For a while anyway," Bill said calmly, as if it were of no consequence.

This was sheerly appalling. Added to the ominousness of it, the menace to her plans, there was the horrible surprise of it. Married to a Legendre, you still had to consider costs. Such a thing had not occurred to Lillian as possible. She had known what Bill's salary was, and the amount of his inheritance from his mother. It had seemed to her that these were vast and inexhaustible riches — and they were not all. They were subsidiary merely. He was a millionaire's son.

Now it appeared that a maternal inheritance of fifty thousand dollars was by no means inexhaustible, and not at all vast, when you began by buying a forty-thousand dollar house, a thousand-dollar trip, and a four-thousand dollar trousseau.

It was also quite clear, by this time, that the fact that Bill was a millionaire's son was a glittering promise, but nothing more whatever. While Legendre, Senior, lived (and he was maliciously hale and hearty) his million would be his to the last dime. Even if he had looked with favor upon Bill's new marriage, it was doubtful whether he would have aided it financially. There might have been a wedding gift, but that was all. Legendre, Senior, believed that money in quantity ruined young people. The salaries he paid his sons were no more — perhaps they were a little less — than he would have paid anyone doing their particular work in his organization. Bill's salary was five hundred dollars a month. Already Lillian had learned how mean and meager a sum that was. A little dress could cost five hundred dollars.

Aside from salary, Bill's assets at the moment consisted of the balance of his mother's money, which would partly, not wholly, furnish the house; and his Hilldale Avenue property, which was for sale. There was hope here, but only hope. No buyer had as yet been found. For the time being Bill and Lillian must live — if you could call it living — on four hundred dollars a month; five hundred dollars less one hundred dollars alimony.

"Don't forget the alimony!" Lillian would shrill. "Your precious Irene — who simply hated to take any thing - gets one-fifth!"

She could hardly bear it. To Bill and even to herself she held that if they had had plenty of money it wouldn't have mattered, she wouldn't have minded Irene's robbing them. But they had not plenty of money. They had not nearly enough. They had so little that Lillian began to feel defrauded. She began to pity herself. It began to seem to her that Bill had induced her to marry him under false pretenses. This she almost managed to believe.

She asked herself: what kind of a splurge could she make on what was left of five hundred dollars a month, after butcher and baker and candlestick-maker and Bill's cast-off wife had got through? Five hundred dollars a month was a pittance to start with. She who had expected wealth beyond the dreams of avarice must scrimp and save and deny herself — and each month she must deny herself a hundred extra dollars' worth of things she wanted badly and needed and had a right to have. And why? For what? So that her vanquished enemy might live in ease! In her mind she magnified Irene's fifth of the salary, until it seemed more than her own four-fifths which she had to share with Bill. Irene's hundred would buy more. Irene would have more than she had. Irene could dress better, and entertain better. It was unfair. It was intolerable.

Now the thought came to her that if she had Bill's divorce to maneuver over again, she would do it differently. She would not be in such a hurry. She would wait, she would bide her time, until she got something on Irene — for surely no one was perfect? — and then she would have Bill divorce her. Bill would be the plaintiff and the injured party. That was the way it should have been.

The advantages would have been incalculable. If Bill had divorced Irene there wouldn't be alimony to pay. There wouldn't be this allegiance to Irene on the part of Bill's family, this refusal to accept Irene's successor. There wouldn't be this universal sympathy with Irene, which already Lillian began to sense and feel.

In all probability Irene would not have remained in Renwood, had she been the defendant in the case, disgraced in court. She would have left town — for good, and that would have been the best of all. "Because I hate her," Lillian thought with primitive simplicity. "I hate the sight of her." And she thought that Renwood was not big enough to hold them both.

They kept meeting, or almost meeting. This was bound to happen — it would happen often, always while they both lived here. Already, in this first few weeks of things as they would be, Lillian had seen Irene at a distance several times. Driving Bill's roadster through the downtown streets, she had glimpsed Irene walking, Irene standing before a show window, looking in; Irene crossing her path on a green light in Peggy Stone's car.

Once in the Bon Marché, while Lillian waited for change at the toilet goods counter, Irene had bought an organdie collar and cuffs at the neckwear, ten feet away. This was the nearest they had yet come to the inevitable face to face encounter, the all-important first one, which Lillian anticipated nervously.

Any day, any moment now, they would round some corner, turn the two knobs of some one shop door - and confront each other. There they would be; and instinctively Lillian knew that in that moment, there and then, a lasting moral supremacy was to be gained, or lost. There would undoubtedly be witnesses on hand. Somehow there always were in Renwood.

She prepared herself. Before her mirror she practiced staring through her own reflection; or she stared at it arrogantly, eye to eye. She tried smiling at it, a little scornful, sidelong smile, with eyes averted — thus she would be brushing by. Whenever she emerged from the hotel, morning or noon or night, she wondered where Irene was, whether she was out and about. It was rather like setting forth with the possibility of seeing some certain man, and of being seen by him. You had the same far eye to the horizon. You were dressed with the same directed care. You felt the same expectancy, the same small inward fluttering. The difference was that that was pleasant. This was not.

CHAPTER NINE

It almost spoiled her pilgrimages, but it did not quite: Nothing could quite do that, as long as she wore the clothes she wore, and drove the cream-colored roadster with the new double L's on the two doors. Her solitary daily rides and promenades to and fro, between the hotel and her new house, between the stores and Sally's — these took the place of parties and receptions in her life, for the time being. They were her important public appearances, her chances to display her bridal finery. She was a fashion parade of one through the midtown streets.

She started out in the roadster, invariably. Bill walked to work. It was a mile, but he agreed that it would do him good. Lillian telephoned the garage when she was ready to leave the hotel. "This is Mrs. Legendre. Listen, send my car around." She liked that. The hauteur and the elegance of that.

She would drive the roadster to Market Square — a block and a half — and park it somewhere. The Square was usually crowded, the curbstones lined with cars, but she did not care. She rather enjoyed parking in small places, scarcely big enough. Stray men were always interested and helpful. They stopped and watched and volunteered advice. "Back up a little more. Little mo— Hold it! Now, swing 'er over to the right as far's you can—"

When it was accomplished she would smile and thank them prettily, but aloofly. They were to understand that though she was grateful for their offices, she was a Mrs. Legendre, of the Coal and Coke Legendres, and had no traffic with the likes of them.

Wherever her errands took her in the course of an afternoon, she almost always ended up at Sally's. Sally was still to be dropped from the list of her friends when there was a list. In the meantime, Lillian preferred being democratic to being lonely. You had to have someone to talk to, after all; and luckily you could visit your hairdresser during business hours without losing caste.

You just seemed a patron with an appointment.

You could even go late in the afternoon when the shop was ready to close, and remain there in seclusion till supper time. Of course Lillian had to be sure to leave a little ahead of Sally. This was easy to manage, since Sally had to change into a street dress. Her first move to do so was the signal for her caller to discover that it was late. "Oh, good heavens! —will you look at the time! Bill will think I'm lost! I'll have to run — "

Sally would nod, with a hard gleam in her eye. "Yeah. You'd better."

"You don't mind, do you?" Lillian sometimes paused to ask.

Sally's retorts varied. "Do I look as if I minded?" she said once, and once she snapped, "Oh, don't be such a fool! Shut up and go, while the going's good."

Sally's shop closed officially at five every weekday except Saturday, when business usually warranted longer hours. At five on other days the final seekers after beauty took their wraps from the painted thorny tree in the corner near the door; set their hats on their heads and pulled them down gingerly over new waves at a wall mirror; paid Sally whatever was demanded by the list of prices tacked over the show case, between a framed beauty school diploma and a fly-specked page of sketched coiffures, and so departed, creaking down the hall and down the stairs. A minute afterward, young Evelyn Kober from the high school, who assisted Sally in the afternoons, also departed, also creaking.

Sally's shop was on the second floor of an old brick house on Market Street, that had been a dwelling once, but that was given over now to modest business enterprises of one kind and another. This was a rear room. The windows, curtained in cretonne, overlooked a dirt yard cluttered with the wooden crates and packing-cases of the Boston store, which had its whitewashed, hugely lettered back turned. The walls that enclosed Sally were salmon pink and somewhat lumpy, due to many patches in the plaster. A stove-pipe hole covered with a plaque of painted tin scarred one wall, and two thin pipes ran up from floor to ceiling in a corner.

The salmon-pink was clean, however, and the cretonne was fresh and cheerful, and Sally's equipment was the best that Joe Gratz's money could buy. A permanent waving machine bristled over a barber-chair in a booth and the manicuring table was a proud one of black glass. Between the windows there was a wicker settee for the ladies in waiting, and a rakish ash-tray stood on the settee's arm. All in all, this was as up-to-date a beauty shop as there was in town; and the thumbed and smudgy appointment book beside the telephone proved it. Here appeared the scribbled names of the select and fashionable. Mrs. Frank Reynolds. Mrs. Jerome Mason. Mrs. Harry Quirk. Mrs. Irene Legendre ...

"Was Irene in today?"Lillian always asked. Or ironically: "Was my girl friend in?" Alone with Sally, settled for the twilight tête-à-tête, it was always almost her first question.

She occupied the center of the wicker settee, and seemed to be supporting its upper rim upon her shoulders, so recumbently she sat, with feet outstretched and ankles crossed. At her sides her coat and hat and gloves and handbag lay flung — eloquently careless. They said plainly: "There are plenty more where we came from." Their owner smoked, using a slim jade holder when she remembered it, and ignoring the ash-tray. The consumed ends of her cigarettes fell on linoleum already littered with powder, with burnt matches, with hairpins, with clippings of light and dark hair.

The shop smelled of eight hours of soap and steam and singeing, and it smelled of tonic and perfume. Sally's white uniform with the sleeves rolled up to the shoulder blades had a wilted look, and Sally herself looked worn, sitting slumped in a chair. But her eyes watching Lillian were alert and lively. They were never tired. They were defensive, critical, annoyed, amused and interested, and even darkly gleeful, by turns; but dull they never were.

It was when Lillian spoke of her predecessor that Sally was most entertained. When Lillian asked if Irene had been here today, and Sally was obliged to answer in the negative, she was privately regretful. When, as had already happened two or three times, she was able to say, "Yes, she was here," she said it with alacrity and launched at once into a full account, needing no urging.

"She was here this morning. She called up first thing for a shampoo and a manicure, and it just happened that I had eleven and eleven-thirty open because Elsie Meyers has the quinsy — did you know it? They say she's pretty sick. Well, anyway: so at ten minutes after eleven she comes breezing in. Irene, I mean. She's always late. She looked awfully cute," Sally continued blandly. "She had a new hat on, black, turned up in the front, with a pin stuck in it here and she had a black dress that I didn't remember seeing. She said it was old, but it certainly was good-looking. It had—"

Sally would describe the dress in detail, with the aid of her hands.

"It don't sound like much," she would conclude, and Lillian's mien would agree. "It was a knockout, though. I told her when she was through with it I wished she'd sell it to me. Well, anyway: where was I? Oh. So first she had an oil shampoo. She said she thought her hair was falling a little — she always thinks that, every once in a while, and then she has the oil. So —"

"Is her hair falling?" Lillian interposed. Sally almost smiled.

"No-o!" she said. Her lips protruded, forming the scoffing emphatic denial. "She just imagines it is. She's got more hair than she knows what to do with. Beautiful hair, she has." Sally's eyes caught Lillian's, consulted them with spurious earnestness. "Don't you think so yourself?"

"Mmm," Lillian said, and then Sally did smile, unobserved. "You can't hand her a thing, can you," she thought.

Lillian said, "Well, go on. So what then?"

Well, so then I put her under the dryer and started her manicure. Say, and what a time I had, too! She was in a hurry because she was going to drive to Youngstown for lunch — I don't know who with. She didn't say. Anyway: so here

I am hurrying the manicure as fast as I can, and she decides she wants to try the real red polish this time. Well, so I get it all on, and I'm fanning it dry—"

Sally broke off, and laughed. "I'm fanning it with that postcard you sent me from Atlantic City! If that isn't a scream! I never thought. But I don't suppose she noticed, I was flapping it so fast. Well — I get all done, finally, and she holds her hand out and looks at the polish, and looks at it—" Sally illustrated, hand outstretched, head on one side. "And if you please, she don't like it! She won't have it! So what've I got to go to work and do in about three seconds but take it all off again, and put on new."

"Why? What was wrong with it?"

"Too red," explained Sally, with a willingness that amounted almost to gusto. "She thought it looked cheap. Vulgar, she said. So I put on the medium for her instead, the same as I always do."

"She's crazy!" Lillian flared, before Sally was through speaking. "That just shows how much she knows! I guess you wouldn't call all the millionaires' wives in New York City vulgar, would you? And you ought to see their nails! Just as red as — as I don't know what."

"As yours," Sally suggested helpfully, with a glance at them. "Well. It's all a matter of opinion."

She wanted to laugh. She was so well aware that against Irene Legendre's opinion, the dictum of all New York would not prevail for Lillian. "When she has her next manicure," Sally said to herself, "she'll be making up some excuse to ask me for the medium polish, —wait and see!"

Sally knew. She did not understand why it was that Lillian, having supplanted Irene, was obsessed and influenced by her as never before; but Sally knew this was so. By intuition she knew that Lillian feared Irene now as she had never feared her, and that she was jealous of her now as she had never been. If Sally felt that this was absurd under the circumstances, she refrained from pointing out its absurdity to Lillian. "It wouldn't be any use," Sally would have said not very frankly. The thing was that it wouldn't have been any fun.

Always Sally had news. When she replied that Irene had not been in the shop that day, she invariably added, "But Mrs. Gordon Saunders was, and she was telling me …" From Irene's perennial companions Sally gathered what she called the dope, invoked it expertly when it was not volunteered, and saved it for Lillian.

Occasional items she discarded. That Irene had sold her coupé, for example, sounded like necessity, whether or not it was. Lillian was not informed of it — not soon, at least, and not by Sally. But of Irene's popularity, of her social goings and comings, of her several escorts and of her marked lightheartedness these days, Lillian heard everything that Sally heard, and more.

Lillian heard of Irene's new apartment ...

There was a twilight hour when Sally's black eyes, resting on her friend, held a very special anticipatory merriment. This increased rather than diminished as Lillian, who upon arrival had announced that she was all in, described her day. She had shopped all morning, it appeared, buying little odds and ends for her house, which she listed for Sally's edification, quoting costs.

"And it was only ninety dollars! You could have knocked me over with a feather. I mean, ship models are usually awfully dear, even the little ones, and this one, well, it's this long! Imagine, for ninety dollars. Believe me, I grabbed it. So then I went over to Maxon's and looked at lamps and picked out a couple, and I bought a cabinet for the piano rolls. Sixty-eight fifty, I paid. It's not so hot, but it was the best they had. Then I bought a cedar chest and some pillows and a few things and on my way out I saw the cutest ash-tray, a standing one — it's a little butler or footman, I forget which, carved out of wood and painted, and he holds the ash-tray up in his hands. Nine seventy-five. So I got that for beside the davenport in front of the fireplace."

The Legendres were to move into their house on the following day. After her arduous morning, on top of it as Lillian said, she had spent the afternoon at the house, supervising the hanging of curtains, directing the disposition of furniture. She had also, with a humility of which she now said nothing, interviewed and engaged Mrs. Emmeline Hoxie.

"Oh, and I hired a maid. You know Mrs. Hoxie, the cateress? Helps at parties — or used to?"

Sally did.

"Her," Lillian said carelessly. "I don't know how she'll be for all-around work, but I told her I'd try her."

"She ought to be all right," Sally said, and was constrained to say further, "If she isn't, you can always pitch in yourself."

"I can always get a man and his wife," Lillian corrected her. "In fact I think I will later anyway."

"Pardon me," Sally thought, but did not say.

Lillian resumed her narrative, to conclude it. "Well. So what with one thing and another, it's no wonder I'm half dead. Such a day! I hope I never have to move again."

She sighed. With her elbows she pushed herself from a reclining position to a sitting one on the settee, having gained strength for a cigarette. She found one in the thin case in her handbag, and put it between her lips. It bobbed as she spoke. Her fingers opened a match-folder. "But it's worth all the work," she said, "because the house is the grandest thing— She struck a match and paused until her cigarette was lighted. "It's really beautiful. Wait'll you see it."

"Oh, am I going to see it?" Sally murmured.

"What?"

"Nothing."

Lillian had understood, however. She looked slightly confused. "Why, of course you're going to see it," she said. "You're going to see it — well, let's see: today's Friday, isn't it. I'll be needing a manicure about Monday or Tuesday. Suppose you come to the house Monday afternoon and bring your things, and I'll have the manicure there — and you can see it then."

"That'll be dandy," Sally said dryly.

She had had enough, her eyes said. It was her turn now. She lowered her eyelids, lest Lillian be warned. From a pocket of her limp white dress she took a stick of chewing gum — Sally's substitute for tobacco — and unwrapped it. She thought of a leading question.

"Well, have you got all the furniture you're going to get?" she asked casually. "I mean, are you all through now?"

"Pretty near," Lillian said. "I have to — "

Sally interrupted. "What style of decoration is it?" she inquired in a connoisseur's tone.

"What style?"

"Yeah. I mean, is it antique, like, or modernistic, or what is it? I hear Irene's is going to be modernistic," Sally said, and bit her stick of gum with a little snap.

"Irene's?"

"Her new apartment."

There was a silence like a soundless ejaculation, and as brief. "What apartment?" Lillian demanded. "What do you mean? She's living with her father—"

"She is now," said Sally. "She won't be long. She's taken an apartment where she can live alone, and entertain, and have a swell time, and it's nobody's business what she does or who she sees."

"Where? Where's this?"

The ghost of a wicked little grin flitted over Sally's face and left it serene again. "Oh, in Renwood, don't worry," she answered. "In the Garden Apartments, right near you. Or right near Bill, whichever you want to say."

The facts came out one by one during the next quarter of an hour. Sally continued to deal them out deliberately and parsimoniously, to sell them for questions, payable in advance. No fact was free; and when such counterfeit coin as a plea to "Go on!" was offered, there was no sale. "I don't know any more about it," Sally would say, looking owlish.

"You do too!"

"Well. What more do you want to know?"

For value received, Lillian became the possessor finally of all the information that had been given Sally by two simultaneous customers — one a close friend of Irene Legendre, the other an acquaintance of Irene and a friend of the friend — this very day. There had been a conversation back and forth between two curtained booths, while a marcel wave by Sally and a henna pack by Evelyn Kober were being administered, as quietly and as laggardly as they could.

According to the authority in the first booth, Irene had leased the apartment three days ago. Of the Garden Apartments, it was the corner one on the second floor front — the one where those people named Keating who started the newspaper that failed had lived, until he lost all his money and they split up and she went back home, and he went goodness knew where. It was a four-room apartment, consisting of living room, bedroom, dining room and kitchen, and bath of course. Irene would convert the dining room into a sort of playroom, with a bare floor for dancing, and with a bar.

The whole apartment would be the last word in decoration - naturally it would be, since Louise Bartlett was advising Irene. Louise had marvellous taste, of course; and coming from Pittsburgh originally and traveling around as much as she did, to New York City and California and every place you could think of, she knew what was what. Irene's apartment was to be patterned after the Park Avenue (New York City) apartment of a girl Louise knew who had married — and divorced — a French marquis. If anything could be smarter than that, you might name it.

Needless to say, all the furniture for such an apartment, all the curtains and carpets and all the incidentals, down to the last cigarette-box, must be imported. There was nothing in the Renwood stores, absolutely nothing (Sally stressed this point) that would do at all. For not only had the Renwood stores no modernistic furniture, no zigzag fabrics, no black glass, no polished chromium: the Renwood stores, Mrs. Bartlett said, had no furnishings of any kind that anybody except the factory workers would have in their houses.

"Of course," Sally added conciliatingly to this quotation, "you know how stuck-up Bartlett is. She thinks nothing's any good unless she gets it in a city — even her manicures and waves. I think they have lovely furniture at Maxon's, myself. I really do, Lil. I'm just telling you what I heard she said."

Even the Lares and Penates that had formerly graced Irene's Hilldale Avenue house had been banned from the new apartment by Mrs. Bartlett — not because they weren't good things, city — bought, but because they were period things, and incongruous. Irene would sell them, or leave them in storage. Someone had suggested facetiously that she give them to Bill as a wedding present, and Irene had laughed, observing lightly that Bill's bride would adore that. "She just laughed," Sally said. "She should worry." Irene hoped to occupy the apartment on or before the first of March. Already Louise's painters — Pittsburgh painters, more like artists than regular painters of walls — were at work in it. They were reported to be striping and stencilling and stippling, in the trickiest way. In the meantime Irene and Louise had gone to Pittsburgh on Wednesday, and to Cleveland on Thursday, and they were in Cleveland again today, ordering van-loads of stuff. Whatever they failed to find in these nearer cities, Louise would buy for Irene next week in New York.

"And that's all I know," Sally said, and this time it was true. "All I know is —"

Summing up, she flicked the sore spots rapidly and accurately, one by one. All Sally knew was that it was lucky Irene had that alimony from Bill, because without that she never could have afforded an apartment — certainly not an apartment like the one she was going to have, that would make other homes in town look like thirty cents. All Sally knew besides this was that Irene and

Lillian — or you might say, Irene and Bill — were going to be neighbors, and could keep an eye on one another. For, queried Sally, how was Irene, at Number 920 Harding Avenue, going to get downtown without passing Number 858? — unless she took back streets, which she wasn't likely to bother to do. Lillian, Sally prophesied, would be bumping into Irene all the time. So would Bill, for that matter.

"It's a good thing you're not jealous of her, or afraid to have him see her!" said Sally, laughing pleasantly. "That's all I've got to say!"

She was still laughing a little later, when Lillian had gone. Alone in the shop, removing her uniform, slipping a tan knitted dress from a hanger and hooking the hanger back onto a peg, she laughed silently all the while. When she pulled the dress over her head she tightened her lips, made them tuck themselves inward, lest her orange lip stick smear the knitted collar; but indentations of mirth remained at the corners of her mouth, and when her head emerged the smile broke out again. She chuckled aloud.

"Fit to be tied!" she said softly. "Honestly, I thought I'd die at her."

Fastening the cuffs of her dress, she spoke again. Now her voice was Lillian's voice, mimicked and exaggerated. Her smirk was Lillian's.

"'And it was only ninety dollars!'" Sally drawled. "'Just im-a-gine, for only ninety dollars!'"

She stopped smiling. Abruptly her amusement became a deep disgust, and her eyes that had rejoiced went cold. She set her lips together again, in a preparatory way, and let a single word project them out.

"Bla-a-ah!" was the word.

CHAPTER TEN

Bill heard about it promptly. There was trouble about it at dinner in the hotel dining room within the hour, with Lillian hissing across the table and some times forgetting to hiss, sometimes raising her voice, so that Bill was embarrassed and wretched. He kept his eyes down.

"Careful. They'll hear you."

"I don't care who hears me! It's the truth! She's just taking that apartment so she can be near you — and the nearer the better! She'd take the house next door if she could get it! And fixing it up like a night club or something, and having a bar put in — what do you suppose she's doing all that for? She's doing all that so she can give wild parties and maybe you'll want to sneak out and come over! That's what she's doing it for! Don't try to tell me!"

In the midst of the meal Bill asked for his check and signed it, and they left. Neither of them had been eating anyway.

Most of their quarrels were one-sided, but this was not. Upstairs in their rooms again, among half-packed trunks and suitcases that would be transported to their house tomorrow morning, Bill fought back. He was very angry. Lillian had never seen him angry, and she was impressed and a little frightened. What would he do? He might do anything, when he looked like that. He might hit her — he wouldn't, though. Gentlemen didn't hit women. But he might walk out on her. He might go, now, and leave her flat. He might go to Irene.

He was towering over her, seeming to stand even closer to her than he did. "Listen!" he was saying. "If you ever again make a scene like that in public —"

He stopped short. He withheld the implied threat, and Lillian waited a minute for it. She watched him, fascinated. "Gee, he's sore," she thought, and she suddenly thought that he was good-looking. He was so big, and his eyes were so fiercely blue.

"Nobody heard me," she said almost meekly.

"Everyone heard you."

"Well, I'm sorry. I couldn't help it. The very idea of her having the nerve —"

"You could certainly help it," said Bill. "And I don't know what nerve you're talking about. Irene has a right to live where she happens to want to. It's a free country."

"That's it! Stick up for her!"

Bill shrugged. "Call it that, if you like."

He turned away. He seemed no longer angry, but merely tired; and Lillian was quick to seize the advantage. She drew herself up, hands planted on her hips. Her voice pursued him.

"Yes!" she said. "It's a free country! Irene has a right to live where she happens to want to — sure she has! And she happens to want to live just as close to you as she can get!"

Bill was across the room now. He had turned again at the windows, and he stood with his feet apart and his fists in his pockets. A small gold football gleamed on the watch chain slung across his vest. He looked at Lillian, thoughtfully. Lillian looked at the football. It had caught and held her falling gaze.

"You flatter me," Bill observed at last.

"Oh, I do?" Her eyes leaped up, and narrowed. "Is that so flattering?"

Bill did not say. He said, "It's ridiculous, and you know it." He said, "If Irene never saw me again, it would be too soon. You know that as well as I do."

"Then why does she want to live so near?"

"She probably doesn't want to. She probably hates it worse than you do. But everything's near in a town this size. She's got to live somewhere, hasn't she?"

"No," said Lillian sullenly.

There was another silence. This time it seemed very long, and full of the echo of her monosyllable. It didn't sound so well, Lillian thought, hearkening to it. She should have done better than that — or else kept still. Now what would Bill say? How was he looking at her? Under her lashes she peeped at him to see.

It was worse than she had feared. He was staring at her intently — curiously, almost. She cried out, "What's the matter? What are you looking at me like that for?"

Bill stirred, and his eyelids flickered. They covered his eyes.

His face was unreadable. "Nothing," he said. "Only let's quit wrangling."

Somehow it was a command.

They had much to do at the house this evening. They remembered now, and in the quiet room they began to move about, preparing to go. Neither of them spoke of going. Bill shut a suitcase to take with them, and Lillian, thus reminded, got a hat from the closet. Putting it on at the bureau, she beheld her still-petulant face in the mirror, and she thought, "I don't care! I meant it! I wish she was dead!" But this pronouncement was private, mute. Bill was obeyed.

They summoned a bell-boy, and loaded him with bags and hat-boxes and coats, and followed him to the lobby, Bill with additional coats and bags, Lillian bearing two books, a box of stationery, a pair of shears and a quart of gin wrapped in the evening paper. The lobby was lined, as it always was at this hour, with salesmen in armchairs, who stared hard at Lillian, as they always did. "Just losing an eye," she noted, "every one of them," and she gave Bill's profile a significant sideways glance. "See?" the glance said. He'd better be careful how he talked to her.

Outdoors it was snowing lazily. Approaching on Harding Avenue, they descried their house through curtains of darkness tufted with flakes of snow. It looked big and dignified and costly. After all, Lillian said to herself, a house was a house. An apartment was only an apartment. Her mood changed, she felt more kindly disposed toward Bill, and as they turned into the driveway she addressed him for the first time since leaving the hotel.

"Did you remember to buy picture wire?" she asked.

Bill nodded. He recited, "Picture wire, hooks, shelf paper, shaving-mirror-damn it, I forgot brass-headed tacks, though."

"Never mind. It doesn't matter a bit."

She could be awfully sweet when she wanted to be, she thought.

Bill stopped the roadster at the edge of the short concrete path that ran from the driveway to the front door. They got out, carrying what they could. On the path Lillian said, "There's that woman again," and Bill snorted under his breath. The house next door was close to theirs, and it had a side bay window containing now, as always when they came, Mrs. Horace Coulter, serene in her belief that shadows were invisible, and that glass and Brussels lace concealed a person.

"You haven't got a brick about you anywhere, have you?" Bill muttered wistfully.

Over their front door a light had been left burning, by which they found the new key among old keys on Bill's ring. The door pushed slowly in upon unworn resisting carpet, carrying a spreading wedge of light in with it. There were two white cards on the carpet, lying just inside the sill, and Lillian's heart jumped. Callers already? She stooped swiftly and picked up the cards; but they proved to be advertisements. If the bearer would apply at Spargo's Cut-Rate Pharmacy, he or she would receive a free trial tube of Peerless Toothpaste.

The house was livable, or nearly so. All important work was done; this evening they would begin the finishing touches. Pictures were to be hung, small scatter rugs were to dot the carpets here and there, at points to be agreed upon. Ornaments, souvenirs and such books as they owned— "Ex-Mistress," "Contract

Bridge," "The Wild Party," "Language for Men of Affairs" (volumes I and II), "Beauty Is Within Your Reach," a booklet of recipes for cocktails, "The Strange Death of President Harding," and a dictionary — were to be arranged in the living-room bookcase.

They would unpack the bags and boxes they had brought along, and put the contents away in bureau drawers and on closet shelves that must first be laid with fitted paper. In the front hall there were objects great and small, some wrapped, some unwrapped, which had been delivered by the stores this afternoon. There was the ship model, and the music-roll cabinet, and the painted wooden footman with the ash-tray in his hands. "What's this business?" Bill inquired, and Lillian said, "It's a smoking-stand. Isn't it cute?" and Bill said, "Oh. A smoking-stand. Well."

They removed their wraps, and Lillian folded the long, loose satin sleeves of her dress until they were half sleeves, wrong side out, with the cuffs on the shoulders. She secured them with safety pins, and exchanged her high-heeled satin pumps for mules. She always wore mules indoors, as her mother always wore carpet slippers. Her mother's mother, in a cabin deep in the West Virginia hills, had gone barefooted.

From the hall closet where the mules had been kept, among paint pots and cans of turpentine and slim depleted rolls of wall paper, Lillian also produced an apron and a pair of rubber gloves. The gloves were to protect her hands. The apron was a dustcloth. She ripped the brown paper wrapping from the music-roll cabinet and went over it with the apron, outside and in. It was very new.

The shelved interior smelled of pine and varnish, and there were little curled-up shavings in the corners.

Bill was irritated because Mrs. Hoxie had gone to the movies. "On a night like this?" he demanded incredulously. "Did you tell her she could?"

"No, she told me," Lillian thought, but she was ashamed to say it. She said, "Well, why not? She's not supposed to stay here evenings."

"She is when we're moving, for heaven's sake!"

"Well, I'm sorry," Lillian said. She added tartly, "It seems I can't do anything right today," but this was lost on Bill, who had started out to the roadster for the rest of the coats and bags. "Shut the door!"Lillian screamed after him. "You fool," she added, low. But he did not hear that either.

They worked for several hours. They did not rest; and beyond brief discussions of decorative problems, or of the whereabouts of things mislaid, they did not talk at all. They were oftener apart than together, working in different rooms, on different floors. Headed in opposite directions, they passed in the halls or on the stairs like hurrying strangers, without glance or word.

As they went they turned on lights and left them on, until all the house was lighted, even to the attic and the cellar. To add to the party effect of this from the street, there was music in the house. Their new player piano played. It played Why Was I Born?, it stopped, it clicked, it rerolled, it played Why Was I Born? They possessed other rolls, but Bill was too busy to change them.

Toward eleven o'clock they met in the living-room, and agreed to call it a day. They relaxed, dropping thankfully into chairs. Lillian's head lolled back, her feet rested on her stockinged heels, toes up, with the soiled mules hooding them. She peeled the gloves from her hands and flapped one of them at the piano.

"Shut that thing off, will you please?"

Fatigue had frayed her nerves. "Hurry up," she added fretfully, "before it starts again. If I hear that piece once more, I'll lose my mind."

Bill attended to it. From the piano he went to the hall for cigarettes from the pockets of his coat, which with his waistcoat and tie adorned the newel-post. Returning, halting at Lillian's listless elbow, he lit two cigarettes, and put one of them between her lips. Solicitously he hovered, surveying her upturned face from which exertion had erased all trace of make-up. She looked gray; and Bill appeared to find the fact alarming.

"Poor kid," he said. "I shouldn't have let you work so hard."

"I'm dead," Lillian agreed. "I ache all over."

She closed her eyes. She was aware that Bill stood there, and she thought, "I suppose I'm a sight," but she did not care. He needn't look at her if he didn't want to.

"I wish I had a drink," she murmured.

"I was just thinking," Bill said. "There's that gin, but there's nothing to go with it. Could you take some with plain water?"

Lillian could try. Bill left the room again, and she lay motionless and waited, and watched the cloudy dark kaleidoscope inside her eyelids. Idly she reflected that Bill probably wouldn't find the gin. She had put it in the cupboard under the sink in the serving-pantry. That was a good place to keep their liquor, she had decided; but it wasn't the best possible place. They ought to have a bar. There was that storeroom in the cellar, where she had lingered long this evening. She would speak to Bill about that storeroom. They didn't need it. They ought to fix it up. They ought to make it over into a sort of playroom, with a hardwood floor for dancing, and with a bar.

She opened her eyes, and contemplated the ceiling and the central lighting-fixture — four electric candlesticks with pointed orange flames, set on a polychrome circle around a chain. On brackets on the walls there were single candlesticks to match; two on this wall, two on that, two over the mantel. There was plenty of light, she thought with satisfaction. There were all the floor lamps and table lamps besides. She lowered her chin to level her gaze. She counted: there were eight lamps, including the little lighthouse on the bookcase that blinked on and off and on and off.

She surveyed the room as a whole. It was finished. Nothing remained to be done. As it was now, it would be when Louise Bartlett saw it, when couples like Peggy Stone and her husband came to play bridge in it; when it was full of a gay and brilliant gathering. ... Sitting up straight in her chair, she scanned this room a little fearfully, darting anxious glances here and there. Could anyone say that it wasn't a beautiful room? Refined — yet rich-looking? Could anyone doubt that it had cost a lot?

No. No one could. She was convinced of this; but she did not settle back again. She was still sitting forward when Bill re-entered.

"Bill," she said.

"Hullo?"

"Do you — don't you like this room all right?"

"Sure I do," Bill said.

He did not look at it. Carefully he picked his way through the crowd of chairs and lamps and tables to Lillian's chair. He bore a small glass of gin and a large glass of water, both full to the brim. He set the small glass down, saying, "There you are." The large glass he wiped with a handkerchief from his hip pocket.

"Don't you think it's rich-looking?" Lillian persisted.

He still did not look. "Um-hmm," he said.

"Listen," Lillian commanded. "The furniture they sell at Maxon's — isn't it the same as what they sell in Cleveland or Pittsburgh? I mean, isn't it all made in the same factories - in New York or somewhere?"

She hung on Bill's answer. For a dubious instant, while he hesitated, his eyes touching things in the room now, she was afraid that he would not confirm her. She was afraid that Sally had told the truth, and that Louise Bartlett was right, and that this living-room looked like a factory worker's living-room to Bill, and would to Louise, and would to all the Hilldale Avenue people. There was that in Bill's eyes, or she thought there was, for an instant.

She must have imagined it. To her vast relief Bill nodded assent. He supplied the name of another place where they manufactured furniture.

"New York — or Grand Rapids," he said.

"Well, there!" Lillian cried triumphantly.

She was vindicated. Sally was just jealous. Sally had just made that up.

CHAPTER ELEVEN

For a month after they moved, nothing much happened. Lillian waited. She had no choice but to possess her soul with what patience was possible to her, until life should begin, until destiny should arrive. The delay and her own enforced inactivity irked her sorely — she would have liked to make things happen, and she knew the way. The big housewarming party was the way. But whenever she said "housewarming" to Bill, Bill said, "Now, please, Red! Don't start in again. I've told you we can't afford to throw a binge like that — not this month. Not with the bills we've got to pay."

It seemed a very lame excuse to her. His credit was good, wasn't it? He was a Legendre, wasn't he? The tradesmen wouldn't worry if he didn't pay those bills for a year! No. That was no excuse at all.

"Sometimes I think you don't want your friends to meet me!" she shrilled accusingly once. "I think you're just stalling!"

There was a great deal more in the same vein. "I guess I'm not good enough for them!" Lillian reiterated again and again. "You're afraid I might disgrace you or something — that's what's biting you!"

This explosion brought results, and quickly. But it was not until late in the month that it occurred. In the meantime, no events and almost no episodes of moment marked the sudden blankness of her days. She had literally nothing to do, now that shopping was over with and the house finished. She wondered what other ladies of leisure did. They had social engagements, of course — but what did they do the rest of the time? She would never have believed that the hours could be so long.

She slept. She read. She took protracted baths in perfumed water. By the half hour she patted lotions and creams and astringents into her skin. With Bill's magnifying shaving-mirror in a good north light, she hunted her face for infinitesimal blemishes to be treated, for eyebrows out of line to be plucked out. She brushed her hair a hundred full-length strokes, sometimes two hundred. She manipulated her scalp till her fingers ached. She gave herself mud-packs and supplementary manicures, and kept her legs and forearms as smooth and bare and hairless as if they had been ivory or shell. In a trailing velvet robe and mules she dawdled through her house, starting mechanical music, looking out of windows. She liked to telephone, and often she called up Bill for that reason. She called up Sally, though Sally was invariably too busy to talk. She called up her mother and asked for news and held the line compliantly while her mother ran to set something back on the stove. She always said to her mother that she was well and happy, and that she was having a wonderful time.

Her mother came to see her and to see the house, one afternoon when Mrs. Hoxie was out. The visit was by appointment. Mrs. Andrews, descending from a streetcar at her daughter's corner and finding that it lacked four minutes of the appointed hour, turned her broad back at once, with admirable tact and presence of mind, and set off on a trudge around the block. Reappearing in due time, somewhat short of wind, she gave the front-door bell a timid poke. She was admitted by an almost overpowering Lillian in turquoise-blue-and-silver tea pajamas, who first closed the door quite firmly and then kissed her on the cheek, saying, "Hello, Momma. So nice to see you."

Mrs. Andrews was dressed as for church, and at first her raiment, as well as her surroundings and her incredible child, affected her. She was solemn and subdued, and her eyes were furtive and even fearful. This was only just at first, however. Then her natural intrepidity asserted itself, and her maternal confidence returned to her. In a quarter of an hour she was upbraiding Lillian for dropping ashes on that lovely carpet, and for smoking like a chimney anyway. "You'll spoil your Looks," Mrs. Andrews prophesied darkly. Lillian's looks, pooh-poohed by her progenitor these twenty years, had earned a capital L and bated breath.

The tour of inspection of the house was long and slow, including as it did the testing of the quality of fabrics and of the weight of silver, the removing and examining and refolding and replacing of the contents of closets and bureau drawers, the pricing of everything, and the ecstatic sighing of,"My!" It was five o'clock before Mrs. Andrews knew it. It was, in fact, five-five. Her son-in-law, whom she designated namelessly as "Mister," would be home at any moment now. Mrs. Andrews observed as she scurried for her coat and hat that she would like to meet Mister sometime; but this was an observation merely. She and Lillian had long since tacitly reached the understanding that it wouldn't do.

She departed lugging a suitcase and two cardboard boxes heavy with largess that Lillian, who in her fashion was fonder of her mother than she was of anybody, had heaped upon her. There were garments in the suitcase, and a clock and a silver cake-dish and a string of beads and a bedspread and six Madeira doilies; and in one of the cardboard boxes there was a baked Virginia ham with only a few minor slices missing.

Generosity, Lillian perceived when she opened the street door, always paid. On the porch of Mrs. Coulter's house adjoining were Mrs. Coulter and leave-taking ladies, three of them. To this group Lillian's mother, burdened as she was, and with her hat askew, and her short skirt and her fat stockings, would seem to be a seamstress or a laundress.

Several other people came to see Lillian during that month. Her sister, the one who was married to a farmer naimed Hoag from down the river, came, bringing three of the younger and more tiresome of her children. Lillian's brother Clyde, home on leave from the Navy, came one morning to pay his respects and to borrow a quart of whiskey and fifty dollars. Well, thirty-five, then, if she wanted to be like that.

The minister came. Sally came more than once, professionally, in the daytime. A Mrs. Gant, of Gray's Ferry, fainted on the street-car and was carried in and revived on Lillian's rose-brocaded divan. A man came selling vacuum-sweepers; another man, an Armenian, came selling linens. A boy came selling magazine subscriptions. No one else came.

She had nowhere to go when she went out. In the evenings she and Bill had nowhere to go, except to the movies. The alternative was staying at home and listening to the radio, and dealing hands of bridge face up for Lillian's instruction.

It would be decided at dinner. Dinner was at six-thirty, or at six-twenty-five, or at six-nineteen.... By degrees, insidiously, Mrs. Hoxie was working toward six o'clock, which she regarded as a proper supper hour and plenty late enough for anybody. The dining-room table was square, and Bill and Lillian faced each other across a stiff new damask cloth, an embroidered centerpiece, and a silver bowl heaped high with artificial grapes and plums, an orange, a pear, a peach and a banana. The wax pear on its under side bore the marks of little teeth. One of Lillian's sister's offspring had believed in it.

Lillian would say, "What'll we do this evening?"

She would lift her eyes and look at Bill, and then look past him. Against the wall behind him was the mahogany buffet, which had a long narrow mirror across its top. In the mirror she could see her face with its colorful circles of eyes and mouth, she could see the two smooth halves of her dark red hair, coiling low on the ears. Behind her head there was a large round tray of beaten brass, that stood upon its rim on a second sideboard. When she sat erect, though not too erect, and when Bill did not get in the way, the mirror showed her her face exactly centering this burnished arc. She said to herself that, if she did say so, it was like a painting. If an artist could see it —

Her eyes would revert to Bill, on the realization that he had spoken. "Hmm?"

This was one of the moments when, gazing at him, she really beheld him. It did not happen often. It happened now as a result of her contemplation of her own images. It was as if she had a curiosity to know what the husband of the beauty in the looking-glass was like.

He was certainly huge, she thought, measuring with her eyes the spread of his shoulders above and beyond the invisible back of his chair. His outthrust elbows — he was carving — made him triangular. His hands were wide and thick on the handles of the carving implements, and they were clumsy with them. He scowled. He hated carving, and always scowled while he did it. He bit the tip of his tongue.

"Don't do that!" Lillian said, annoyed.

It always annoyed her. Once or twice at first Bill had queried, "Don't do what?" But now he knew.

"Sorry," he said.

His scowl relaxed. He was without expression, and Lillian noticed then that he looked tired, and that his face was thinner lately — this last she remarked with approval. His face had been too full. She liked lean triangular faces, sallow rather than ruddy like Bill's, with the cheeks slightly concave as if sucked in. She liked lines across male foreheads when they were faint lines, and Bill, she discovered now, had two — a long one and a shorter one just below it. She had not seen them before. "He looks older," she thought finally. "More serious." He was growing up. Well, it was time.

She watched him spear a potato from a smoking silver dish with the carving-fork and transfer it to the dinner plate before him. The plate already held a hacked uneven slice of lamb and a sprig of parsley. Bill added two spoonfuls of peas, and he and Lillian exchanged plates, using four hands, across the table. This nightly self service commemorated one of Mrs. Hoxie's earliest victories. "If it's a waitress you want—" Mrs. Hoxie had said, and balefully she had paused, until Lillian assured her that it wasn't.

Bill filled his own plate. They began eating, and Lillian said, "What did you say about this evening?"

"I don't know. What would you like to do? Movie?"

"What movie?"

"Why, any one."

"We've seen the Bijou," Lillian reminded him. "And I saw the Strand this afternoon. And the Alhambra has that Western picture, and I hate Western pictures."

Bill, who rather liked them, said that some of them weren't so bad.

"Terrible," said Lillian. "I'd rather stay home than go see that."

"Well, let's stay home, then. Unless you'd like to take a ride?"

It was too cold to take a ride. They would freeze, Lillian averred. And besides, where would they ride to?

Bill didn't know.

The point had now been reached at which Lillian habitually said, "We might call up somebody." A verbal nudge, accompanied by a quick and covert glance at Bill.

Bill made her furious, she always thought in the next instant. He gave her a pain. Why couldn't he ever say, "Yes, let's call up Louise and Johnny Bartlett?" Or why couldn't he say, "That's a good idea. Let's have the whole crowd in. Let's not wait till we can afford a house warming — what's the sense? Let's just have them in informally."

Bill said no such thing. As often as not he said nothing at all. He just ate, as if he had not heard. Again, he urged her to call up any of her friends she wanted when he knew perfectly well, he must know, that it was his friends she meant.

Just because she hadn't met them yet, Lillian said to herself, was no reason why Bill shouldn't ask them down for an evening. Why should he stand on ceremony, who had made mud-pies with all of them? What ailed him, anyway? Was this stubbornness on his part —"orneriness" was the Renwood word -- or plain stupidity?

Of recent evenings, Lillian had had a new, concrete suggestion to supplement the tentative one that they call up somebody. Small thanks to Bill, names entered in. "Jerry und Miriam Mason!" she added now, in the bright exclamatory tone of inspiration. "Maybe they're not busy. Let's phone them."

The Masons were young, they were exalted, they were ideal. Next to the Bartletts, there was no couple that Lillian so much desired to know, and to know well. There were no potential intimates — the Bartletts always excepted — who would better serve as a nucleus for the reorganized clique that had been Bill and Irene's crowd, that was to be Bill and Lillian's. Half the battle would be won if the Masons took her up. It had seemed to her that at least a quarter of it had been won when she met the Masons and sat with them for an hour or more in a movie.

This extraordinary bit of good fortune had befallen her, quite without warning, on an evening early in the current week. Its unexpectedness bothered her at the time. At first she could only think of the particular hat and coat and frock, and even shoes and hose, that she would have worn if she had known. ... The momentary cloud lightened when a swift appraisal convinced her that Mrs. Mason's costume could not touch hers as it was for lavishness. Mrs. Mason wore a hip-length gray squirrel coat above a rust-colored dress of some sort, with a hat to match. There was nothing to the hat but its color and its shape, and the coat was last year's coat cut short. Lillian remembered its earlier incarnation going along a street - pulled along, she recalled irrelevantly, by a leash and a German police dog.

Mrs. Mason's eyes were dark and a little sleepy, though they were direct. She said, "How do you do?" in four separate sounds, not slurred together. She did not smile. Her right hand held her coat together at the throat. If she noticed Lillian's instinctive notion to shake hands, she did not seem to.

"And Bill," she said, turning to him, her lashes lifting. "How are you?"

"Stranger," Lillian expected to hear her say. There was that note.

They were in the lobby of the Bijou Theatre, which was empty at the moment save for them. Bill and Lillian, entering through the storm doors from the street, had found the Masons at the ticket window. Jerry, an angular, tall young man with brown hair and a derby clasped jauntily on it, was pocketing change and picking up tickets; removing a cigarette from his lips and annihilating it under the toe of a large glossy cordovan shoe.

"It's the boy!" he exclaimed jovially at sight of Bill. "Hey, wait a minute, Mimi —"

Mrs. Mason, surely because she had not recognized the Legendres, had started inside.

She halted and came back, murmuring, "Oh. Hello there. I didn't see you." She addressed Bill, and her eyes were on him; and Lillian, watching, was reminded that she had been one of Irene's witnesses, that she had testified in court to Bill's "gross cruelty." Not that it mattered, of course — it was just funny. All of Irene's witnesses had been chosen by Irene and Bill, and asked to serve as a favor to them both.

"You know Lillian, don't you," Bill said.

There was Miriam Mason's, "How do you do?" and Jerry's hearty acknowledgment: "Awfully glad to meet you, Mrs. Legendre." He smiled warmly, pumping Lillian's hand. He was nice, she thought in a flash. He was nicer than his wife. Well, naturally. All husbands were nicer to you than their wives, when you were good-looking.

The introductions over, Miriam turned to Bill, and Jerry wheeled to the ticket window, demanding two more tickets. "Here!" Bill protested. He also wheeled. Lillian said to Miriam that it was cold out, wasn't it, and Miriam said that it was.

"Yes," she said.

They filed through a door into the darkened auditorium, and down the center aisle behind an usher with a flashlight. Lillian went first. She would have preferred to let Miriam lead, so that Miriam would take the seat farthest in; it was the second girl who sat between the men.

This could not be managed, however. There could be no jockeying for position at the head of the aisle, or at the mouth of the row, with Miriam Mason, as there could and would have been with Sally. Lillian did hesitate at the row, but it was no use. The other three waited, and Bill touched her arm in a way that meant, "Go on."

The feature picture had started. It was a musical extravaganza— "All-Talking! All-Singing! All-Dancing!" the advertisements had proclaimed — and

Lillian had looked forward to seeing it. Now, however, she gave it scant attention. It danced across her vision, and sang and talked against her ears, but her mind was full of the Masons, of things to do for their benefit — things like holding Bill's hand, which to Bill's surprise she was firmly doing; things like whispering affectionately to him.

Her mind was full of plans for the rest of the evening. After they left the theater, where should they go? To Deems', where everybody would see them, where every body would say, "I didn't know Bill Legendre's new wife was so clubby with Miriam Mason?" Or should they go to Lillian's house?

At Lillian's house no one would see them; but the Masons would see the house, and be enthusiastic about it, and all the town would hear that they had been there. Besides, at the house they could have real drinks, which warmed you up and made you friendly.... Here Lillian glanced thoughtfully at Miriam Mason's profile, beyond and below Bill's profile in the gloom.

On the whole, she concluded, the house was the place to go.

She was impatient for the end of the picture, eager for the lights to flood the theater, as they would for a minute before the second show. The Masons and the Legendres, having come late, would keep their seats, while the seven-to-nine-o'clock audience flocked past them up the aisle. The whole throng would remark the quartet, they could not fail to do so; and to heighten the effect, when the lights came on and the exodus started Lillian meant to lean over and engage Miriam in conversation. She did not know what she would say, exactly, but she would say something — some confidential, laughing little thing that would look well.

But these plans miscarried. In the first place, Miriam did not care to stay for the second show; she whispered to Bill, who whispered to Lillian, that they were leaving.

"You want to stay, don't you?" Bill added. Bill was so dense sometimes.

They all left. They left, moreover, before the picture ended, before the lights came on. On the screen the company was singing the final chorus when Miriam, then Jerry, then Lillian, still struggling with her coat, and Bill, still helping her with it, trailed up the aisle. Beyond the doors they confronted the nine-to-eleven-o'clock spectators, awaiting admission. That was something, Lillian felt; but it wasn't much, especially since she somehow lost the Masons in the crowd.

She and Bill rejoined them on the sidewalk, where they had lingered — for the purpose of saying good-night, it appeared now. Miriam said it at once. Jerry said, "Got your car, Bill? We'll run you home if you haven't."

"We've got it, thanks."

"Oh, but listen!"Lillian cried, in a tone more dismayed than she had intended. She flushed, and stopped. They were listening. They were all listening, and Miriam was eying her enigmatically. She couldn't ask Miriam. She couldn't even ask Jerry.

She turned upon Bill. "Aren't you going to invite these people home for a drink?" she demanded of him. Self consciousness made her manner tart, rebuking.

"Oh, no, really," Jerry said instantly. "Thanks awfully, but —"

"Wish you would," said Bill.

Jerry looked at him, and was silent. He looked to Miriam. They all did.

"We can't, Bill," Miriam said gently. "Not tonight. My mother's visiting me, and we shouldn't have left her even for this long." She put four fingers on Bill's sleeve and held them briefly there. "Some other time we'd love to come, if you'll ask us."

"Sure," Bill said.

"Yes, absolutely!" Jerry was emphatic. "Let's get together soon."

"You bet," Bill said. Somehow Lillian felt excluded. It was time she said something. "Yes indeed!" she said effusively. "We'll have to do that. I'll call you up," she promised Miriam.

Once more the cool dark eyes regarded her. "Do," Miriam said.

"They told us to call them," Lillian reminded Bill now, across the dinner table.

"Yeah. I know. ""Well, then, why don't we?"

"Tonight's a bad night to get anybody," Bill said. "Saturday night. All the boys'll be playing poker some where."

"Do they always? Every Saturday night?"

"Always."

"I think that's so funny," Lillian said. "I mean, why do they have to pick Saturday nights?"

Bill said he didn't know. They always had. It was traditional. He thought about it, for the first time evidently, and half smiled. "As a matter of fact," he said, "it probably dates back to the days when our grandfathers were mill-workers and celebrated pay-day."

"Whose grandfathers were mill-workers?"

"Almost everybody's in town." This was interesting.

"Whose, exactly?"

"Oh — I couldn't begin to name them."

"But for instance? Not yours!"

"Well, no, not mine, as it happens," Bill said, and Lillian thought, "There you are." Not his — and not the grandfathers of any of his equals. It wasn't interesting after all.

"Well, anyway," she resumed, "I think it's the limit. I should think the wives would hate it, being ditched like that every Saturday night. I would, I know. Saturday night of all nights, to have to sit home alone and read, or else give a hen-party or something! That's not my idea of the way to spend the big night of the week, I must say!"

"They don't seem to mind," Bill said.

Lillian's face hardened. "Irene didn't mind," she translated, "—is that it? Well, I'm not Irene."

Bill said nothing, and anything additional that Lillian might have said was averted by the entrance of Mrs. Hoxie with two plates of salad. Mrs. Hoxie's entrances often turned away wrath. Mrs. Hoxie was still new. Her mistress was still anxious to make a good impression.

"You look tired, dear," she informed Bill tenderly now. "Was it a hard day?"

"Why, no. Not specially."

Mrs. Hoxie spoke. "There's no dessert," she announced contentiously.

Lemon pie had been ordered, but Lillian did not bat an eyelash. "There's no dessert," she repeated to Bill. "Just the salad."

Mrs. Hoxie strode out.

"She might take the plates, at least," Bill grunted. "What's the matter with her, anyway? She's getting worse and worse. I didn't think it was possible."

"We need a couple," Lillian said. "That's what's the matter. There's too much work in this house for one lady to do."

"'Lady' is right! She's practically royalty."

Lillian was nettled. "I meant 'woman.'"

It was a recurrent slip. She must remember not to make it again.

She placed her salad plate before her, setting her dinner plate aside. She took up her fork. She remembered not to use a knife, though the heart of lettuce was compact and tough and slippery with pink dressing. She was getting on — she really was. The long postponement of her social première had this consolation. When she thought of these weeks of waiting as weeks of training, they seemed a good thing.

In this moment of meekness, it occurred to her that her stand of a moment ago on the question of Saturday poker parties had not been well taken. You showed your ignorance when you inveighed against the customs and credos of the Hilldale Avenue dwellers of the world. She said to Bill in quite a new tone, "What were we saying? Oh, about the poker. I was kidding about that. I won't really mind if you want to play Saturdays — later on, I mean. I won't care, when I know all the wives and have something to do."

Bill did not thank her. He did not even look his gratitude, and Lillian became plaintive. "You wouldn't," she pouted, red-lipped, "want to play yet, would you? And leave me all alone here, when I'm all alone here all day?"

"No, of course not." She smiled then. "Well, I didn't think so." He smiled faintly back.

"You love me, don't you?" Lillian concluded comfortably.

Bill nodded, somber eyes upon her face. "You're beautiful," he said.

That was settled. Lillian, content, attacked her salad. She mopped up dressing with a loaded fork, and propped her elbow. "By the way," she said conversationally, "I saw Irene again today."

Bill's "Yes?" was polite, and nothing more.

"On State Street," Lillian said. "She was coming out of the music store when I was parking. That Montgomery fellow was with her. Is he sweet on her, or something?"

Bill shrugged. "Why ask me?" his shrug inquired indifferently. He sipped coffee, and replaced the cup in the saucer, moving the spoon with it, fitting it into its precise depression. "I wouldn't know about that," he said, and he said as a casual statement, "I don't even know which Montgomery you mean."

He learned which one. "Stuart Montgomery," Lillian said promptly. "I think. Isn't he the dark one? Sort of cute-looking? Drives a black car with red wire wheels?"

"Yes."

"Well, him. He had his car there, and they got in it. I guess he'd been buying her a present of a victrola — he had one of those portable ones, and she had a big pack of records. So they stowed the stuff in the back seat and off they went. I don't think they saw me — anyway, they didn't let on. Believe me," Lillian averred with sudden relish, "she doesn't see me if she can help it! She knows better, since that day in Deems'!"

"In Deems'?" Bill echoed absently.

Oh, I told you! Don't you remember? Last week it was. Remember I told you I ran smack into her and laughed right in her face?"

"Oh," Bill said. "Yes." He said he remembered now.

"Since then she keeps those funny eyes of hers to herself when I'm around — believe me!"

Bill made no comment upon this. He consumed his coffee, and reached backward to the buffet, where cigarettes reposed in a china box with a china golfer in a green cap on the lid.

"It's queer you don't run into her," Lillian said, chewing. "She's all over the place, it seems to me."

Bill tapped a cigarette on the table. He slid it in his fingers, and watched the fingers. "The fact is," he said, -"I forgot to tell you: I saw her the other day."

An instant's electric stillness followed this avowal. Long though she had anticipated it, Lillian stared wildly, jaws arrested, fork arrested. He had seen her! Bill had seen Irene!

The fork sounded on her plate. "To speak to? When? When was this? Where were you?"

"On the street," Bill said. "On the sidewalk in front of her father's drug store. She came out as I was passing by."

"She would!" Lillian sneered parenthetically. "Well, and what happened? What did you do? Did you speak?"

"We said hello. Naturally."

"Just, ' Hello?'" You said more! What else did you say? What did you say exactly? Tell me!" she besought him feverishly. "Tell me the whole thing!"

Somewhere behind Bill's forehead with the new lines showing in it, behind his eyelids that were down like blinds, there was the memory-picture of the meeting on the side walk. He could see it. He was looking at it even now. "Look at me!" Lillian cried out, not clearly comprehending why.

She must make him show her what he saw.

Bill looked at her. "There's nothing to get all steamed up about," he said. "Honestly, Red. There isn't really much of anything to tell —"

He stopped abruptly, and seemed to reconsider. Reticence left him. He began again, still fingering the thinning unlit cigarette. "We didn't say much," he said. "We didn't stop and talk, if that's what you mean. That is — we only stopped a second. We said, 'Hello,' both at once, and then we both said, 'How are you?' — and Irene put her hand out, so we shook hands. Then I picked up a little package she dropped — and she sort of laughed and said, 'I'll give you three guesses what this is,' and I said, 'Lime drops'. She was always crazy about them," Bill explained a little stiffly, catching Lillian's eve.

"Go on."

"That's about all. Oh, she asked me how I was, again, and I said fine. And then she said, 'Bill, I haven't congratulated you.' And I said, 'Thanks, 'Rene. ' And she said she hoped I was awfully happy-and I said I was."

"You did!" A paean in two words from Lillian. "How?" she demanded avidly. "How did you say it exactly?"

"I don't remember exactly. I guess I just said, 'Yes, I am. '"

"But as if you meant it?"

Bill's glance was level. "Certainly," he said.

"Well, go on. How much longer did you talk to her?" Lillian inquired with returning asperity. "I thought you said you only stopped a second!"

"A minute. It wasn't long."

"And I suppose in the meantime everybody you knew came along and saw you?"

He shook his head. "I don't think so. I didn't see anybody."

"Did you look?"

"Yes."

"Well, go on. What's the rest of it? What did she say when you told her you were happy?"

"She said she was glad."

"Oh, she did, did she?" Lillian laughed shortly. "Big hearted Bessie. And what did you say?"

"Nothing."

"Well, what then???

"That was all. Irene said, 'I suppose we ought not to stand here like this,' and I said I supposed not. And that was that. We said good-bye then, and went on."

"Too bad you couldn't have done that in the first place!" Lillian thought, but she withheld the arraignment. There was a tantrum coming later, when it would fit in when the full enormity of Bill's misprision would be shown him, and all the reasons why he should have walked straight past Irene and never stopped at all would be made plain.

She said instead, on a delayed recollection that now smote her, "Look! When did you say this was?" 'The other day,' you said, didn't you?"

"Monday or Tuesday."

"And will you please explain why you didn't tell me about it before?"

"You didn't ask."

She glared at him. "That's a fine explanation, that is! Is that the best you can do? I want to know why you didn't tell me you saw her!"

"If I said I forgot it," Bill rejoined simply,"you wouldn't believe me."

"I most certainly would not!" He shrugged. "I should have tied a string to my finger."

He was disarming. He was even credible, in his utter imperturbability. Lillian was given pause. She studied his face, squinting slightly for keener discernment. Was he such an actor? Or was it true? Could seeing Irene have meant so little to him?

She said, "How could you have forgotten a thing as important as that?"

"That's just it, you see," said Bill. "It wasn't. You're the one who's making it important."

"You mean it didn't mean anything to you, seeing her again?"

"Not a thing. Why should it?" Lillian's eyes glinted. "Did she know it didn't?"

"She had no reason to think it did, at any rate."

"You didn't say anything that — well, anything complimentary? You didn't say you were glad to see her, or —"

"I've told you what I said."

Lillian thought a minute. "And you left her then? You didn't walk on with her?"

"I did not."

"Where did you go from there?"

"Post Office — where I was headed."

"And where did she go?"

The frayed fabric of Bill's patience gave. "Oh, good God!" he almost shouted. "Is this the third degree, or what? She went on up to the corner and turned left into High Street — she might have gone anywhere! How do I know where she went? I didn't ask her!"

Lillian might have said, "Just how do you know she turned left into High Street?" Remembering the location of Irene's father's drug store, midway of the block, she might have said, "Just how could you know that, unless you stood there staring after her?"

She did not say these things. In her instant umbrage at Bill's exasperation, she missed the inadvertant revelation he had made. All she said was, "Don't you dare to yell at me like that! Shut up!" And all Bill said was, "Gladly."

Early in April, in the society section of the Herald, there was this item:

"Mr. and Mrs. William H. Legendre will be host and hostess to 30 friends at an informal gathering this evening in their new home, 858 Harding Avenue."

It was inadequate, of course. Lillian, at breakfast at nine o'clock that morning — early breakfast, because she had so much to do today — read it somewhat fretfully, in spite of her elation. She had herself typed out and mailed to the Herald a list of the "30 friends," beginning with Mr. and Mrs. John Bartlett and Mr. and Mrs. Jerome Mason, and winding up with the Messrs. Richard Hendricks, Philip Brown, and Stuart and Jock Montgomery, unattached. Where was that list? Miss Carolyn Baynes must have counted the names, else she would not have known that there were thirty; but what had she done with them then? Consigned them to the wastebasket?

It seemed unlikely. They were Miss Baynes's favorite names, editorially speaking. Perhaps, thought Lillian, Miss Baynes was saving the list for tomorrow. Probably that was it. Tomorrow morning there would be a real account of the party. "There'd better be!" This she thought grimly. To date, the Herald had not done well by the second Mrs. Legendre. One more such over sight, and they would see - they would regret it. Mrs. Legendre would cancel her subscription.

She wished the list to be published because of the names that were on it, but almost more because of the names that were not. Her omissions were proud ones. Mr. and Mrs. Frank R. Reynolds (née Jane Legendre). Mr. and Mrs. Byron Legendre, Junior.... It was not enough that she had not invited them, and that they knew it. Renwood must know it. The possibility that Renwood might confuse the knowledge, might make a wrong deduction from the absence of Legendres, did not occur to Lillian, whose mind was full of many things these days.

Sitting at breakfast, with the folded paper propped before her, she contemplated the rectangle of print that was her paragraph, looking steadily at it while she fed. The adjoining paragraphs — the one above, that said that the Girls' Friendly would meet this afternoon, and the one below that announced the birth, at the City Hospital yesterday, of an eight-pound son to a Mr. and Mrs. George Elkhart of School Street — were rectangles of equal size, impertinent, encroaching. With a Chinese fingernail Lillian made four incisions around the real news, and removed it. She would keep it. Entering into the swim tonight, she would keep all future clippings. Mrs. William Legendre does this, Mrs. William Legendre does that. "Among those present was Mrs. William Legendre. "... She must buy a scrapbook.

Lifted out of the paper and placed by itself on the tablecloth, today's paragraph might be short, but it was momentous. She smiled to herself. There it was. "Mr. and Mrs. Legendre will be host and hostess" There it was at last. She had put it over. She could have put it over long ago, she thought in passing, if she had had any sense at all. She might have realized that accusing Bill of being ashamed of her, afraid to introduce her to his friends, would turn the trick. Of course he would deny it — and of course he had. He had denied it instantly and hotly. Then all she had had to say was, "All right! Prove it! Call them up! Call them all up and ask them down here to a party! Then I'll believe you."

Clever, she thought now. Very cagey, that. She really had a good head when she used it. Over the rim of her coffee cup she indulged in a self-congratulatory glance at the buffet mirror. The glance held. She had nice eyes, too.

Clever of her, she thought, coming back to the point again duly, to have made Bill telephone the crowd himself. They couldn't refuse him. They had all accepted then and there. "Friday evening? Why-yes, I think we can, Bill. We'd love to." Lillian had heard them through the upstairs telephone. She wondered: would the acceptances have been unanimous, if the invitations had come from her? The risk involved in finding out had not been worth taking — still, it would be interesting to know.

She shouldn't be sitting here, she said to herself. She must get going. One more cup of coffee — she poured it now from the nickel percolator — one more cigarette with it, and this day of days must begin. She must confer with Mrs. Hoxie, first of all. She viewed the prospect with unprecedented equanimity. Today she felt equal to Mrs. Hoxie, and more than equal. Today she could tell Mrs. Hoxie where to head in.

She must dress then, and drive downtown and do her errands. Flowers for the house, a corsage for herself, ginger ale, lemons, candy — Better write these things down. She kept a stub of pencil in the silver bowl on the table, underneath the artificial fruit. She dug for it, bringing to light a lipstick and a safety pin and the key to the liquor closet and several burnt matches. The stub of pencil had no point, and she rang for Mrs. Hoxie. "Sharpen this," she said, and forebore to say, "please."

On the back of the circular that had been her morning's mail she jotted swiftly, pausing betweentimes, speculating. Should she buy confetti? Confetti and serpentines made things gay. And how about paper hats, pretty ones for the girls, silly ones for the men? They were fun too.

Once officially begun, the day sped along. It was eleven o'clock, and Lillian, returned from shopping, was guiding the roadster to the kitchen door to be unloaded. It was noon, and she was off to the station to meet the twelve-ten train, upon which cakes and patty-shells from LeGatta's in Cleveland were arriving by special messenger. It was one o'clock, and after, and she was thrusting cut flowers into vases. She was pressing the gown she meant to wear.

She was at the telephone, calling Bill; calling Deems' about the ice cream; calling various numbers for Washington Wilkins, to remind him that he was due at her house not later than six o'clock. Washington Wilkins was Renwood's journeyman butler. A window-cleaner by day, by night he opened doors at parties, served refreshments, and shook up cocktails, all for eighty cents an hour, plus ten cents car-fare, plus a laundry charge of forty cents if you wanted his starched white coat. Of course, if you wanted his black alpaca, you could save the forty cents; but at a glance your guests would know your penury.

Three o'clock brought Sally Holtz, with paraphernalia in a rattling box. To Lillian this was as the beginning of the evening. Everything had been made ready now, except herself; and making herself ready was a part of the festivity. With a sense of sheer delight, of excitement free to mount as it would from now on, she relaxed and awaited Sally's ministrations.

"Well?" Sally said, when her wraps were removed and her box was open on Lillian's bed. "What'il it be? What're you going to have? The works, I suppose," she added, for some reason eying her client coldly.

Impervious, Lillian said, "Um-hmm. Everything."

"Shampoo first?"

"Oh, heavens, no! No shampoo. You know how my hair acts!"

"Well, you said, ' Everything,' didn't you? You don't need to bite my head off!"

Clearly, Sally was not in a very good mood. "What time's this wonderful party of yours supposed to be?" she inquired, although she had been told.

"At eight."

"I thought it must be in about two minutes — as nervous as you are."

"Who's nervous?" Sally's lip curled. "Listen, will you," she said, aside. In any mood, however, Sally was a conscientious artisan. She had once, and knowingly, beautified a rival for a rendezvous with her own Joe Gratz — literally without harming a hair of the hussy's head. She did her dutiful best for Lillian now, massaging her face first of all, with creamy slaps only a little vicious. She removed the cream, and applied a series of hot towels only a little too hot. She removed the final towel and exclaimed,"Tch!"

"What?"Lillian moaned.

"This hicky on your chin here. You would," said Sally, "crop out with that, just when you want to look nice! Isn't it always the way, though? I never knew it to fail."

"What hicky?" Lillian was indignant. "You mean that tiny little wee bit of a red spot-like a pin-prick or something?"

"It don't look like a pin-prick to me," said Sally from above. She looked again. "Tch! Too bad."

She felt better. A little retribution went a long way with Sally. It was now possible for her to interrogate Lillian about the party, her appetite for the details overcoming her unwillingness to give the hostess-to-be, who was already smug enough, goodness knew, that satisfaction. Spreading a paste like mayonnaise over Lillian's face and the front of her throat, leaving it there to dry and harden and craze in a lattice of tiny lines, she said, "Who-all's coming tonight, besides the ones you told me?" and saw Lillian's glad fingers, counting them off.

"Stuart Montgomery, eh," Sally echoed at the end. She stretched a strip of cloth under Lillian's chin and up the sides of her head and tied it tightly on top, like a toothache-band in a comic picture. "Isn't he the one who's running around with Irene all the time? Sure he is. I'm surprised you're having him."

Lillian's lips from the mayonnaise mask spoke carefully. "Why not? Belongs to the crowd."

"But does Bill like him?"

"Um-hmm. Sure."

"I thought maybe he didn't," Sally said. "Any more, I mean. ... Here, lie still!" she added, timing the command with accuracy. "And don't try to talk. You'll spoil your face."

Lillian subsided, her protests perforce confined to an irate mutter that sounded like, "Craziest thing I ever heard in my life." Sally smiled, unseen. She thought, "It got a rise, though, didn't it?" It had served its purpose. Covering Lillian's closed eyelids with bits of cotton soaked in lotion, Sally winked her own right eye jocosely. Her good humor was now quite restored.

"I'll start your manicure, Lil," she said almost fondly, "while that's drying."

There was the manicure and the application of two coats of medium polish and one coat of light. There was the removal of the dried egg, and the substitution of a compound of lettuce and almonds. There was a call to the kitchen for pieces of ice. The call being unanswered, Sally went down for the ice, while Lillian sat and smoked, and rejoiced to perceive that it was four-thirty already.

Sally was gone for the ice an unconscionable time.

"Mrs. Hoxie showed me the cakes," she explained, returning finally. "And the jellied salads. They turned out fine, didn't they? Cute, the way she's got the slices of olives and pimentoes in there, like eyes and eyebrows looking up at you. I suppose the dressing'll hide 'em, though," Sally said, and continued, "Mrs. Hoxie wouldn't give me but this one little piece of ice. She said there was a hundred and twenty-five pounds of ice in the ice box, but none to spare with all the drinking she supposed was going to be done around here tonight."

"She said it!" Lillian affirmed with enthusiasm.

"She tells me you're not going to have any kind of music, after all. I thought you were going to have a six piece orchestra from Cleveland."

"We were, but we decided not to," Lillian said, as matter-of-factly as if there had been no controversy, no pleas, no threats, no tears. "You see, it would have meant that we were giving a dance, really — instead of just having some of the crowd come in. We'd have had to ask a lot more people, and we didn't want to. We didn't want any more," Lillian repeated, enjoying the arbitrary sound of this.

"Oh, I see," said Sally. "You didn't want any more."

"No. We decided thirty was enough, for a small party. This isn't our real housewarming, of course," Lillian added. "We'll have that a little later on."

"Oh, you will." Sally nodded gravely, with pursed lips. "Well," she said, "when you do, get somebody else to doll you up."

"Why? What's the matter with you?"

"The matter with me," said Sally crisply, "is, I'm losing my mind. What's more, I won't be here. I'm going to retire from business. I'm going to marry the Prince of Wales and give housewarmings in the palace, just small parties — just the Queen of Romania and the Holy Ghost and some of the crowd. So now you know. And now," concluded Sally, "will you please stick your swelled head back here on this pillow again while I ice your face?"

Bill got home at a quarter after five. The front door shook the house, announcing him, and upstairs and down stairs the electricity blinked once with the turning on of the player piano. Formerly Bill had shouted,"Hey!" from the hall when he came home, but he no longer did. It had been the left-over habit of another era, and once he had shouted, "Hey, 'Rene!" through this house — a catastrophe.

Sally was just leaving. To the downstairs music, and in perfect time — Sally had rhythm, and silver cups from the Cloverleaf Ballroom to prove it — she accepted her money, counted it, folded it, slipped it into her handbag, said "Thanks for the tip," morosely, took up her box and stepped to the door. There she paused and glanced back.

"Well, so long. I suppose I'll be seeing you."

Lillian was binding her new coiffure with hairpins and a veil. There were hairpins in her mouth. "So long," she said through them. "Thanks a lot, Sal."

"Oh, don't mention it."

"I'll call you tomorrow, and tell you all about the party."

"Goody, goody, goody," Sally said to the hall outside.

Alone, Lillian remained before the mirror a little longer. Her hands completed their task and fell, and the painted fingertips caught on the rim of the dressing-table and clung there. She looked down at the little clock. Five twenty.

Two hours and forty minutes more, and nothing to do but bathe and dress and have a bite to eat if she could eat. She probably couldn't, and she didn't want to take the time; but Bill, of course, would insist on a meal of some sort. He would even have an appetite, as usual. Men were so funny.

Leaning forward a little, she studied Sally's handiwork, going over it optically, grading it point by point. Eyebrows very good. Eyelashes excellent — that eyelash curler was a great invention, probably the greatest since the lipstick, or since rouge. She liked her eyelids too, shadowed like that with a purple-bronze pigment; and her skin, save for the pin-prick that a beauty spot would cover, had never looked better. There was no doubt about it: Sally knew her business. This was a gorgeous job, this face. Now if it only lasted through the evening — It must. She would make it last. She wouldn't put her hands to it, she wouldn't touch it. Her bath would be a sponge bath, not a steamy one.

In the mirror she saw the chosen evening gown, the Patou copy in aquamarine-blue satin, hanging on the closet door on wooden shoulders. It should be spread out across her bed. The aquamarine-blue slippers with gold heels— $ 28.50 and $ 2.00 extra for dyeing — should be taken down from the closet shelf and out of their tissue paper, and set side by side nearby. The coq-feather fan that she might or might not carry, the hose that she would wear if she wore any, the shaped, exquisite bits of lace and ribbon — these should be assembled and disposed conveniently. On a night like this, you wished you had a lady's-maid: a French one named Germaine, like the one in Greta Garbo's picture, or a white-capped one named Victoria. "Victoria, my slippers!" The command rapped in Lillian's mind, and her eyes were imperious and they stayed so. She would have a lady's-maid some day. Some day she would. Some day her Patou gowns would be originals, not copies.

The piano was still pounding when she went downstairs, having laid out tonight's raiment for herself. In her temporary costume of brown veil with dangling ends, blue velvet robe and old black pumps, bare-legged, she descended to the living-room to see what Bill was doing. She was distressed to find him calmly reading — or calmly sitting there, with the folded evening paper on his knees.

"Bill!" she expostulated. "For heaven's sake! Do you know what time it is?"

"Hullo," he greeted her. "It's early, isn't it?"

"What under the sun are you doing?"

Bill had been thinking. He looked oddly guilty. "Nothing," he said. "Just playing a couple of tunes. Is there something I ought to be doing?"

There was not; but his inactivity, in such an hour, was a damper, somehow. "Plenty of things," said Lillian, and she discovered one. "You've been opening windows again! And who turned that gas-log out? What do you want to do — freeze your company to death?"

"It was sweltering in here."

"No, it wasn't," Lillian said. "It was just nice. Other people aren't such fresh-air fiends as you are."

She left him closing the windows, and moved into the dining-room with its table laden with towers of plates and platoons of forks and glasses. There were salted almonds in a silver dish and she ate an almond and took a chocolate from another dish, but put it back again. She brushed her finger-tips on her robe and crossed to the dining room windows and raised the drawn green shades part way. She would lower them again later, before eight o'clock; in the meantime it would be a pity not to let Mrs. Horace Coulter, from behind her Brussels curtains, view the table.

She returned to the living-room after a detour into the kitchen and the pantry, both of which seemed simultaneously full of Mrs. Hoxie. Everything was going well, Lillian told Bill. Did he want something to eat? Oh, dear. Well, what? Would crackers and milk do? They would have to eat off a card-table. There was a job for him — he could set up a card-table somewhere and find a cloth to go on it, and put some newspapers underneath to catch any crumbs that might fall. Would he like some dried beef, too? There was probably a jar of it. She'd look. She'd look in a minute, when she got these flowers fixed right. She hadn't had time this afternoon to really arrange them — she'd just poked them any old way into the vase— Ouch! Damn it! Thorns. ... What time was it now? Well, what time ought Bill to start mixing the cocktails? Oh, not till then? But he'd be dressed up then! Still, he could put an apron on, couldn't he. He could let Washington Wilkins do the mixing, while he advised. Where was Washington Wilkins, by the way? Wasn't it six o'clock? What time had Bill said it was, again?

"Two minutes of," Bill repeated.

He sauntered towards her as he spoke, leisurely but purposeful. He captured both her darting hands and brought them down to her sides and released them. By her shoulders he faced her about and pushed her gently into a chair. "There," he said. "Now you're going to rest a minute, and smoke a cigarette. You're absolutely jittering, did you know it?"

She admitted it readily, since he was sympathetic, sweet to her. She smiled at him. "Well, of course! Do you blame me? It's different for you-you know all these people. But it's my coming-out party-and my wedding reception and everything, all in one!"

Bill nodded. "And it's going to be fine," he stated, as if maintaining this against argument. "Everything's going to be fine. Don't you worry."

"I'm not worrying," Lillian said in some surprise. "Did you think I was worrying? What about? About meeting them all, you mean?"

"I thought maybe."

"Why should I worry about that?" she asked him, searching his face with her eyes. "Is it going to be so hard to meet them? What do you mean? Do you mean you think they won't be nice to me?"

"Nothing of the sort!" Bill said. "Of course they'll be nice to you. Why shouldn't they be?" He sounded wroth, but not with her. He bent and kissed her on the cheek. "They'll like you a lot," he said. "And — I'll be very proud."

"Careful of my face! It's all made up. ""It's grand," Bill said. "It's a grand face."

He was not so sympathetic, not so sweet, about the Patou dress. This was somewhat later. They had had their milk and crackers, they had put everything away, and Lillian had driven Bill upstairs. "You know how long it takes you to shave! And it's better to be ready. Some body might come early, you can't tell."

He was removing his tie in the bedroom, tugging at the knot, when he noticed the dress on the bed. His fingers slackened, and he lowered his chin to look.

"Red," he said, over his shoulder. Lillian was back at the dressing-table.

"What?"

"You're n— Is this the dress you're going to wear? And the fan and everything?"

"The dress, yes," said Lillian. "I don't know about the fan."

"I don't know about the dress," said Bill. "Are you sure about it?"

"What's the matter with it?"

"Maybe I'm wrong. But isn't it a little too elaborate?"

"If you mean it hasn't any back to it," Lillian said, "it hasn't. But aside from that it isn't elaborate at all, that I can see. It's perfectly plain. It's all line and color," she supplemented, recalling the saleswoman's phrase.

"Elaborate for this particular party," Bill explained. "We said, "informal, you know. We didn't even say it was a party — we just told them to come in. I'm afraid the other girls won't think to wear evening dresses, Red."

"Well, they should!" Lillian cried. It had taken her mind but a fraction of a second to race through her wardrobe and to return, twice resolute, to the starting point. "I don't care if they don't — they ought to!" she continued hotly. "Other places, people wear evening dresses in the evening — no matter what! They wear them just to have dinner alone at home! Why, in New York —"

"But they don't here," Bill said patiently, when she had finished.

Her eyes hated him. "Oh, you! You're always taking the joy out of life!"

She wouldn't let him, she thought, seeing him shrug and turn away. She wouldn't listen to him. She would wear what she wanted to wear tonight — she didn't care what he said. She looked to the aquamarine-blue dress for reassurance, and found it. The men would approve, any way, if the women didn't.

CHAPTER THIRTEEN

Always she was to remember that first party — that first and last — as a sequence of animated pictures, ordered but disconnected, like excerpts taken from a film to advertise it. There was the picture of the headlights of the cars arriving. Two headlights, two more head lights, then two more.... All the cars arrived in a procession: a coincidence that might have been fortuitous if they had been on time. They were not on time. They were all twenty-five or twenty-six minutes late.

"Dinner party somewhere, I imagine," Bill answered when Lillian asked.

Only Stuart Montgomery, Irene's admirer, was later than the rest. He appeared at a little after nine, and someone said, "Isn't he wonderful?" and someone else said, "Two blocks in under an hour. It's a record," and every one laughed a little and several people glanced at Bill and two or three of them changed the subject smoothly.

There was the picture of the hall when they first came. From the living-room, where Lillian stood beside Bill and nudged him urgently — unconsciously, convulsively, in the stage-fright of this moment — she saw them all, beyond the doorway. They seemed a multitude. The hall was full of them, and of their forward trooping, and of their voices finishing light things they had been saying. Cold air rushed in with them; and from behind them somewhere Washington Wilkins made and remade obsequious suggestions. If the gentlemen would kindly rest their coats at the end of the passage, please; and if the ladies would please kindly walk upstairs?

There was the great Mrs. Johnny Bartlett in the hall. There was a passing glimpse of her, and always afterward that glimpse was a photograph superimposed on the scene as a whole. "There's Louise Bartlett!" Lillian breathed ecstatically, pressing Bill's arm again. She had never really believed that Louise would come.

The ladies were long upstairs. For many minutes, the living-room was dark with men — young men in business suits — surrounding Lillian in all her glory. This was a picture rather like a musical comedy tableau. Here was the star, supported by the male chorus. Lillian thought of the simile, and thought it deserving of utterance. "I feel like a leading lady with a lot of chorus men!" she laughed to them — presently, after a moment or two, when she knew them well enough.

Bill had presented them one by one as they entered. He had stood there, very erect and grave and dignified, and a little forbidding, saying, "My wife," or "This is Lillian" to them. To all but one of them, Lillian had said, "How do you do?" — distinctly, in separate syllables, as their own Miriam Mason said it. Only once, during the seventeen or eighteen introductions, did her tongue slip, and she covered that lapse quick-wittedly. "Pleased to meet you," she had begun to say, but she changed it to, "Please — I didn't get the name?"

She knew all the names, of course, by heart; and all the faces. Here was Phil Browne, who had gone through grammar school a grade ahead of her. "How do you do, Mr. Browne?" Here was Harry Quirk, with whom for years she had exchanged prolonged half-smiling glances on the street. "How do you do, Mr. Quirk?" Here was Gordon Saunders, who had been the high school football captain and her hero when she was thirteen. She had written him a letter in purple ink on lavender paper, once. "Please — I didn't get the name?"

Here was Jerry Mason. Jerry she had met, and she hailed him like the old friend that, comparatively, he seemed. "Jer-ry!" she carolled. "How are you? It's grand to see you again! Where have you been keeping yourself — you and Miriam?"

She had regained composure. She felt no stage-fright now — there was no occasion for stage-fright when your audience was strictly stag, and when you had red hair and no back to your dress. Men were all alike, she thought. These were more mannerly, less bold, than other men who had admired her, but the difference was a surface thing. The admiration was the same. Their eyes were on her, all their eyes were on her, weren't they?

They were. It was enough. For them she became the coquette of the sidewalk groups of former days, the bright witch of the old steamboat excursions. She was lively. She was provocative. She was facetious, even roguish. She mentioned Irene right away.

"I know you're all friends of Bill's "ex"," she said to them gaily. "But I'm broad-minded — I won't hold it against you!"

She sparkled, saying this, and her smile went circulating, collecting due responsive smiles from them. "Well, that's good, one young man rejoined amiably. Only Bill failed to enter into the spirit of the thing. Lillian giggled outright at Bill's expression. "Look!" she exclaimed, pointing at him. "Look at Bill! He thinks I've opened my mouth and put my foot in it!"

Here the picture blurred somewhat, and the sound accompaniment became confused, as if the retrospective reel was speeded up. She remembered that Bill said some thing to Washington about drinks, and that he himself left the room to see about them. She remembered wondering why everybody didn't sit down, and inquiring why; and she thought she remembered adding some humorous line, some wisecrack — she thought perhaps it was, "The seats are free!" She remembered a pause; then Jerry Mason had held a chair for her, saying, "Won't you, Mrs. Legendre?" And she had said, "I don't mind if I do."

They were all seated when Bill reappeared with Washington Wilkins and drinks on a tray. Everybody took a cocktail or a highball, and there was another of the puzzling little pauses that seemed to be peculiar to this crowd. What were they waiting for now? Were they thinking up toasts to the bride and groom? Just as Lillian fluttered inwardly, certain that that was it, Bill spoiled it all. "Well, over the river," he suddenly said, and everyone looked relieved and drank. Bill drank straight whiskey from a highball glass.

Then the ladies were heard on the stairs, their casual voices floating. Lillian spilled her cocktail, setting it somewhere, anywhere, as she rose; hours later she found the dried splash down the side of her gown. She knew a return of panic, and she started forward - she must be near Bill. No, near the door, where Bill would join her. She signalled him with frantic eyes and saw him put his glass down. She hurried across to the door, to the very sill.

It was too far. She had arrived too soon, so that she witnessed in a flash a pantomime never intended for her. On a step midway of the staircase Louise Bartlett, leading the feminine line, had halted, halting them all. They were to observe the wall paper. As Lillian looked, Mrs. Bartlett indicated for her followers a large bouquet of blue wall-paper roses and cerise ones. Mrs. Bartlett then covered her eyes with a slim white hand.

There was that picture, always afterward.

There were the snapshots of the dresses, coming singly through the door. Louise Bartlett's black net dress with long tight sleeves. Connie Quirk's brown velvet, with cuffs and collar of coffee-colored lace. Jean Saunders's dull green silk-crêpe with a cape around the shoulders. Peggy Stone's black chiffon.... Bill had been right. Lillian's was the only evening gown in her living-room, and this was Renwood, and New York was infinitely far away and foreign. Who knew what they wore there, anyway? Not she, who had been there once to Mrs. Bartlett's hundred times.

"You dropped your fan, Mrs. Legendre," a man behind her said.

She had thrown it, but she took it, stammering her thanks. She tried to hide it in the full folds of her skirt.

"What a pretty fan," said Mrs. Bartlett softly.

Mrs. Bartlett had green shining eyes with lazy fringes. She had a long, grown-out black bob, a cloud of ringlets caught back from her face by the delicate barettes of her small ears. She had a liquid voice, cool and murmurous. Everybody listened to it, everybody always made for it a little silence like a groove through which it slid.

"Lovely," Mrs. Bartlett said. She motioned toward the fan. "May I see it, Mrs. Legendre? I haven't seen one for so long."

There was that.

The ensuing hour or more was all one picture of the living-room with people sitting in it. It was a talkie rather than a movie. They just sat. They did not dance —the best dance music on the radio, the newest rolls and records, did not tempt them. Lillian had Washington Wilkins clear a square of floor, and you would have thought that they would take that hint. But no — they didn't. They were polite, perhaps: they would not start until she started. Or they were shy; no one would start till someone else did. She tried to catch Bill's eye across the room, but Bill was talking. She turned to Jock Montgomery beside her.

"Listen," she said, and he inclined his head to the confidential angle of hers. "Don't these people like to dance, or what's the matter?"

Mr. Montgomery considered the room from under his eyebrows. "Well, yes, sometimes," he said. "But they like to talk."

"But they can talk any time!"

"Well, yes, that's true."

"I'd like to get this party going," Lillian said anxiously.

"But it's going very nicely," Mr. Montgomery demurred, "don't you think?"

Maybe it was, she thought dubiously. Maybe it was from their standpoint. It wasn't from hers. This wasn't her idea of a party, of a gay and brilliant gathering — not by a long shot. This was just talk, talk, talk. Just sitting like bumps on logs, conversing. Brilliant it might be, but it wasn't gay. They didn't even raise their voices high above the music. They didn't even shout and interrupt.

Mingled with her concern and perplexity, there was a kind of wistfulness. She had never, she thought, seen anything like these people. They had had — she counted back — three rounds of drinks. At least, they had been offered three; it was their fault if they'd missed out. On three rounds of strong stimulants, any party she had ever known or heard of would by this time have been going, and going like mad. "Looping," the word was. Couples would have been dancing — one couple would have been clowning, doing a Bowery dance or something comical like that. Somebody would be turning on the radio while the piano was playing, or the piano while the victrola was playing, or both, or all three; and you wouldn't be able to hear yourself think. Glasses would have been broken — always a jolly sign. One of the men would have put on a girl's hat, and maybe her coat, if he could get into it, and the girl would be laughing and chasing him all around. Couples would be missing, by this time. A group at the piano would be singing through it all, harmonizing, with their faces red and very serious, and with highball glasses in their hands; and on the piano a girl would be sitting, swinging her legs, and leading the songs. That would be Sally. Lillian could just see her.

Well, this was different. These were society people, and this was their kind of party — naturally, it would be as different as day was from night. Look at Louise Bartlett, for example; and look at Sally. Look at these young men who sat about with coats and vests on, and who leaped to light your cigarette; and having looked at them, think of Joe Gratz and George Beauvais and Bones Jones, and just think of Tuffy Lascari.

No. There was nothing alarming in the decorum of this party. Because these guests didn't cut capers like garage-mechanics and hairdressers at play, she need not feel that they were not enjoying themselves. They were. Hadn't Jock Montgomery said they were? This was just their Hilldale Avenue way. She understood now. The town was wrong. The town believed that Hilldale Avenue parties were as wild as wild. There was a laugh for you! They ought to see one.

She understood, and if she was a little disappointed, that was her fault, that could only be a lack of taste in her. She would learn to like this sort of party, she supposed. She would learn, in time, to get a kick out of this talk, which must surely be both wise and witty. She thought that she might even get a kick out of it now, on this first try, if she only knew what it was about. It didn't sound too highbrow — that wasn't the trouble with it, although it might have been. The trouble was that they talked about places that she hadn't seen yet, things she hadn't done, people she hadn't met. They reminisced of parties and excursions in the past. "Bill, do you remember—?"

Bill remembered. Irene would have remembered too.

They had familiar little flippancies, jocular allusions, that were quite meaningless to Lillian. She laughed, but she did not know why, and once or twice they looked at her as if they didn't, either; and once or twice their laughter died before hers. When she failed to laugh she felt that she seemed disapproving. It was hard to know just what to do.

They weren't very polite, she thought at last, for all their breeding. She was their hostess, and they left her out. Didn't they realize, didn't Louise, who led the conversation, realize that she took no part in it because she could not? Topics like golf and tennis, winter resorts, roulette, horse races called the Preakness and the Kentucky Derby, betting, the stock market, astrology and horoscopes, the stadium at Ohio State, and Somebody Hemingway's novel — what could she say of these, or of their endless reminiscences, save, "Yes!" when yes was indicated, or, "Ha-ha! That's a scream!"

Was it because she knew so little that they never seemed to hit on anything she knew and could discuss? Or — she began wondering — was this intentional? Were they deliberately leaving her out, showing her up? She thought they were, she thought they weren't. She couldn't decide. Sometimes her sense of her own conversational limitations refuted the suspicion, for a time. After all, she thought, what subjects could she talk about if Louise or someone were to introduce them? Renwood. The movies. Shorthand and typewriting! A little about New York, a little about Atlantic City. ... The range was far from wide. It was no wonder that they missed it. They could miss it without trying, and doubtless did.

They were the intelligentsia: she did not forget that. If they had really meant to talk over her head, she told herself, they could have talked so far over it, it wouldn't have been funny. Athletics and resorts and gambling weren't by any means the best they could have done or the worst, rather. Even books were not. She read a lot of books herself. "Has anybody read ' Ex-Model?" she inquired at large, but no one answered. Evidently no one had.

"It isn't very good," she muttered, reddening.

Often they did not seem to hear her when she spoke. Her voice got lost among the surer voices. It was curious that Bill, who was way off across the room, was frequently the only one to catch it, to reply to it, to smile appreciation and encouragement. Perhaps his ear was more accustomed - maybe that was it. Or maybe not.

Sometimes he helped her. Things she could not know about — things like their reminiscences — he would some times explain, hearing her vague, punctilious mirth. While the others listened patiently, or didn't listen, while they lit fresh cigarettes and gazed around the room, he would recount the incident that clarified the jest for her. "This was one weekend, Red — we were all up at Bedford Springs, you see, and Sunday morning—"

When he finished they would take the conversation back again, taking him with it. "Oh, Bill, that reminds me! Remember Hugo Davis? Tell Bill about poor Hugo, somebody!" Forgetting her again.

She suffered, but she learned, sitting hearkening and absorbing on the sidelines of her own bridal reception. The part of her mind that always learned worked hard. It was a part detached, impersonal, unaware of her suffering — a sort of mental ear-trumpet to catch things. It caught pronunciations. It caught new words, four-dollar words, and some idea of how to use them. "Provincial" for "small-town." "Banal" for "ordinary." "Gourmet" — definition not given, but Louise was one. Somebody was "repressed" and somebody had "delusions of grandeur and Connie Quirk was accused of a "father fixation." "Frightfully" sounded more intellectual than "awfully", and "revolting" was a lovely word. You accented the "ex" in "exquisite". You said "if I were." When somebody held a match to light your cigarette, you didn't blow the match out afterward. You let him blow it. When somebody sneezed you didn't say, "God bless you," in society. Bad luck or no bad luck, you let it go.

She learned these things and many more by listening and observing; and by asking she learned one or two highly important things. She said to Jock Montgomery, tapping his knee to get his attention, "Look. Loui— Mrs. Bartlett goes to New York City all the time, doesn't she?"

Mr. Montgomery said yes, Louise went very often. "What hotel does she stay at, do you know?"

He didn't know. "I'll find out," he said matter-of factly. "Louise—"

"No!" Lillian begged in a whisper, but it was too late. Louise's head had turned. Louise's green eyes, noncommittally flicking the bare arms and neck and the burgeoning purple orchids of her hostess on the way, had come to rest inquiringly on Jock.

"Where do you stay in New York? What hotel?"

Thank goodness, Lillian thought, he hadn't said that she had asked. And thank goodness Louise didn't say, "Who wants to know?" It was between them, and she breathed again. She looked away, pretending not to hear.

The hotel had an unfamiliar name — a name in French. Louise supplied it glibly, with what Lillian could not guess was a strong New England finishing-school accent. "Whereabouts is it?" the helpful Mr. Montgomery pursued, and Louise told him. She added that she always stopped there: that she had for years. "I adore it. The most divine food, of course, and slews of atmosphere. It's full of celebrities—"

She mentioned a singer, a playwright, a motion picture actress and a gentleman pugilist who lived there. "It's too amusing, really," she concluded.

"What was the name of that, again?" Lillian breathed to Jock when she could.

He repeated it for her. "How do you spell it?"

He spelled it. Lillian was unaware that her lips moved, memorizing it.

"I just wondered," she said indifferently at the end.

She learned, also by asking, something about the perfume that Mrs. Noel Currier had on a chiffon handkerchief. Mrs. Currier, a small blonde with a snobbish nose and hair as brightly gold as new gold money, sat just beyond Mr. Montgomery. Lillian said, "That's frightfully nice perfumery, Mrs. Currier. I've been smelling it all evening. What is it?"

She heard herself with pride, for this was progress. She would have said "awfully nice" an hour ago.

"It's exquisite," she added, for good measure. Mrs. Currier was glad she liked it. "I'd like to get some. What's the name of it?"

Mrs. Currier smiled a little. "It hasn't any name," she said. "It's a blend, you see. It's three different perfumes mixed."

"Oh, is it?" Lillian said with interest. The idea was new to her, and though she felt it was a good one, the point of it escaped her altogether. "I'll have to do that," she observed, and continued innocently, "What three perfumes? And how much-a third of each?"

It was a mistake. She saw that instantly. Mrs. Currier's azure eyes upon her were incredulous at first, and then they were indulgently amused.

"I mean — if you wouldn't mind telling me," Lillian faltered.

"My dear," Mrs. Currier said, "I'm so sorry. It's my own prescription, you see. I'm afraid I should mind telling my best friend."

One lived and learned.

The party in its second hour split up, to Lillian's dismay. The men deserted — gradually they drifted off and out, to congregate in the room at the end of the hall that was called Bill's study because a desk of his and two great slippery leather chairs and all his golfer's magazines were in it. Lillian watched the exodus with a sinking heart, inevitable though she thought it. "I was afraid of this," she kept saying to herself mechanically. "I was afraid of this."

Well, there they were. Bill, and Jock Montgomery, so nice — and all the men. There they went, and here, among these formidable, these remote, these suave cool Hilldale Avenue girls, they left her. Oh, they mustn't! Stop them! "Bill!" her mind moaned after him. "Bill, you stay! Stick with me!" But only her mind moaned. Bill did not hear.

In time to come, remembering that desperate unease, she would believe that it had been a premonition. She did not know now what it was. She said to Jock Montgomery, when she felt him start to rise, "Oh, now, don't you go! Please! I won't have anyone to talk to!" That was it, she thought. Who would she talk to, and who turn to now?

It was too bad that Louise Bartlett overheard. All evening Louise had failed to hear the things she said — it was as strange as it was hapless that this suppliant under tone of Lillian's to Jock Montgomery reached her. "But you have us, Mrs. Legendre," Louise's purling voice said. "Won't you talk to us a little while? I'm sure the boys won't be so very long."

"Just try and talk to you!" Lillian thought with sudden anger. But outwardly she was craven, flushing wretchedly, stammering that that would be nice, that she would like that.

"Run along, Jock," Mrs. Bartlett murmured. "We really don't need you, after all."

"I guess I'll have to," Jock said to Lillian. "Who am I to sit in on a sorority meeting?"

Then they were all gone, all the men. This was another picture of the living room, with vacant chairs and chairs with dresses in them. Around the spot of floor that had been cleared in case of dancing there was an irregular border of silk slippers with high heels. Black silk. Brown satin. Black again. Beige. Gray. ... Lillian's were the only vivid slippers. They looked big. She drew them in, and smoothed and stretched her skirt down.

Louise saw her. Louise saw and heard everything she cared to see and hear: that was becoming evident enough. "We owe you an apology, Mrs. Legendre," Louise said pleasantly, "for not having dressed. Do forgive us, won't you? It's all Bill's fault, of course. The wretch
pretended that this was to be informal!"

Louise's little smile remarked the vagaries of men.

"We're dreadfully sorry, really," she continued. "We ought to have known — in fact, I did know! I said to the girls, 'I'm perfectly sure Mrs. Legendre will be dressed!' Don't you remember my saying that?" Louise appealed to them all.

§§

"And I was right," Louise sighed. "And here we all are in our little Mother Hubbards! And our hostess so —so soignée! It's too sad for us, really."

She smiled again, and Lillian smirked back uncertainly. Soignée. Soignée. What did it mean? Was it nice, or wasn't it? All these things Louise was saying — were they flattering, or insulting? She didn't know. She wasn't sure. How could you tell?

They spoke of her house next. Louise spoke of it. "I adore your house, Mrs. Legendre. It's fascinating — so colorful. Tell me, did you do it all yourself?"

"Well, yes, I did."

"Not really!" Louise said. "All of it?" Her green eyes, widened slightly, made a little circuit of the room. "My dear, how could you?... Unless you've had experience," she supplemented blandly. "Perhaps you've studied interior decorating, Mrs. Legendre?"

"No, I nev— no."

"I thought you might have," Louise said, "before you were married. So many young girls nowadays take it up, as a sort of stop-gap-after all, life is very dull if one doesn't do something, isn't it? But of course, there are all sorts of other things that one can do," Louise observed.

She gestured with a cigarette in a short holder. "That Chinese corner is particularly interesting, I think. Have you been to China, Mrs. Legendre?"

"Who, me?" Lillian said involuntarily. "Why, no. No, I haven't."

"But wherever did you find all those enchanting objèts d'art? Such unusual ones? The incense burner-and the Buddha?"

"Why — I don't know, I—"

Louise continued to admire the Chinese corner with her eyes. "A breath of the Orient," she murmured, "here in Renwood! I do think that's so nice. Renwood needs more of that sort of thing. It's really terribly insular, Renwood. Don't you find it so, Mrs. Legendre?"

Lillian found it so. "Yes, I do. It certainly is. It it's terrible that way."

"The people," Louise sighed. "The people are so bigoted, don't you feel they are? So really insufferably dogmatic?"

Lillian felt that they were. They must be. She said, "Aren't they." But it was not enough. Louise, she saw, expected her to say more. Louise was waiting for her to say more than simply, "Aren't they." ... Lillian heard herself emit a nervous hiss of laughter. "And how!" she said.

"Exactly," said Louise.

So it went on. Louise talked, and deferred to her, and waited; and Lillian replied. She must reply. The room kept still for her, absolutely still, as it did for Louise. All the bright, polite eyes in the room came swarming toward her. How did she like the Country Club? She had been out there, of course? Did she like the clubhouse? Had she walked over the links? She played golf, did she not? Oh, really, no? Hadn't she ever? But surely she had played Tom Thumb golf, on one of those cunning courses — the one at Avalon Park, or the one back of the freight station? But surely!

So it went on, and on. Lillian thought it would never stop. This was what she had wanted, she reminded her self — vainly; this was attention, and a chance to talk. These were simple topics, local, chosen specially for her. This was interest and assistance from Louise. Why should it torture her, why should it numb her lips and dry her throat, and force the terrible slow scarlet up her face? Why should she remember, every time Louise spoke sweetly, the little scene on the staircase, the remark about the fan? Why should she recall all the wrong things about Louise — that Louise was Irene's great friend, that Bill had never liked her, that many people did not like Louise and that they said that she was cruel, that she was hateful, that mercy was not in her?

Louise, waiting again. The bright, polite eyes coming swarming. "Wh-what?" Lillian queried. "I didn't g— I didn't hear that."

"I was saying," said Louise, "that you ought to take some lessons at the Club when the season opens. From the pro, you know. The golf professional. He's very good."

"Is that so?"

"He used to be a caddy," Louise said. "I'm sure you'd like him."

"In other words, we're both bums," Lillian thought.

She knew, she understood, then and thereafter. Her mind made swift and shattering translations. She could not delude herself, she could no longer, with the thin veil of Louise's subtlety, hide from herself Louise's meanings. Now she knew what all this was — deep in her mind she must have known it from the start, to know it so well now, to see it with such clarity. They were kidding her, these girls. Of course. Of course. They were giving her a ride. They were making fun of her, making a perfect fool of her, laughing at her behind the bright polite glaze of their eyes. They were collecting ludicrous quotations and descriptions, to take away with them; enough to last them for a long time. They were Irene's great friends, and this was sport and it was vengeance. So they had come. Now she knew well why they had come.

This was what happened, then. This was what you got. You were the red-headed Andrews girl from Renwood Falls, from the railroad crossing, and you stole a rich husband and bought a big house, and a Chinese Buddha, and a naked dress, and you tried to crash Society — and this was what you got. Never mind what you expected, hoped for. This was what you got. This was what Society did to you, to make you understand. You couldn't crash it in a million years.

All right. She understood. They needn't keep on telling her. "All right, all right," she thought monotonously. "All right. I get you." They could quit now. They could lay off. Louise could save her precious breath. They could go home now, any time. They could go jump in the river. ...

"Go on away," she thought. "Go on. You've done your stuff. Why don't you go?" And suddenly, gritting her teeth, she thought, "Get the hell out of here!" But she said nothing.

It was Louise who suggested their departure, ultimately. Louise grew weary of the little game. She let a pause fall, and her face made a controlled contortion, not entirely imperceptible: Louise was yawning.

"Where are the boys, I wonder!" she exclaimed brightly then. "They've been gone quite long enough, it seems to me. Call them, somebody."

One of her minions ran to call them.

"Because it's time we thought about going home," Louise observed. "It must be late."

It was a little after ten. Lillian stood up. "You've got to eat," she said tonelessly. There was all that food. ... She started for the dining-room and kitchen. As she went she felt that they were looking at each other, commenting behind her back upon her vulgar choice of words. Well, let them. She didn't care. She didn't care how they looked, or what they did, or what they thought. Not any more.

The party was over before eleven. The guests departed as they had arrived, in a procession. Later Lillian would hear from Sally where they went. They did not go home. They had said that they must, that it was late, that tomorrow was another day — but they did not.

As Sally put it, "It seems they wanted to see Irene — I suppose to cheer her up. Anyway, so they went on to her place, and stayed there till three in the morning."

CHAPTER FOURTEEN

There was a Country Club dance in April, but the William Legendres did not attend it. The announcement came during the week following their party. Bill brought the printed card home and gave it to Lillian, silently. Lillian read aloud:

"The Seventh Annual Spring Frolic of the Renwood Country Club will be held on Saturday evening, April 20th, beginning at eight p.m. Dancing.

Entertainment. Supper. Music by Juby Cole's Collegians. Tickets (including supper) $8.00 for members, $10.00 for guests."

Lillian smiled sardonically, lip curling. "I bet that'll be hot."

Bill watched her toss the card aside.

"You don't want to go?" he asked, though without surprise. She was like this now. She was bitter now, and arrogant, and scornful of the town and of the people of the town. In a week she had become a different Lillian. In less. Overnight she had adopted a new rôle.

"'Go?'" she said. "I should say not. You couldn't hire me."

She was not afraid to go. Fear was not part of this new rôle, timidity was not, humility and diffidence were not. This rôle was boldness. Nerve. Often and often in those days and weeks she played it publicly, that none might miss it, that all might know and feel her new disdain. She went out more, not less. She let herself be seen more frequently: herself, alone and proud, aloof and insolently gorgeous, driving her cream-white roadster all around. She smoked as she drove — a cigarette for Renwood, crimson at the tip, burned cocked between two thin gloved fingers on her steering wheel. Renwood, as Louise Bartlett had maintained, is insular. Only brazen women smoke in public in broad daylight there, and blow sly, silent toots of smoke at pious ladies passing.

She dressed the part, moreover. She who had dressed to win the town sought now to startle and annoy it. There was the way she put her hats on — the same hats, become extreme. There was the way she deepened the red of her mouth and whitened the white of her skin, and sometimes let her hair show in flamboyant patches on it, and sometimes hid her hair and bound her face with a black turban. There was the Russian-looking frock, bought in New York, that she had never worn because it was too dramatic, too bizarre — "too wild," she said. She wore it now. There was the tight black satin dress trimmed with monkey-fur, with the monkey-fur collar that sprayed from throat to shoulders like a fountain of black ink. Now she wore that.

There was the Chow dog she acquired. In this sartorial connection he must certainly be mentioned. He completed all her costumes. He was an accessory, like a muff with feet. He was a color note — a color repetition in the scheme. He matched her hair almost exactly.

His name was Rufus when she got him; she would think up a cuter name than that. He had a pedigree, or he was said to have one; and he had belonged to a man in East Clinton, a customer of Joe Gratz ',

"You mean Gratz the bootlegger?" Bill asked when she explained this

"Yes. He's a friend of Sally's," Lillian said. "Sally told me about it. Said he'd taken this dog for a bad debt, and wanted to sell him. So I told her to tell him to see me."

"Looks like a good Chow," Bill observed. "Good curly tail." He snapped his fingers. "Here, fella! Come 'ere a minute. Let's see your tongue, old boy."

"It's black," Lillian said, "like — as it should be, I mean."

"Yeah. He's all right," said Bill. With his fingers in the dog's dull fiery coat he raised his eyes. "Wha'd you pay for him?"

"Oh, not much." Bill waited.

"You ought to know I didn't pay much," Lillian said with sudden acrimony. "How could I? I haven't got much — have I?"

"Practically nothing," Bill said drily. He was so informed with increasing frequency these days; and he never disputed the contention. He said now, "That's why I asked. Good Chows are usually pretty expensive."

"Well, this one wasn't — or he wouldn't be here!" Bill still waited.

"I got him for fifty dollars," Lillian lied, obliged to risk this guess. She had won the dog with a pair of dice in the back room of Joe Gratz's place on Union Street, where she had gone with Sally. She had no idea what he was worth. "Fifty dollars is cheap enough, isn't it?" she demanded crossly.

Bill nodded.

"I didn't pay it," Lillian said, for the sake of verisimilitude. "I didn't have it — naturally. But fifty's what I told him I'd pay when I had it. When, as and if."

"I see," Bill said.

It turned out very well. Lillian knew that it was going to when, after a moment's pause, Bill got up and crossed the living room to the Chinese desk. There he seated himself again, and uncapped a fountain pen, and drew his checkbook from a pigeonhole.

"Shall I make it out to Gratz, or to you?" he inquired over his shoulder.

Lillian was casual. "Oh — you might as well make it out to me."

Behind his back as he wrote she made a little rueful face. Fifty was fifty — but she could have said a hundred.

Rufus was a great success. He was a gaudy possession, he was becoming to her; and like herself, he created a stir on the streets. He was the only Chow in Renwood, and women edged away from him, and little children thought he was a lion. He himself thought he was. His prancings on the leash she bought for him diverted male spectators, who liked to say, "What kind of a dog is that?" even when they knew. At home Lillian ignored him, banishing him to the yard or the cellar; but where she walked, he walked, and in the car he rode beside her.

Everything was effect. Everything she did was a gesture of defiance, a snapping of her varnished fingertips in Renwood's face. She dared anything now, having nothing now to lose. Let them hate her. Let them hate her even as she hated them — or let them try to. Now let them talk of nothing else, who had always loved to talk about her. She would supply them with new things to say.

There was the April evening when a musical comedy, a real one, not a movie one, played Renwood. This was an event. Real shows, real, tangible, three-dimensional actors and actresses, came only once or twice a year. When they did come, the Bijou Theater bragged for weeks beforehand on its billboards, and for days beforehand in the Renwood Herald; and people who had bought their tickets said to other people, "Got your tickets yet? You haven't! Well, you'd better hurry up! They're going like hot-cakes,"— adding proudly, "It's the original New York company, you know."

Even people who didn't believe it was anything of the sort, cosmopolitans who went up to Cleveland to matinées all the time and had an annual week of theater-going in New York — even these bought tickets, although they laughed about it, saying that they were sure they didn't know why. "I've seen the show, of course. Oh, yes. Will and I saw it year before last, over East. Marilyn Miller was in it then. I have the program at home."

The day of the performance was to certain young men of Renwood as Circus Day was to the little boys. Gentlemen who but a few years back had met the circus train at dawn now loitered about the station to meet the afternoon "Flier" from Pittsburgh. Once the magnet had been elephants, now it was chorus girls; but the procedure was much the same. One gazed at them with dazzled eyes. One followed them to their encampment. One dogged the footsteps of the man who seemed to be their keeper. One learned their names. One fed them, if allowed.

The curtain rose at eight-fifteen. It was scheduled to do so, and within the memory of the oldest living inhabitant it had never once gone up ahead of schedule. This time it might, however — or such was the general feeling. Families rushed through early suppers, and housewives stacked the dishes; and ticket-holders reaching the Bijou lobby simultaneously fought at the gate for precedence, though it wasn't yet eight o'clock. At eight, or at five minutes after eight, the curtain could have risen. Such seats as were still empty then were not enough to matter.

On the night of the performance of Maybe It's Love, at five minutes after eight, a pair of seats in the fourth row of the orchestra, on the aisle, were among the half dozen still unoccupied. It was not known whose seats they were, but it was taken for granted that they belonged to members of the Hilldale Avenue younger married set who thought they were smart and citified, said Renwood with a sniff, when they came straggling in the last of all.

The auditorium was bright with light. You could read your program, that was a single paper, long and narrow and barred with rows of dots, like a laundry list. You could, as the program advised, look about you NOW and choose your exit. You could study the advertisements painted on the asbestos curtain, remarking as you always did that there was that Vega's Butcher Shop ad, when there hadn't been any Vega's Butcher Shop for years and years. Stretching your neck and tossing your head and shoulders this way and that, you could locate your friends and wave to them, and note what they had on and whether their seats were as good as yours or not.

By ten minutes after eight, the patience of the second balcony was exhausted, and a rhythmic steady clapping came from there. This continued until the musicians appeared in the pit, when it ceased, satisfied. Everyone listened respectfully to the tuning of instruments, the general flutter subsided into an attentive hush, and the "Sh-hs!" from various quarters, though stern, were unnecessary. Now the music would play. Now Vega's Butcher Shop and the Renwood Business College and the rest of the curtain would furl and disappear.

What actually happened next was to go down in history as one of the major outrages perpetrated, from first to last, by the red-headed Andrews girl, Bill Legendre's wife. It would never be forgotten. It would never be forgiven. Years afterward, when Lillian had been long gone from Renwood, the recollection of it would still infuriate whole tea-parties, whole bridge clubs, whole Tuesday sewing circles. Someone would say, "Remember the night she came sailing into the Bijou—" and a chorus of voices would join this first voice, crying, "— in evening clothes!" And someone would always add, "Dressed up like Astor's pet horse" and someone else would snort, "Undressed, you mean!"

The usher for the left aisle of the orchestra, Miss Hildegarde O'Brien, did her best to warn the audience. Miss O'Brien's face, as her feet thumped down the aisle in double time, heralded sensation, and her rolling eyes said, "Look behind me!" Once before, in her seven years of service at the Bijou, Miss O'Brien had ushered an evening dress and an evening wrap; but on that occasion dress and wrap had contained a female impersonator, whose entrance via the aisle had been part of the show. This was utterly different, and Miss O'Brien looked as flustered as she felt. She had never expected, she afterward said, to live to see the day.

The heads of the audience turned. They need not have hurried so about it, for Lillian was not hurrying. She was giving them time. She came as leisurely as if the aisle had not been steep — in second gear she came, to let them see her. She was all in white. Some said her white fur wrap was ermine, some said nonsense, it was rabbit, and others said they didn't know what it was, unless old Mrs. Haverhill on Fairview Boulevard had lost her cat. Everyone agreed that the way she wore it was the limit: as tight around those hips of hers as the paper on the wall, and all but falling off one sleeveless shoulder. Sleeveless? Bare! There was nothing over that shoulder, nothing for some distance below it, except a string of rhinestones and a row of four white flowers. According to Mr. Nickerson, the State Street florist, whom many consulted in the next few days, the white flowers were gardenias. Real ones. They cost $1.50 apiece by the time Mr. Nickerson got them down here from Cleveland. Four times one-fifty equals six - six dollars, if you please! And half a year ago Lil Andrews didn't have six cents. ...

But these and all Renwood's incisive animadversions belonged to the future. For the moment, shock followed shock, and there was no time to think them up. The Bijou audience could only gape at Lillian, confining its remarks to sibilant ejaculations: "She hasn't got any stockings on!" and, "Look! Look at her hair!" For Lillian's hair —as if the color of it wasn't wild enough! said Renwood later — was arranged in some new-fangled and outlandish way. Specifically, her hair was all brushed to one side, the left side, of her head, where it formed an immense flat rosette low over the ear. On the right side the coiffure was plain and slick, the right ear was exposed, and a single earring dangled from the rouged lobe to the shoulder. Well, honestly! Renwood said later. Talk about your sights!

Finally, there was her escort. Of the series of concussions felt by the Bijou audience, this was the most severe. Descending the aisle two paces behind Lillian was a tall young man whom everyone at first, engrossed in her, took to be Bill. It was not Bill, however. It was not Bill at all. It was a dark young man with glossy hair and a slightly surprised expression. It was a total stranger, never seen before.

Just as those whose seats were in the orchestra discovered him, the second balcony discovered Lillian. You heard it do so. For leading ladies, for love scenes, for anything sentimental, spectacular, audacious or risqué, the Bijou's second balcony has a genial and appreciative whistle, which it makes with its teeth, its tongue and its two forefingers. It made it now. At the same time, shoes in the second balcony — masculine shoes, from the High School, caught step with Lillian's measured tread and thunderously accompanied it during what remained of her progress down the aisle. The confusion was further augmented by the rapid circulation of the news that Bill Legendre was out of town ... was away on a business trip ... was in Toledo with Legendre, Senior. This highly significant and illuminating intelligence, transmitted from lip to ear to lip to ear throughout the downstairs rows of seats, gained emphasis and volume and created generally a sound somewhat like steam, somewhat like bees.

But Lillian was shameless: serene and imperturbable. As far as anyone could tell, neither the whispering nor the whistling nor the stamping disconcerted her one whit.

Indeed, there were those who afterward maintained that she had enjoyed it, and that the demonstration from on high had flattered her. Certain it was that when she reached the fourth row and turned into it, her head that should by rights have been bowed down, lifted instead, and her glance went brightly, sweetly, to the second balcony, as a stage star's might have, in acknowledgment. Falling again, the glance for the fraction of an instant rested idly upon Jane Legendre Reynolds, seated with her husband two rows back.

"Hello, Frank," Lillian was heard to murmur.

She faced about, and languidly sat down. The strange young man also sat down, and Lillian said something to him that no one caught — though Mrs. P. B. Wittmack, in the seat behind, tried hard, feeling herself the hope of Renwood in this moment. Mrs. Wittmack later confessed her failure, but tempered it by adding that she was almost sure that Lillian had called the stranger "dear. "... Mrs. Wittmack told her conscience that a woman like that would.

The strange young man responded with a swift and transient smile. At once his face resumed its aspect of perplexity, which the happenings of the past few moments had but served to deepen. Plainly, the more the young man saw of Renwood, the less he understood it. His eyes in his motionless countenance made covert sorties to the sides, and an unseasonable moisture was noted on his fore head. These manifestations, combined with the fact that the young man was attired in a business suit like anybody else, won the audience to him. Unanimously it was felt that he was probably quite nice; he was probably much more sinned against than sinning.

To be sure, it was he who now assisted Lillian to remove her wrap; but this was manners, not connivance. It was not the young man's fault that with his aid, surely unwitting, Renwood's worst fears were realized. The back of Lillian's gown proved to be even more indecent than the front of it had led the pessimistic to expect. That there might be no doubt of this, Lillian leaned forward, on the pretense of an interest in the tootling musicians; and there was no doubt of it. Her gown was composed of a skirt and a bib. Save for the rhinestone straps, which curved and met behind her neck, the back of the bodice and sections of the sides were non-existent.

Mrs. Eustace R. Longstreth, of Monument Street, was the first to recover. Mrs. Longstreth, the president of the Renwood Woman's Club, the guiding spirit of the Renwood Parent-Teachers' Association, and the founder and chairman of a committee of lady censors who labored night and day for purity and the protection of the morals of Renwood's young, adult and old — Mrs. Longstreth, accompanied loyally, if sheepishly, by Mr. Longstreth, rose up and left the theater. Though her gait and her manner suggested that she went to fetch a policeman, Mrs. Longstreth was not coming back. She was going home. She was renouncing the performance - four dollars a seat or no four dollars.

Under the circumstances, Mrs. Longstreth could do no other.

CHAPTER FIFTEEN

Bill and his father, in his father's big car, rode into Renwood late in the afternoon of the next day. Bill was driving. Legendre, Senior, never drove if he could help it — and he usually could. People who had ridden with him usually helped him help it, saying, "You don't want to bother, do you? Shan't I take the wheel?" Only Irene had ever dared be more direct. "Darling," Irene had said, "I'm sorry, but you are the world's worst driver. You're simply hair-raising. I'd rather walk."

Legendre, Senior, had loved that.

He rode now at Bill's side, with his hat tipped low over his nose, and a cigar with a long, surprisingly substantial ash on its end, between his fingers. The car was a touring car. Bill had insisted that the top be down, and it had been down when they left Toledo; but Legendre, Senior's, hat had blown off so many times that finally they had put the top up again. Besides, it had begun to rain. "There, you see?" Legendre, Senior, had remarked with satisfaction. "Now it's raining."

In the seat behind them there was the equipment necessary for a four-day business trip - two suitcases, two bags of golf-clubs, and a brief-case which contained rye whiskey. There was also a smooth white cardboard box with the name of a lingerie shop lettered on it. Lillian had told Bill to be sure to bring her something. The box, though new this morning — it had been the afterthought that had delayed their scheduled departure from Toledo — looked a little battered, having already a bashed-in side and a fracture along the edge of the cover. Legendre, Senior, digging for the brief-case before luncheon, had handled it perhaps a trifle roughly.

Bill drove up Spruce Street toward his father's house. "You drop me at home," his father said, "and take the car along to your place. Bring it down to the office in the morning."

Bill nodded. "Ride down, for once," his father said.

This peevish little thrust at Lillian he evidently felt was not quite worthy of him, for he altered it, saying amiably, "Arrive in state, the way you used to. You might even get there on time."

"I never used to do that," Bill reminded him.

They were almost home. Legendre, Senior, threw his cigar at a neighbor's tulip bed, and sat erect with the aid of both his elbows. He cleared his throat. "About this trip to New York. You tell her we talked it over, and that I'm going to lend you a thousand dollars — at six per cent interest, tell her — pending the sale of your house on Hilldale, when you're to repay me."

"Right."

"I'll give you the check in the morning. "

"It's damn nice of you, Dad."

"It's nothing of the sort," said his father briskly. "It's business." He paused and clutched the door at his side as Bill made the turn for the driveway. Then he continued, "When do you think she'll go?"

"I don't know. Just as soon as she can get ready.

She'd go tonight if she could," Bill said, "I know that. She's crazy to go."

This was putting it mildly. Lillian talked of nothing else. "It's a kind of obsession," Bill added, more to himself than to his father.

He had stopped the car at the porch steps. Now he shut the motor off. For a meditative moment they both sat there.

"Does she know anyone in New York?" Legendre, Senior, asked, very casually.

Bill shook his head. "No. Not a soul. It's more a matter of getting away from here than anything else," he said. "You can't blame her. And then of course she wants to shop, and see some shows —"

"Yes," said his father. "Well. She'll probably go tomorrow night, then, you think? And how long do you think she'll stay?"

"I don't know. I suppose a week or ten days."

"Will she spend a thousand dollars," his father inquired mildly, "in a week or ten days?"

"Well," said Bill, "she wants to buy some clothes."

"I see."

It went without saying that Lillian would stay while the money lasted. Legendre, Senior, briefly considered making it two thousand dollars. Would an extra thousand mean more weeks away — or merely more clothes? Legendre, Senior, decided to postpone deciding.

"Well," he said lightly, "I hope I'll see something of you, son."

"You will," Bill said.

His father looked almost shy. They both did. They gazed ahead through the windshield at the far garage doors. "You wouldn't want to come home here and stay for a week or so?" said Legendre, Senior. "And close up your house? That is, if you feel like it," he added hastily. "It's just a suggestion. You do as you like."

"I'd like that," Bill said. "I was thinking of that, myself."

His father nodded matter-of-factly. "We'll shoot a lot of golf."

"You bet," said Bill.

That was all they said. "Where's Ephraim?" Legendre, Senior, demanded abruptly in a scolding voice. He glared at his silent house. He bellowed Ephraim's name. "Blow the horn," he directed Bill. He bustled out of the car on one side,

3333

333333

33333333

 langendre climbed out on the other, and they dragged one bag, one golfbag and the brief-case from the back, and Bill carried them up and put them on the porch. By this time, the danger of their admitting or betraying in some fashion their deep and moving fondness for each other was safely past; and they shook hands unemotionally, even almost indifferently, as American sons and fathers should. Legendre, Senior, said, "Good trip," and Bill said, "Yeah. Thanks for taking me along," and he said, "See you in the morning," and his father said, "Watch out for my new hedge, there, son." And so they parted, and Bill drove on home.

He was admitted by Mrs. Hoxie, who seemed to rebuke him optically for being neither friend nor foe nor even book-agent, but only the master of the house without his key.

"How are you?" Bill said.

Dropping his suitcase in the hall and leaning his golf bag against the newel-post, he did not listen to Mrs. Hoxie's plaintive reply, which was that she was well, excepting that her feet hurt her. "Come spring," said Mrs. Hoxie, "they always —"

"Where's Mrs. Legendre?" Bill interrupted. "Upstairs?"

Lillian was upstairs. "On the little porch. She's resting," Mrs. Hoxie said further, with peculiar emphasis and relish. "I guess she's tired."

Mrs. Hoxie lacked the courage to say, "— after being out gallivanting last evening," greatly though she desired to say it. Her thin lips folded reluctantly, and her glance at her employer glittered. Who would tell him, if she didn't? Nobody.

"You'll find some shirts and things stuffed down in this golf bag," Bill was saying. "Better take everything out. What time is it?"

"Near six."

"Well, dinner in half an hour."

He started upstairs. It was now or never, Mrs. Hoxie knew; and she said suddenly, addressing his mounting back, "There's cold chicken, left over from last night, when company was here. Will that be all right?"

"That'll be fine," he said, not even turning. He was a cool one, Mrs. Hoxie later declared.

Lillian lay reading on the chaise-longue on the sleeping porch that she had

33

— 124 —

furnished as a sort of boudoir. This was her favorite nook, but Bill disliked it with a special dislike of which he was conscious whenever he crossed the threshold. It always smelled of stale smoke, for all its dozen windows; and there was always this and that — a comb, a brush, a bitten chocolate, a little loop of lost red hair, a nail buffer, a hand-mirror, a box of aspirin tablets, an empty plate, a green hot-water bag, quite cold — lying here and there, among the books and magazines and ash-trays and crumpled sofa-cushions that belonged.

Furthermore, the curtains at the windows annoyed Bill. They were made of a white material figured thickly in dark crimson with Statues of Liberty, Eiffel Towers, Atlantic Oceans, eastbound monoplanes, and Colonel Charles A. Lindberghs in medallions. There were also dates — or a date, repeated countless times. There were yards and yards and yards and yards. Lillian felt that the curtains were not only novel and timely, but patriotic, and even pretty. Bill felt that they were awful, and that Lindbergh himself would agree.

Lillian wore maize velvet pajamas that the dry cleaner had ruined in a misguided attempt to remove stains of liquid mascara, which he took for ink. This costume, despite its visible discolorations, was decorative, as was Lillian herself, with her hair unloosed in a blaze over the cushions; and Bill said involuntarily, "Hullo, beautiful." He hardly ever said that any more.

"Hello," said Lillian. "So you're back."

His light kiss touched her cheek below the corner of one eye. Her kiss for him, though her lips formed it, missed entirely. She had not stirred except to close her book upon one finger, and with the other hand to hold her cigarette aside. Now when Bill stood erect she lay regarding him lazily. She remarked that he was sunburned — or was it that his face was dirty? Bill said it was both. He had got a good burn yesterday, playing eighteen holes of golf. It had been hot as summer in Toledo.

"What's that box?" said Lillian. "Is that my present?"

She sat up then, and dropped her book, and set her cigarette on the edge of the little table within reach, where so many cigarettes before it had been put down and forgotten that their grooves made an almost regular design. "Here!" she commanded, wriggling the fingers of both outstretched hands.

Bill slid the cardboard box across her lap, and she jerked at the string and threw off the cover and attacked the layers of tissue paper, loosening them noisily. In the past Bill had noticed that Lillian opened glossy white boxes like this one with a far greater fervor than she ever displayed when she saw what was inside. Her enthusiasm always seemed to die abruptly then, so that he knew that, whatever it was, it should have been something else. His latest offering was no exception.

"Oh," said Lillian. "Nightgowns. How nice."

There were three nightgowns, hand-made but rather unimaginative ones, of pink silk and coffee-colored lace. Lillian looked underneath the third, but there was no fourth. She allowed the three to fall back into place and gazed at the top gown a moment. "Pink," she remarked reflectively.

"Would you rather have had some other color?"

"Well," said Lillian, "I like black. Black chiffon. And odd colors I like. But these are very sweet," she concluded politely. "Thank you."

She replaced the cover, and lowering the box to the floor, lay back on her pillows again. She reached for her cigarette. "Well, go on," she said. "You were telling me."

"Was I?" Bill's forehead wrinkled quizzically. "Oh, yes," he said, "I was telling you that it was hot in Toledo. Are you sure you want me to go on with that?"

He loafed back to the chaise-longue as he spoke and seated himself on the foot of it. He had been unostentatiously opening a window. "No," he said, "you tell me, now. Let's get this weather straightened out. How was it here?"

"Oh, it was all right, I guess."

"And how were you?"

"How do you think?"

"That's too bad," Bill said. "I'm sorry. Didn't you have any fun at all?"

"Do I ever? In this town?"

He thought of his news and would have communicated it then and there; but Lillian's petulance turned into gaiety in the next instant, so arrestingly that he got no farther than, "Listen!" — It appeared that she had not altogether meant what she had said: not this time. This time she had complained from force of habit.

"Last evening I did," she admitted now. "I had the most fun I've had in ages. ... Guess who blew into town yesterday, Bill, and called up? Friend of yours. Used to go to Ohio State when you did."

"Who?"

"Guess!"

"Well, there were two or three guys in school at the time."

"Alec Fairfax," Lillian said.

"No!" exclaimed Bill, grinning immediately. "Old Pooge Fairfax! Well, what do you know about that! The old hyena! Is he still around?"

"No, he left this morning. Or I suppose he did. He said he had to. He was just here a day, looking over the Putnam-Williams plant. It seems he's some kind of an engineer."

"Oh, Lord," Bill said. "An engineer. He was a piccolo-player when last seen — and a lousy one at that. I'm getting old, there's no doubt about it." Lillian blew smoke at the ceiling. "You know what he said about you? He said you were the most popular man in college — far and away. And he said you were one of the greatest backs he ever saw play football. He talked a lot about you. All the time, in fact," she supplemented. "I couldn't get him off the subject. He described whole games, and touchdowns, and everything."

"What a thrill for you!" Bill said, amused. "I thought you said you had fun?"

"Well, I did," Lillian maintained. "Wait till I tell you."

She lit another cigarette, and sat up straight to tell him, clasping her arms around her trousered knees. "In the first place," she narrated - quickly, for this was the unimportant part, "—when he called up and talked to me and told me who he was, and all, I invited him to dinner here. I thought you'd want me to."

"Absolutely! Of course."

"Well, that's what I thought," Lillian said.

She omitted to mention that Alec Fairfax's voice on the telephone had sounded more exciting than its owner had turned out to be; nor did she disclose the fact that, in an excess of hospitable spirit, engendered by the voice, she had driven to the Harding Hotel in her roadster, with Rufus beside her, to get him. She had called him from the lobby, saying,"I'm waiting downstairs," and young Mr. Fairfax had said, "How will I know you?" or words to that effect, and she had laughed and answered, "Well I have red hair, for one thing."

But of all this she said nothing now. "So he came," she said, "and we had dinner."

The unimportant part ended here. "And then, after dinner," said Lillian, sparkling again, "we went to the show at the Bijou!"

"Oh, that's right," Bill remembered. "That was last night. And it was good, was it?"

"You should have seen me!" Lillian returned rapturously.

She described herself. It took some moments, and many illustrative motions of her hands, which dressed her in last evening's dress for Bill's visualization, and pinned last evening's flowers on her left shoulder. "And my hair-" said Lillian, and the hands showed how her hair had been arranged, and even how one earring had been fastened to one earlobe. When it came to the donning of the wrap, Lillian got up from the chaise-longue, and stood; her hands pulled air around her shoulders loosely, and drew it tight around her hips and waist; and one hand clasped it there. She walked to the door and turned, and the space between the door and the chaise-longue became an aisle, and Bill became the Bijou audience.

He did not look it. He was not astonished, not incensed. He even smiled, although his eyes were grave.

"And what did everybody do?" he asked, when Lillian, laughing, dropped back against the cushions once again.

She told him, with gusto. The wild salute from the peanut gallery, the consternation in the seats of the mighty, her sister-in-law's face, Mrs. Eustace R. Longstreth's flatfooted departure — she dwelt upon all these, and upon the ludicrous bewilderment of Mr. Alec Fairfax, and upon his droll confusion.

"He didn't know what it was all about," said Lillian. Mirth overcame her at the memory.

Bill chuckled too, but briefly. "Poor old Pooge," he said. "That was a hell of a thing to do to him. After all, Red!"

"Oh, well — "Lillian dismissed this, "— what's the difference? I'll never see him again."

"No. Very probably not," Bill said.

This was ignored altogether. Lillian lit a new cigarette, and continued her gleeful recital. There was a good deal more of it; the fine first turmoil caused by her entrance had not, it seemed, alone sufficed for her. Accordingly, when the curtain fell on the first act of Maybe It's Love and the men of Renwood adjourned to the lobby to smoke, she had adjourned likewise. She had waited a moment or so, until all the men had gone who were going. "If I hadn't," she explained to Bill, "they'd never have gone at all, of course. Their wives would have pulled them back into their seats by the coattails."

Bill didn't believe it.

"Oh, you don't?" said Lillian concisely. "You should have been there."

She had waited a moment or so; then, when it was quite too late for the wives to do anything but fume, she had swept up the aisle and out to join their escaped and unchaperoned husbands. In order that her destination might be unmistakable, she had opened her cigarette case as she went and extracted a cigarette from it. She had been attended by young Mr. Fairfax. In a word, no Renwood wife could have fancied for one soothing instant that this notorious home-breaker, in her movie-vampire's costume, was merely — harmlessly - bound for the dressing-room.

"Well," said Lillian to Bill,"did they burn up! I wish you'd seen them. I give you my word, if I'd been some kind of a rattlesnake or something, going out to bite their boy-friends, they couldn't have looked any different! And to make everything just lovely for them, it was a long time between acts. It must have been fifteen or twenty minutes."

"And what happened?"

"Well, nothing much happened," Lillian said. "It was all in their minds, don't you see? They just sat inside there, wondering what was going on. And thinking the worst, of course! One woman —"

Here again convulsive mirth interrupted Lillian. She could scarcely proceed. "Oh, Lord," she moaned. "One woman — Mrs. Henry Ives — couldn't stand it any longer, so she sent her little boy out to get Henry and bring him back in again! It's a fact! She did! I hadn't any more than gotten out there and started smoking, when out comes this kid, saying, ' Poppa, Momma wants you'—"

"Oh, now, listen!" said Bill. "You're just making this up as you go along."

"I'm not! I swear it! You can ask what's-his-name Alec. It's only the truth. I tell you," Lillian told him, earnestly now, and patiently,"you don't know these women in this town. They're scared to death of me. They don't trust me any further than they could throw me."

"But that's ridiculous!"

"Isn't it?" Lillian readily agreed.

This proved not to be the modest assent it seemed, for she added smilingly, "As if I wanted any of their funny little husbands! I wouldn't take one as a gift — if they only knew it."

Bill said, after a slight pause, "It's the older women you're talking about, isn't it? I mean, I can't imagine the younger ones getting into a lather — not," said Bill, "if Sheba herself was loose in the lobby."

"No, I don't suppose they minded so much," Lillian acknowledged. "I don't know. They wouldn't show it, anyway.

I know this, though!" she said, brightening. "I'll bet you anything you want to bet that Louise Bartlett minded what I did to her!"

"What did you do to her, for heaven's sake?" Bill said. "I never heard of such a busy evening."

"I sent her one of my gardenias," Lillian said demurely, "from the lobby."

"You what?"

"Well, in a way, I did," Lillian said. "I sent Johnny Bartlett back to his seat with one of them in his button hole — and everybody in the theater looking at it, and looking at Louise to see how she was bearing up."

Bill in his mind looked at Louise being looked at. He guffawed suddenly. "Oh, that's swell!" he said. "That really is."

His inflection suggested that he had not altogether appreciated the previous revelations. He added, "You mean to tell me he let you put a flower in his buttonhole, though? Old Johnny?"

"What could he do? We were standing there talking to him," Lillian said, "Alec and I. He couldn't be rude, could he? And then when I got it fixed, he couldn't take it off again, because I stuck right by him then for the rest of the intermission."

"You didn't, by any chance," said Bill, "rub powder on his sleeve, did you?"

Lillian did not smile. "No," she said. "He had a light suit on."

Promptly at six-fifteen, Mrs. Hoxie in the lower hall lifted her voice and shouted, "Supper's ready!" She was firm. Twenty minutes had elapsed since Bill had asked for dinner in half an hour. Mrs. Hoxie, though ever disposed to grant the requests of the head of this household when they were reasonable, had not seen fit to grant this one, which was not. Twenty minutes, Mrs. Hoxie felt, was ample time for a shower and a change of clothes. Or if it wasn't, it ought to be. Mrs. Hoxie was due at her sister's at seven.

"It's on the table!" she shouted additionally.

There was no assenting sound from upstairs, and it occurred to Mrs. Hoxie that she was supposed to say, "Dinner is served" —of all the highfaluting nonsense and to say it, moreover, to somebody, rather than broadcast it into space. This was a new rule, recently laid down by Lillian, whose sudden hard-eyed arrogation of authority had for the time being left her servant speechless. Now for a moment Mrs. Hoxie suspected that the silence enduring upstairs was intended as a reprimand and a reminder; and truculently she said to herself that she just hoped it was. Mrs. Hoxie would not be speechless this time. Retorts formed in her mind, and recriminations marshalled themselves. Among other things, Mrs. Hoxie would state that for thirty-three years as a lady helper thirty-four years come June — she had been saying that suppers were ready; and it had been good enough. "And," Mrs. Hoxie would say to Lillian, "what was good enough for Mrs. K. J. Matthewson, and for Mrs. Roland Hendricks, and for Mrs. Doctor Means, and for all those ladies — well! ..."

— Mrs. Hoxie even held a muttered rehearsal.

Then she became aware that the silence was not absolute. Remotely, in the upper regions, a conversation was going on. That was it, then: they just hadn't heard her. Mrs. Hoxie drew in her figurative horns, and planted her flesh-and-blood fists on her hips. She again announced supper, this time at the top of her voice.

Still they did not hear her. The distant talking, which Mrs. Hoxie now referred to under her breath as "gabble, gabble, gabble," still continued.

Mrs. Hoxie mounted the stairs. There was no help for it; and it must be said for her that, despite her principles and her aching feet, she accepted the necessity quite philosophically. She hustled up; and a beholder, had there been one in the hall below, might have thought her somewhat more than willing. This, in point of fact, Mrs. Hoxie was. She had decided suddenly that so prolonged a dialogue wasn't usual, and that the chances were that it wasn't friendly. It was probably a fight. It was undoubtedly a fight. Mrs. Hoxie's haste was a promoter's eagerness.

It brought her to the upstairs hall in no time, and along the hall to a point acoustically satisfactory. Here Mrs. Hoxie tarried, standing still yet straining forward, rather like a statue of a runner. This pose she maintained for an interval, though it took her less than ten seconds to learn that her swift ascent had been a waste of breath and energy. They were not fighting. Mrs. Hoxie's mistress— "She" to Mrs. Hoxie — was not getting Hail Columbia, Happy Land, or anything like it.

On the contrary, from the way She was squeaking and squealing and carrying on in there, you would have said that somebody had just left her a million dollars. "God forbid," thought Mrs. Hoxie devoutly; and she had other thoughts, such as that there was no justice, and that the way of the transgressor was not hard so you could notice it And as for that other saying about a word to the wise being sufficient, whoever said that ought to try it on Mr. Lengendre.

Of the squeaking and squealing itself, Mrs. Hoxie could make nothing at all, though there were words to it as well as noises. It ran: "Why didn't you tell me? Oh, I could kill you! Imagine sitting there letting me talk and talk and— Oh-h-h, I'm so happy, I could die!"

Mrs. Hoxie was very soon bored with it. She rounded the corner into the guestroom that the sleeping-porch adjoined, and would have advanced to the threshold to say for the third time — and for the last, Mrs. Hoxie vowed privately — that supper was ready. She was half way there when the apparition of her mistress, coming flying through the doorway, brought her to a standstill. This was most unexpected, and Mrs. Hoxie, who had a weak heart, clutched the region of it. "Mercy!" she said. "You scared me."

Then a simply astounding thing happened. It happened before Mrs. Hoxie had any idea what was happening, it was all over before she understood clearly what happened, and as she said at her sister's later much later — what could she do? She could do nothing. She could only stand there, petrified, gaping at the hall door, through which the flying maize velvet quickly vanished. She could only stand there and let the truth dawn on her ....

Mrs. Hoxie's mistress, crying, "I'm going to New York, I'm going to New York, I'm going to New York!" had thrown her arms around Mrs. Hoxie, hugged her, twirled her once like a top — and Mrs. Hoxie was not sure but what She had even kissed her.

CHAPTER SIXTEEN

The Limited that roars through Renwood early in the evening stops when signalled, and it stopped for Lillian. There was a moment on the platform when she thought it wasn't going to: the giant locomotive loomed, came on and pounded past her at such terrific speed that she thought the engineer didn't know... But the cars slowed down, and one of them had a porter in its open door; and they ran for it — Lillian and Bill and the boy who was carrying the luggage that Bill couldn't carry, he having only two hands and two arms, after all.

They ran, and the train hesitated, and Lillian stepped on the porter's wooden step and felt his boosting hand under her elbow and heard him say, "There you are, Miss." She was up the steps of the car, and her bags were thumping at her heels; she was turning into the corridor, still going on her own momentum. Then she remembered Bill, and she ran back to wave to him. It was almost, not quite, too late; the train was beginning to move again. She had a quick photograph of him, standing below her, big and bareheaded; of his face, laughing at her; of one of his eyebrows lifted. He made her a nonchalant little salute with his hand, and he called something to her. She didn't know what it was. She thought it was, "Be good," most likely.

She went into the car. She went through it, between the open Pullman section to the other end. For all her breathlessness, her progress was deliberate. It might have been titled, "Enter the Lady Who Has the Drawing Room." She trailed a luxurious perfume, and presented to plebian eyes a fitted black cloth back, with a silver fox fur dangling down it. She was followed, not too closely, by the porter with pieces of luggage that were obviously made of rare and perishable leather, since covers of heavy fabric, snapped with snappers, shielded them.

Reaching the drawing room, the lady who had it flopped down in a corner, and became Lillian with her nose all but pressed to the window. Outside in the dusk, Renwood was being left behind so rapidly that she must look now, at once, if she wished to see the last of it. She did wish to. Smiling a little, she watched the ultimate outposts — the Hendricks Foundry, the rows of identical houses where the workers lived, the power station, the ball park and the woods beyond it - go. Not until they were gone did she settle back and unfasten the fur which choked her, and remove the tight suede gloves with the wrinkled wrists, and find a cigarette. She stretched out her feet to the opposite seat, and leaned her head back, and rested. She was still smiling. She couldn't seem to stop.

The porter arrived with his second load of her luggage, and she smiled at him. "What time do we get in in the morning?" she asked him, though she knew. She was pleased when he said, "In New York, miss? We git in New York at nine-ten." He couldn't say, "New York" too often for her.

"Is that all now, miss?" he added.

Lillian could think of nothing more. The porter limped to the doorway, and paused in it. "You want this door left open, miss," he remarked rather than queried. His experience had been that misses who looked like this one usually did.

"Open, yes."

The porter nodded sympathetically. "I'll bring you a paper bag," he said, "for to put your hat in."

Lillian said that he might as well bring two, while he was about it. There'll be another lady in here with me," she explained. "She's getting on at the next station."

This was Sally. At the telephone last evening, sitting gazing fixedly at it, Lillian had considered long and well a burning question: should she, or should she not, take Sally to New York with her? And ultimately she had made up her mind that she would. She had been then, and she was still, aware of the disadvantages, and a little troubled by them. There was the financial disadvantage (Sally only had a hundred dollars) and there might conceivably be social ones as well. Lillian admitted that socially, she herself was perhaps no ball of fire; but certainly she had learned a thing or two in the past few months, and she had the clothes. Sally, on the other hand, had never learned anything and never would; and the only evening dress Sally owned was that old beaded chiffon with all the beads gone. In the event of a swell New York party — Well, there was no use being silly, Lillian thought. In that event Sally would just have to go to a movie.

The financial disadvantage was as obvious. A double hotel room would cost more than a single one, needless to say; and Sally's appetite had long been the marvel of every beholder. As against these inevitable entries on the debit side, however, there were Sally's accomplishments, professional and other. It seemed to Lillian that in New York, where you wanted to look your best night and day — where, indeed, you had to look your best to be even noticeable — a companion who was a beautician by trade might earn her salt. Moreover, Sally was clever with a needle, and she could get spots out of things. It would be almost like having a lady's maid along.

Finally, it would be fun. The chief and clinching argument in favor of taking Sally had been this simple one, that it would be more fun than going alone. "At least until I get to know some people," Lillian had thought; for somehow she thought of her fortnight — or less — in New York as indefinite, as longer than any fortnight ever was.

Sally's, "Will I!" of acceptance over the telephone had been of a pitch to shatter an ear-drum unprepared for it; and from that moment on, her gratitude — her humility, indeed — had been all a benefactor could desire. In twenty telephone colloquies in the twenty-four hours intervening, Lillian had been cheered to note that Sally was a different girl. This had been manifest in many ways. For example, the suggestion that she entrain at another station had come from Sally herself, who had said without rancor that it would "look better." It was also Sally's suggestion, it was even her plea, that she be permitted to bring her business implements along for daily gratuitous service to Lillian. "It's the only way I can even begin to make it up to you," Sally had said. "So if you wouldn't awfully much rather have New York facials and things — of course I imagine the work they do there is much better —"

Reassured on this point, and promised Lillian's loyal patronage, Sally was happy. "Now don't you even bother to pack cold cream or anything," she said. "Don't you worry your head. I'll bring the works."

To Mr. Bones Jones, who owned his own taxi, had fallen the honor — unremunerative, but distinguished none the less — of driving Sally thirty miles to take the train. Mr. Joe Gratz, to whom the honor rightfully belonged, would have none of it. This had been reported by Sally to Lillian during the second or third of the series of their telephone consultations. "Well," Sally had announced, "I just told Joe, and Joe is hopping. He's frothing at the mouth. He says, 'Go ahead — but don't come back.' Can you imagine that? 'Don't come back,' he has the nerve to say to me."

"And what did you say?"

"I just said, 'Who do you think you are, —the Mayor?'"

There had been no reconciliation up to five o'clock, when Sally, on the point of setting out, had last called Lillian. The hopping Mr. Gratz had not been heard from. This obduracy on his part was felt to be regrettable, but not permanent, and not — from any standpoint except one —at all important. As Sally said, "The only thing is, it would have been nice if he'd snapped out of it before I left." Since he had not, Sally still had only a hundred dollars.

She had never seen New York. In fact, the Sally who boarded the Limited when next it stopped had never been east of Pittsburgh, nor west of Cedar Point, nor south of Wheeling; and she had never before set foot in a Pullman car. For these reasons, and others that were temperamental, there was about Sally's entrance nothing of the histrionic calm, nothing whatever of the hauteur, that had characterized Lillian's. Sally entered in a rush and a flurry from the near end of the car, preceded by cries of, "Where? Which way? This way?" in the vestibule, and by a staccato salvo of heels in the corridor. She whisked into view, stopped dead, stared wildly in all directions, and discovering the drawing-room door behind her, wheeled and darted in. Further cries ensued. To the listeners in the station lull, it must have seemed that friends long lost were reunited — albeit to the far greater exuberance of one than of the other.

"For heaven's sake, pipe down," Lillian was obliged at last to murmur. "They'll think we're a couple of hicks that've never been on a train before."

This dire possibility quieted Sally, for the moment at least. "I forgot," she whispered meekly. "I'm so excited."

She forgot again when Bones Jones walked past below the window, with his spectacled gaze directed toward some window down the car. The sight was too much for Sally, who rapped frantically on the glass, calling,"Bones! Here! Here we are!" before Lillian could stop her. It was then too late, for the attention of Mr. Jones had been attracted; he returned — nor could good-byes send him away. He stood until the last, expecting to be entertained, and enjoining the harassed Sally to talk louder. Mr. Jones was no lip-reader, he shouted wittily.

"Some day you'll learn!" Lillian hissed to Sally.

The train pulled out. Mr. Jones, lost to view, was as if erased from memory's slate entirely; and in the drawing room of Mrs. Legendre and Miss Holtz, a kind of hysteria of relief prevailed. Here they were. They were off. Nothing could stop them now — except, of course, a railroad wreck. (Sally knocked the wood of the window sill.) Neither of them had missed the train, neither had lost her ticket, none of the catastrophes that might have occurred had occurred — and New York was ahead. Sitting facing each other, they smirked inanely. They giggled outright. Sally, who never smoked, said, "Give me a cigarette-quick!" When she tried to light it her convulsive breath extinguished matches, and they giggled helplessly at that.

They could talk now, they could say what they pleased, and without shutting the door. No one could hear them: no one could think mortifying things. There was much to be said. There were their telephone talks to enlarge upon and to link together, and there were their emotions of last night and today to compare. It developed that neither of them had been able to sleep a wink. "But the funny thing is," said Sally, "I'm not a bit sleepy, are you?" And Lillian said that she should say she wasn't. She said that she never wanted to sleep again.

They spoke of what they would do tomorrow; of what they would do tomorrow night. They would doll all up, they decided, and dine somewhere, and see a show. The decision made them pensive. They were silent, momentarily.

"It's too bad we don't know anybody over there," Sally said from the silence. She might as well be frank. "Any men," she said. "You don't know any, do you?"

"No."

"Maybe we'll meet some."

This hopeful observation seemed to strike Lillian as stupid. "Of course we'll meet some," she said shortly. "What do you think?"

"Well, I didn't know."

"You can't get any place without men," said Lillian Andrews Legendre.

It was during the next little pause that they thought of going to the dining-car. "Are you hungry?" Lillian asked, and when Sally said, "No," she said, "Neither am I." Still, they thought they would go to the dining-car. They rang for the porter — Sally had been wanting an excuse to ring — and they inquired of him where the diner was. The porter said that it was three cars back, but that it was crowded. Finding that this did not at all dismay these red-haired ladies, the porter went further. The diner was full up, he said, and folks were standing in line.

"It'll be about twenty minutes, half an hour," the porter added. "I'll come an' tell you. Unless you'd like your dinner serve 'right here?"

But they wouldn't like that. "Thanks just the same," said Sally warmly.

They settled down again. Sally was for freshening her makeup for the imminent expedition, but Lillian said to wait. There would be time when the porter called them and besides, you couldn't do your eyelashes when the train was going. She spoke from experience: you had to do them at a station. This raised the anxious question of whether or not there was a station soon, and Sally solemnly produced a time-table. There was. For their eyelashes there was Ashtabula at seven-forty.

Restoring the time-table to a very large black patent leather handbag, a sort of knapsack full of tickets, bills, cosmetics and clean handkerchiefs — not to mention an address book with virgin pages, purchased just today, Sally found and fished forth a scrap of paper with a scribble on it.

"Our hotel," she explained. "I wrote it down when you told me. I'll have to learn it, won't I? — or I'll be out of luck! Lost in New York City, imagine me. How do you say it, now?"

It was Louise Bartlett's New York hotel with the French name. "I never heard of that hotel," Sally said, when the lesson was over. "But then, I wouldn't've, I don't suppose." She looked at Lillian respectfully and eagerly. "I bet it's grand, isn't it?"

"Wait till you see it," said Lillian, safely enough. "The most divine food," she quoted from memory. "And lots of atmosphere. It's just full of celebrities."

"Of what?"

"Celebrities. Famous people."

"Oh, celebrities!" Sally said. She laughed happily. "Well, that's us all over."

Sally, Lillian thought in the intervals of her own twitterings, was very naïve. She was so ga-ga she was positively childish, and she made you feel, by comparison, blasé. It was not a bad feeling. You could sit back and smoke and smile your compassionate amusement while Sally bounced up to explore the drawing-room and the little washroom inside. You could hearken goodhumoredly to the exclamations of admiration that the shiny nickel basin and the soap gadget called forth from her. You could explain the upper berth, and whence it came and where it went — you could even take a sort of pride in upper berths. When Sally said with awe, "It's wonderful, the things they think of," you could nod with what was almost modesty.

In your benevolence, you could refrain from all allusion to the fringed silk dress, the red straw tricorne hat and the Easter Sunday coat of light gray flannel trimmed with light gray, something certainly not fur — that Sally wore. Lillian did mention Sally's luggage, but that was different. That was just too awful to be borne. There were four pieces. There was the implement case, which had been on its last legs for two or three years; and there was a cardboard hat-box marked, "Beatrice —56 State Street, Renwood, 0 .— 'Beatrice for Bargains.'" There were also two suitcases, one of them rattan. Lillian pointed a scathing finger.

"Where'd you get that?"

"It's my aunt's."

"It looks it."

"I know," said Sally, who hadn't known. "I guess I'll h- I mean, I'm going to buy me a new one in New York."

"Well, I hope we get in the hotel with it," Lillian said. But that was all she said. There was no use risking hurting Sally's feelings, on a night like this.

They were pink and white for the dining-car, they were waiting only for Ashtabula, when the first little adventure of the New York trip occurred. There appeared in the drawing-room door a gentleman who had passed it several times — as Lillian, who faced that way, was aware.

The gentleman was followed closely by another gentleman, to all intents and purposes just like him. Both were rather fat. Both were middle-aged. Both held cigars between two fingers. The leader had his left thumb hooked into a waistcoat pocket; the other wore no waistcoat. This was the one conspicuous difference.

The second gentleman eyed Sally, who returned his friendly gaze in kind. The first gentleman was the spokesman. Coming far into the drawing-room, begging as he came, he halted beside Lillian. He smiled confidently down.

"Beg pardon," he said again. "But haven't I seen you in Cleveland?"

"You have not," said Lillian, with a positive promptness not quite kind.

This closed the incident. The second gentleman's now piteous glance was ignored by Sally, and no one appeared to hear the first gentleman at all when he said, still jauntily, "Oh, now, listen here! Don't be like that!" There was a slight pause, during which the profiles of Lillian and Sally were outlined purely against the hurrying dark beyond the windows. Then the gentlemen, mumbling, turned. They retired, in a body.

The ladies commented. Lillian was righteously indignant. "The nerve!" she snorted. "Those fat old fools as if we'd look at them!"

But Sally, though she agreed that the gentlemen had been fat old fools, was gratified.

"Still," she said, "it just goes to show you."

CHAPTER SEVENTEEN

Their hotel room was large and high, and it had three windows in a row — three views of Central Park, interrupted by bright glazed-chintz curtains. At night the park was lovely to look down on: black, mysterious, for all its moving motor cars and its multiple festoons of lights. Sally said that it always reminded her of the summer sociables they gave on the lawn of the parsonage of the Unitarian Church at home. "With the Japanese lanterns, and the trees and all,"

Sally said defensively.

On the inside their room had buff-colored walls and olive-green beds and tables, and chintz-covered chairs; and it was spacious enough to contain, besides the essential furnishings, a day-bed and an extra dressing table, of the tall-mirrored type called "vanity." This was Lillian's at sight. Sally's dressing-table was the smaller one across the room, with the photograph of Joe Gratz in a folding leather frame standing on it and — in due time - the calling cards, the speakeasy cards, the theater ticket stubs, the printed admonition that had collared a bottle of ginger ale, and other souvenirs rimming the mirror. Sally was an insatiable collector. In the little drawer of the telephone table, trophies too bulky for the mirror were rapidly accumulating; by Friday — they had arrived on Tuesday morning — the exhibit included theater programs, menu cards, two night club hammers and a clacker, the program of a fashion show at a department store, a stolen fork, and the silver ribbon bow from a corsage sent on Wednesday evening to Lillian by Lillian, and worn with intent to edify and to shame a Mr. Spud Koehler.

"He might as well know right now," Lillian had said, "that I like orchids." Mr. Koehler, who was of Manhattan, had been a windfall. He had been a gift from the punctual gods on Tuesday afternoon — no later; and by Friday, Sally was already saying, "What would we have done without him?" To which Lillian was replying that they would undoubtedly have done just as well, "—if not better." Lillian was not entirely satisfied with Spud, who told you the plots of plays and musical comedies and movies, and who called all waiters, bus-boys, bell-boys, doormen and drivers, "George," and all coat-room attendants and cigarette-girls, "Baby."

But even Lillian was obliged to acknowledge that Spud had been very useful, and that he had simplified and expedited everything. Thanks to him, they had not had to spend a single evening by themselves, not even Tuesday evening. And Spud had his good points. He knew New York as the visiting ladies knew Renwood, and he could always get second-row-aisle seats and ringside tables — at least, he always had so far. He spent money freely, if overtly, and he had a variety of friends. He produced a new one for Sally every evening.

There would be formal introductions in the hotel lobby. Lillian and Sally, issuing in the order named from an elevator, would discover Spud and the inconnu in armchairs not far off. Simultaneously Spud would discover Lillian — and Sally, of course. He would be heard saying, "Here they come!" in a boastful undertone. Spud was very proud of them, as well he might have been. Sally had a new evening gown, bought in desperation on Wednesday; and Lillian was Lillian, even in New York.

She was "Miss Legendre" in New York. On the hotel register she was

"Miss Lillian Legendre, Cleveland." Sally had said, "But suppose Bill writes to you? You won't get the letter," and Lillian had said, "Why won't I? How many 'Legendres' do you think they have in this hotel, besides me?" So that was all right, or it would be. Bill hadn't yet written.

"This is Miss Legendre," Spud would say, "—and Miss Sally Holtz. My old pal Eddie Macauley. Eddie, give these little girls a hand."

By Friday they had met five New York men. They were not displeased with this record, and they were even a little smug about the propriety of the meetings. They had not picked anybody up - not they. Even Spud, in the beginning, had been presented to them, and by a friend of Bill's. Well, not a friend of Bill's, exactly, but an acquaintance — a Mr. Luigi, who ran Bill's favorite New York speakeasy. It amounted to the same thing.

Mr. Luigi, peering through an inset of dense grill-work in his locked front door, had recognized his card, with his signature on the back of it, whether or not he recognized Lillian or remembered her name. He had unlocked the door and bowed them in. "We're so dead tired from shopping," Sally had explained to him, "— we thought maybe we might have a little cocktail." Sally had been anxious not to be misunderstood. Though she had Lillian's word for it that New York speakeasies were perfectly respectable, especially in the daytime, and that unescorted ladies of the nicest sort repaired to them, Sally was still dubious. It sounded pretty funny, she said, to her.

Her explanation to Mr. Luigi had been truthful, in any case. They were very tired from shopping — or from exploring shops; they had tried hard not to buy anything today. "Whatever you do," Lillian had said to Sally as they were setting out, "don't you let me buy anything, will you, Sal? No matter what I say. Because that's the trouble with New York — you want everything you see the first day, and you just go haywire, and then you're sorry every day after that. I know, believe me!"

Sally had done her best. If her fatigue was greater than Lillian's now, her rôle of guardian was perhaps the reason. Vigilance and remonstrance at counters, at millinery mirrors and in trying-on rooms, Sally had found, took a lot out of you; and the saleswomen who glowered at you, inquiring with their New York eyes why you were butting into this, and what you knew about it? — you in your little fifteen-dollar-and-ninety-eight-cent dress made you feel badly. Moreover, Lillian had glowered. She had sided with the saleswoman, and in their absences in quest of more and more irresistible temptations, she had demanded tartly of Sally whose funeral, please, this was? "I know what I said — but I guess I can change my mind, can't I?"

They had left the hotel at noon, after they had unpacked and got settled, and after Sally had treated Lillian's face and fingernails and hair. There had been a slight delay just as they started from their room. "Wait a minute till I slap some make-up on," Sally had entreated, and Lillian had waited, with the door open and one hand on the doorknob, rattling it. Then they had been ready, they had dropped twelve stories in an elevator, they had entrusted their key to a man at the desk, and wedging themselves into one tight quarter of a revolving door - Sally's fault, of course — they had reached the sidewalk. "We turn left," Lillian had said, and they had turned to the left and proceeded at a brisk clip to the corner of Sixth Avenue. "This is Sixth Avenue, you see," Lillian had said. "Now the next will be Fifth Avenue"; but the next had been Seventh Avenue, and the next beyond that had been Broadway. After a period of indecision, during which Lillian kept saying that she couldn't understand it, they took a taxi.

At half-past one, in the novelty jewelry department of a store that they thought was Hellman-Jacques' — it turned out later that it had been Ernst and Zoller's — they thought of lunch. Intermittently in the ensuing hour, Sally thought of it again, and at quarter of three she spoke of it, observing that she was starving. They were just then approaching a misses' dress department. "What's going on?" Lillian rejoined abstractedly. "Look at the women."

Sally looked. There were women seated on velvet chairs in rows as far as the eye could reach. The rows —there were two of them, facing — formed an aisle, through which at this very moment a girl like a bisque doll taken from a show-window downstairs and given life and lissomeness was moving.

"It's a fashion show!" Lillian cried, and she began to hasten toward it. "My dear, can you imagine the luck?"

Sally couldn't. It was a procession of French imports for the summer.

You had a program, a stiff white one with a tasseled pencil attached, and you could write down "Louiseboulanger" and "Paquin" and "Molyneux" and names like that, if you knew how. They were announced for you, in clear and carrying voices belonging to black crêpe-de-chine personages stationed here and there. When the mannequins swayed past you — one by one, and long minutes apart you could stop them, if you dared, and ask them what the dresses cost. To your surprise the mannequins also had voices.

"Three hundred and fifty," they said. "Our copies will be one hundred and seventy-five."

Repetitions of this annoyed Sally, and made her irreverent. "I'll take a dozen," she whispered to Lillian, who whispered, "Shut up."

They sat on a little gray velvet seat for two, where a slow and stately gentleman, dressed as if to be married in a cutaway coat and striped trousers, had placed them. Lillian smoked cigarettes and looked intense. She held her program against her knee and kept the pencil pinched in her fingers, and from time to time wrote busily. Reading over her shoulder, Sally was impressed by such notations as "fuchsia slippers-contrast," "white suede hat," "turquoise jewelry tan lace eve. dress" and "yellow sport outfit black belt & buttons." There was even a detailed analysis of a mannequin's coiffure, with the word "Try" written after it and underlined.

"She doesn't miss a trick," Sally thought. "I never saw anything like her."

Sally's own program was blank except for the little cat with whiskers that Sally, given a pencil and a minute, always drew. She was moved to add something, and she wrote down "black lace dress, pink slip," and in a corner she traced Joe Gratz's initials.

They had one whispered exchange that both of them were to remember. Lillian began it. "I could do that," she said, without preamble.

"What?"

"That."

Sally's eyes followed hers. The blondest of the mannequins had just gone by, in pale blue chiffon ruffles and a bluer velvet jacket. A little way beyond them she was standing now, displaying the velvet jacket's sleeves and lining, and untying its bow. She was slipping the jacket off and holding it away, while she turned and turned again, displaying the gown. She had a beautiful figure, "—but so has Lil," Sally said to herself. As for their faces, there was no comparison.

Wherefore Sally nodded. "I see what you mean. Sure you could. But what of it?" she continued, sotto voce. Lillian looked so solemn and so scheming. "For crying out loud!" Sally whispered. "What would be the big idea? You — with a rich husband —"

"Yeah!" said Lillian. "Oh, yes, indeed. He's rolling in it."

Sally was shocked into momentary silence.

"Well, at least you don't have to work," she countered then, reproachfully. "You know how you hated working. You oughtn't to forget that, Lil."

"I hated it in Renwood. I wouldn't mind it here."

"What makes you think you wouldn't? Modeling dresses all day-

"Listen," said Lillian. Sally listened.

"The way I feel this minute," said Lillian, "I'd scrub floors — to live in New York."

That was the way she felt this minute, thought Sally.

Mr. Luigi's speakeasy had been a private house, and it still looked like one — it looked so much like one to Sally that she had a sense of guilt going up the stairs. "Did he say to go up?" she asked before she would start. Mr. Luigi was busy locking his door again.

The second floor was reassuring, however. This was no home, Sally guessed. In the hall a small square bar enclosed two bartenders, both active, and the rooms at left and right were full of benches, chairs and tables. Before the bar, with his elbows on it and his foot on its low rail, stood a short, well-fed young man in gray, with pasted brown hair and a welcoming blue eye for Lillian. Mr. Spud Koehler. They saw him first, as he first saw them, in the bar mirror.

They passed him demurely and entered the room at the right — the larger, front room. Here there were booths, and the tables had colored cloths and little modern lamps with conical shades, and the walls had amusing silhouettes painted on them. In the corner near the two blind windows, a Negro in a dinner jacket was playing lazy jazz on a small piano. There were a number of people, ten or a dozen, sitting about. There was a couple in love, and there was another couple, and there was a party of four in a booth — three young men, and a girl who looked married to one of them. There were two iron-gray gentlemen, like fathers, in a corner. Everybody was quiet enough, every table was minding its own business; and the dare devil light that had been in Sally's eyes in the taxicab en route to her first Manhattan speakeasy now dimmed and disappeared. A glint of pride replaced it. The little back room at Joe's on a rainy Monday evening was wilder than this.

They had been at their table perhaps a quarter of an hour when Mr. Spud Koehler came into their lives officially. It had been only a question of time, and of Mr. Koehler's ingenuity. Out of the corners of their eyes they had watched him pondering ways and means.

Once or twice he had seemed to believe in Lillian's sedate imperviousness; he had seemed on the point of giving up, of paying for his drink and going. When these symptoms were marked — then and only then — Lillian had turned her face toward him. Mr. Koehler had decided to tarry longer.

He was presently seen to detain Mr. Luigi for private conversation. Mr. Luigi at what he heard first hunched his shoulders and spread his hands out wide; then, as Mr. Koehler spoke more earnestly and at greater length, the shoulders shrugged, the hands descended to Mr. Luigi's sides. Mr. Luigi nodded. Lillian and Sally, in whose own conversation there had been a lull, fell to chatting animatedly of the fashion show of this afternoon. They were engrossed when Mr. Luigi and his client reached them. They looked up with small starts of surprise.

"You remember Mr. Koehler," Mr. Luigi said to Lillian. "Mrs. — Miss- Ah-h, for names I am so bad!"

So it was done. Miss Legendre remembered Mr. Koehler very well, she said, in a voice a trifle raised in case there were any skeptics present. She asked how he was, and how he had been. Mr. Koehler had been fine, just fine.

"How about yourself? ... You're looking swell," said Mr. Koehler feelingly.

Even Mr. Luigi was convinced, or nearly so.

Spud — he was Spud with almost no delay — was a self made man. He was in the mirror and plate-glass business. He had a plant in Jersey, and a showroom here in town. Lillian and Sally must come and see it. Spud had a car, the make of which he mentioned, together with the year (this very one) of its manufacture, the number of its cylinders, and the interesting fact of its current presence outside the speakeasy. The mounted policeman in this street, whose name was Maguire, was a friend of Spud's, as well as of Luigi's; and Spud could park as long as he liked between the no-parking signs without getting a ticket. Not that getting a ticket would have mattered at all to Spud. The Police Chief was another friend of his.

Spud lived in West Fifty-fifth Street. He had a big apartment — too big; he had rattled around in it, he had been like a lost soul in it at times, and so now he shared it with two other fellows, Skeel and Runyan. Runyan was away a lot. Away now, in fact. Skeel was a broker. Lillian and Sally would like Skeel. He was a great fellow, greatest fellow in the world. He was one of Spud's best friends — a noteworthy distinction.

"Tell me about yourselves," said Spud in conclusion; and indeed, it did seem only fair.

They told him all they felt he ought to know. This wasn't much, but it served. Spud was not a very good listener. He was given to interruptions, relevant and irrelevant, and to leaning back in his chair and snapping his fingers and calling for Luigi or George. In the interims, while he heard who his ladies were and whence they came, he looked at Lillian. It was evident that as long as she looked like that, he didn't care.

"D'you get over to New York often?" he asked her.

"As often as I can."

"'Atta baby!" said Spud. "You like my town, eh?"

"I adore it."

"Like the theater?"

"Mad about it."

"What are you two little girls going to do this evening?" said Spud.

When you were with Lil, Sally thought with a fleeting sigh, it was that easy.

They met Skeel. They met Spud's second cousin, Roy Somebody; and on Thursday evening they met Eddie Macauley. Mr. Macauley, like his predecessors, was Sally's escort — a fact which unfortunately kept slipping his mind. He seemed to think that he was Lillian's. From time to time, set right by the most unfriendly glances from his host, or by cheerfully candid complaints from Sally, Mr. Macauley became abashed and did what he could about it. His atonements usually took the form of brief turns on the dance floor, during which he plied Sally with questions full of the third person pronoun and noticeably barren of the second. Eddie, in short, was Sally's in name only.

"Well," said Sally in the dressing room, "another one bit the dust, I see. It's a good thing I'm in love with Joe. I might get sore some evening."

Mr. Macauley's infatuation was unrequited. Lillian said, "He's the type who breaks his neck to pay the taxi and then sits on his hands when they bring the dinner check." But he played his brief part in the prologue of the drama that was imminent, and in retrospect she would think of him kindly. For with him, the progression away from the original Spud began — that ended where it ended. The next man they met was a man Eddie knew, one Harry Fletcher. And it was Harry Fletcher who knew Gaerste.

Leaving Spud behind them was pleasant enough, per se. They were very gay on Friday evening, without him. Attended by the Messrs. Macauley and

Fletcher, they felt increasingly festive. Things were looking up. This new man, Harry, wasn't bad at all. Even as Eddie, for all his faults, had been an improvement on Spud, so Harry Fletcher was an improvement on Eddie. "If this keeps up," said Lillian, "one of these days we might meet some really attractive men," — a bit of divination that was later recalled and applauded.

In the meantime, they were enjoying themselves. They couldn't complain, they agreed. They were getting around a lot — as they had always. The scratch-pad on the little telephone table in their room was growing blacker and mussier and more competitive daily, and the mementos in the drawer were mounting so that when you opened it, a champagne cork or a doll or something fell out. By the end of the week, their clothes — their evening clothes especially — bore telling evidence. There was the smear of grease from the axle of Spud Koehler's car on the hem of Lillian's green velvet wrap, which Sally wore. There were the pin-holes and the stains of stems on Lillian's left shoulder-straps. One of a pair of pearl slipper-ornaments — also Lillian's — had been lost at the Casino, or at the Club Montmartre, or possibly in the taxi in between; and wine had been splashed on Sally in her new lace gown when a pair of black adagio dancers in Harlem on Friday night, very late, had whirled too fast and a little too close to the table.

Their evenings were always prolonged. Sometimes physical weariness assailed them, but they were never sleepy — they never wanted to go home. A thought for their escorts, due at downtown offices at nine, never crossed their minds. Nor were they ever surfeited. Though they were always restless, always moving from place to place, from hotel roof to grillroom, from one night club to another — piling in and out of cars and taxis all night long, it was not because the places ever for an instant palled. Simply it was because there were so many, many of them, and they had so little time for seeing them all.

Wherefore evenings begun at seven o'clock or seven thirty lasted till four and five — Saturday night lasted till seven. Entertainment ceased and dancing ceased and bands walked out on them, and cabaret girls wearing ordinary clothes, like shop-girls, came through smoke-foggy rooms, past empty tables and their tables, and were gone. Then it would be decided that they might as well go too; and their bill, face down in shame, would be brought by a newly alacritous waiter. They would gather cosmetics together, they would retrieve from the girl at the coat room two ebony sticks and two oval black pancakes that opened up — "Plopp!" — and were hats. High hats. ... There was always a swift and secret meeting of smiling feminine eyes when the hats went, "Plopp!" Renwood was never so remote as then.

They would emerge under an awning, exclaiming at the dawn, and chorusing, "Good-morning!" when the door man said good-night to them. They never went direct to the hotel from this last dancing-place. They were always hungry: Sally was always hungry, and Lillian always said she was, because it was the New York thing to breakfast before bedtime on scrambled eggs — invariably on scrambled eggs, with bacon — in some democratic restaurant, in your plutocratic garb. It was the New York thing to take an early-morning ride in Central Park: to get the smoke out of your lungs, New Yorkers said. So you took a little ride, in Spud's car, or in Harry Fletcher's car — once you engaged a silly open carriage, with a horse and all, and rode in that.

They were really seeing New York, they felt. They were getting to know it really well. They could have told you a good deal about it. New York was enormous, endless, and as tall as it was wide, with buildings reaching to the clouds and the most famous people — actresses and song-writers and band-leaders and such — living in penthouses on the tops of the buildings. New York had six million inhabitants, who were said to work all day, and who certainly played all night, because you saw them. In between times they went home to Park Avenue, if they were rich and social, or to Greenwich Village if they were artistic. Poor people lived on the East Side, tough people in the Bowery, the Chinese in Chinatown, of course, and the black people up in Harlem. That disposed of everybody, more or less, except the young men-about-town, like Eddie and Harry — and they were no problem. They lived on the side streets, among the speakeasies.

These things Lillian and Sally knew about New York, and could have told you. What they felt about it, the glamour that it had for them, was inexpressible, was beyond any words of theirs. They had no real belief in it as a place where there were households, for all their list of residential sections. They had no sense of normal lives, of family meals, of firesides, of reading-lamps and easy chairs, of children going to school. Behind the lustrous windows in the tall apartment houses, New Yorkers dwelt — and New Yorkers were the people at the theaters at night, the other couples dancing on the dance floors. New Yorkers were the sleek, dramatic women at whom you stared and stared, and their attendant gloomy millionaires. New Yorkers were the Great Ones who were invisible, but whose proximity you felt and thought about and thrilled to. You might see one any time. You might meet one anywhere. Your favorite movie star. Your favorite aviator. Your favorite radio voice, at last embodied.

These were New Yorkers. New York itself was Broadway. It was Fifth Avenue until the cocktail hour — then it moved over, it put on jewels and spangles by the billion, and was Broadway. It was the packed auditoriums of playhouses. It was the traffic in Times Square. It was the gaudy midnight view from a glassed-in roof. It was the Tango. It was a trumpet with a gilded derby hat on the end of it, screaming anew the old St. Louis Blues. It was a night-club hostess with yellow hair and a big, skin-tight red dress. It was the jingle of hammers against glasses in applause. It was the "Twee-twee" sound that orchestras made when a dance was over. It was the stutter of little silver tap-shoes on a golden floor.

It was New York. It was champagne cooling in a sweating bucket. It was an orchestra-leader's face on the skin of a lighted drum. It was a dozen dancers, girdled with ostrich feathers — red ones, green ones — doing a dance to drums. It was a sullen girl with a strange, disturbing voice, singing, How Long Has This Been Going On?

CHAPTER EIGHTEEN

Their excitement over everything, which they dissembled much less well than they hoped they did, was one of the things about them that charmed their several swains. By its contagion, jaded gentlemen like Eddie and Harry, who had lived in New York for five years and three years and a half respectively, were enabled to recover, for an evening or two, some of their own lost out-of-towners' gusto. During the sightseeing parties of Friday and Saturday nights, Eddie and Harry were indefatigable guides; and Harry was a prodigal one. They made a good team. Eddie had the inspirations— "Let's look in at Belle Livingstone's a minute," — and Harry had the wherewithal.

The exception to this rule occurred on Sunday, in the afternoon. Gaerste was Harry's inspiration. Lillian would remember just when and where he had it — they were in his car, and they were on Riverside Drive, and it was not quite five o'clock. They had left the hotel about two. They had lunched at a squat stucco inn, in what Eddie and Harry had described as "the country": a suburban town the size of Renwood, it had proved to be. They were returning now. They were still sightseeing. Grant's Tomb had been pointed out, and politely regarded by Lillian and Sally, and a battleship anchored in the Hudson and droves of its sailors strolling on shore had been duly called to their attention. Eddie and Harry were now concerned with the question of what to show them next. They conferred, Eddie leaning from the back seat to the front, so that his head in its slanted gray hat was at Lillian's shoulder. As the guest of honor, she rode beside Harry.

"There's that 'speak' in the Village," Eddie said, "with the little roof garden. We might drop down there and have a drink outdoors. It's too nice to go in yet."

"I've got a better idea than that," said Harry suddenly.

"What?"

"We'll go calling."

"Lillian, who had been meditatively returning the scrutiny of a pair of passing ensigns, looked around now. "Calling? Who - on whom?"

"Friend of mine has a place I'd like you to see."

"Who's that?" asked Eddie.

"Chap named Gaerste."

Eddie had heard of him.

"What kind of a place?" Lillian wanted to know. "You wait," said Harry.

They turned up a side street and started across town. Sally's plaintive voice was promptly heard from the rear: "Hey, where we going? Nobody tells me anything!"

Eddie sat back, and reported.

"'Gaerste,'" Sally echoed disapprovingly. "Funny name."

"It rhymes with 'thirsty,'" Eddie said. "And how have you been?"

"Where is this place?" Lillian inquired of Harry.

"Clear across. Over by the other river."

"But that's the East Side, isn't it?"

"Smart little girl."

"But isn't that the slums? The East Side? I always thought it was."

Harry smiled. "Well," he said, "it is and it isn't. You see what you think."

Twenty minutes' driving and halting for red lights brought them down a numbered street bridged twice by Elevated structures. It was a broad street, and the farther you proceeded on it, the less like the East Side as in the movies it became. There was not a pushcart anywhere, and not a sign of airing bedding. On the contrary, what remained of the street after you passed the second Elevated looked enough like Park Avenue, Lillian thought, to be Park Avenue. It wasn't, of course. But here were more of the same apartment houses — high, wide, handsome — with doormen to match, with elongated visors of awning protecting the sidewalk. Here, in the fronts of the buildings, all the way up, were the broad casement windows that you liked particularly; that particularly made you wonder whose they were.

Lillian sat up. She reached to the top of the wind shield and tilted down the little bar of mirror in which Harry was wont to note, sometimes in time and some times not, the approach of goggled Doom on motorcycles. In the mirror now were Eddie and Sally, looking at opposite buildings — Eddie at left-hand buildings, Sally at right. Lillian concentrated upon her own near face. Lipstick wouldn't hurt. She opened her handbag hastily, and plunged her fingers in.

"Who is this man?" she said. "What's his name, again?"

It was too late for other questions. They were there.

At the end of a reddish-brown awning a doorman opened the car doors for them, and Lillian and Eddie and Sally got out. "Just a second," Harry said, "till I pull along, out of the way."

"Pull up behind that Rolls, sir," said the doorman matter-of-factly.

In the dim and vaulted Spanish lobby, the doorman's hatless twin made motions at a switchboard and said into a transmitter that Mr. Fisher was downstairs for Mr. Gaerste.

"Fletcher, Fletcher," said Harry, "— not Fisher."

But it appeared that it did not matter. Mr. Gaerste wasn't in.

"That's too bad," Harry said tentatively. He glanced at Lillian, and turned again to the doorman's twin. "Let me talk to his man."

He was connected. "Hello," he said, "is that you, Henning? This is Mr. Fletcher. Where's Mr. Gaerste — out of town?"

He listened. The answer was protracted, and Sally, losing interest, whispered to Eddie that there wasn't any Gaerste. "Yes, we have no Gaerstes. ... Look!" added Sally. "Look through that door down there the little courtyard, with the fountain. Isn't that the darlingest thing?"

They were inspecting it at closer range when Lillian's voice recalled them. "Come on, you two! We're going up anyway."

"Gaerste's horseback-riding," Harry explained, "over in the park. But he ought to be home any minute now, he said about five. So we'll go up and wait."

On the way to the elevator, Lillian linked her arm into Sally's and drew her somewhat ahead of the gentlemen. "Hm'm?" said Sally; and their new hats came together, brim to brim.

"It's a penthouse!" Lillian's breath exploded.

"What is? Where we're going?"

"Sh-h. Yes! Harry just told me."

They could speak no more, but they could exchange a delirious glance, and did. Only this had been lacking. Their New York trip was complete.

In the elevator, shooting smoothly to the roof, Lillian said to Harry conversationally, aside, "How old a man is this Mr. Gaerste? Old?"

Harry, who was himself twenty-five, said that Gaerste wasn't so terribly old. He didn't know how old exactly. Under forty, though.

"And he isn't married?"

"No. I believe he was once," Harry said. "But that was long before I knew him."

"How long have you known him?"

"Couple of years."

The elevator stopped. Its sliding panel revealed a second panel marked "P. H.," and this in turn disclosed an entrance hall. They confronted a circular window, like a monstrous porthole broken into panes, with a quarter circular window-seat full of silken cushions below it. Or perhaps it wasn't a window. Perhaps it was only a painted scene.

The criss-cross frames of the panes, the zigzag crescent of the cushions, the terrace just outside, the fan-backed chairs and the sun-umbrella, and the evergreen trees against the parapet, and the sky above it, and the aëroplane in the sky - all these looked real, or almost real. But they probably weren't.

"Golly!" breathed Sally. "Great, isn't it?" Eddie said.

Harry noticed the aëroplane. He smiled slowly. "There would be a 'plane up there," he said, "all nice and shiny." But only he knew the point of this remark.

He rang a bell beside a door like a checkerboard of tan and silver squares. "Now watch," he said over his shoulder. "Don't miss the gentleman's gentleman."

Sally was puzzled. "The which?"

"His valet, Henning. Formerly with the Duke of Wheresis — and all that."

Not until Henning opened the door did Lillian turn from the window. She had not said anything at all.

There was first a foyer that Sally thought must be the living-room, so very big it was, so beautiful it seemed to her, all done in black and white and green and silver. This was modern decoration. Sally recognized it for herself and, pleased, told Lillian. The young men were surrendering their humble hats to Henning.

"Modernistic," Sally muttered. "This is like Irene has."

But Lillian did not concur. "Oh, is it!" she said witheringly. She spared a glance for Sally. "Irene," she said, "never saw anything like this — and never will."

There was a doorway next: a plaster arch, with metal gates, waist-high, wrought of dull silver in an odd design of trees and peacocks. Henning opened a gate and held it open and they all passed through. Here was the living-room. Sally grew secretly sheepish over her secret misconception. Here was a room four times the size and twice the height of that first room, with twelve long windows in two walls, with a fireplace like a cavern, with rugs like great rafts floating on a marble pool of floor. The marble pool was black and the far-off walls were white, or near-white. Everything else — the rugs, the furniture, the books and cushions, the decorative screens, the twelve foot window draperies — everything else was brilliant blended color.

It was Eddie, swallowing his unpalatable awe, who found a simile. A modern salon so huge was like an automobile showroom. "All it needs," said Eddie, "is six or seven Cadillacs." But nobody heard, nobody was listening to Eddie.

They wandered on. Their shadows that their feet had anchored to the polished marble began to move along again; to vanish over rugs. You could not see this room by standing still. You made a round trip — a grand tour, with excursions to the corners. The corners were especially picturesque. In one of them an enormous V-shaped couch with mirrors behind it was built upon a platform up three shallow curving steps. Upon a similar platform in the corner diagonally opposite, two grand pianos, twins, stood end to end, with their lids rearing.

"This fellow Gaerste plays, I hope?" said Eddie, eyeing them.

Eddie was becoming rather cross. "Or doesn't he," he said.

Harry said he did, sometimes. "To amuse himself. He plays jazz by ear

— he's not bad, either. And he likes this two-piano stuff. He gets a guy named Spider James who used to be with Lopez up here, or somebody else like that, and they do an Ohman and Arden for hours."

"But he doesn't play professionally."

"No. Hardly!"

Lillian turned her head. "What does he do, Harry?"

"Well, well!" Harry said genially. "Another county heard from! Where have you been all this time?"

"I've been looking."

"You haven't said a word."

"Well, I am now," said Lillian. "What's his business?"

"He hasn't any, honey. He's retired."

They were proceeding toward the next corner a moment after that when Eddie said moodily, "I bet that's his picture."

He referred to the largest of the large paintings in the room, and the only portrait. This hung over the fireplace. It was a full-length portrait of a middle-sized young man in a naval officer's blue uniform. The young man stood with his arms folded and with his feet apart, as if the painted rug beneath them rolled. He looked sternly and responsibly off over the East River. There was a light above him, on the frame, in a gold tube.

"Yeah, that's Gaerste," Harry said.

"Is it? He's nice-looking!" Sally cried in great amazement. This was plainly the last thing she had expected. Indeed, it was too much; and Sally's tact, which was ever wayward, went on one of its holidays. She beamed at Lillian; and when Lillian ignored this optical congratulation — for such it seemed to be — Sally prodded her with words. "Don't you think so, Lil?"

"Don't I think what?"

"He's nice-looking?"

Lillian glanced casually at the portrait again. "Um hmm," she said.

She turned away. It was the only thing to do. She and Harry sauntered on, leaving Eddie and Sally lingering. "Quite à ping-pong," Eddie was saying. "Four more of those in a row, and we'd have a rough idea what the guy looks like."

Lillian murmured irritably, "He gives me a pain."

"Who?"

"Eddie. What did he come up here for if he was going to razz everything he saw?"

Harry smiled his slow smile. "Oh, well," he said. "It strikes some people that way."

"What does?"

"This place."

"They're just jealous!"

"Probably," said Harry.

"He doesn't look a bit old," Lillian said. "He looks about twenty-three or twenty-four."

"Eddie?"

"No, no! This man. In his picture, I mean."

"Well, but you saw the uniform," Harry reminded her. "It must have been painted during the war, or just after."

"Oh," said Lillian. She thought about it. "Still," she thought. "Here's the bar," Harry said. "Take a deep breath."

It was another corner: one that, in effect, had been filled triangularly with plaster and then scooped out to make a small round room within the room. A submarine scene: green water, strings of silver bubbles rising, little flashing vivid fish, adorned the curved wall of this alcove. There was an arc-shaped bar, a rather lovely green and onyx thing, like a mermaid's mirrorless dressing-table. There were also four long-legged black stools with bright-green leather tops. These, though they somewhat spoiled the illusion, were useful.

Eddie and Sally were called to come and look, and they came and looked.

"We can have a drink," Harry said, and he rang a fish's opal eye. "We can have it here, or on the terrace, either one."

"I don't want a drink," said Lillian. But the others did.

"Where're you going?" they demanded.

Her voice trailed back to them. "Nowhere. Just out here."

Harry, following her after the bell had been answered and the drinks ordered, found her standing near the fire place in the outer room, confronting the low bookshelves at one side. She had a framed photograph in her hands, picked up from the top of the shelves. She said, "Who's this, Harry?"

"That's a Mrs. Johnson."

"Who's she?"

"Well, let's see," said Harry, "who is she? She isn't anybody specially. She's a little divorcée. Friend of Gaerste's."

"A friend of his?"

"That's all," Harry said, twinkling.

"Why?"

"I just wondered."

"As a matter of fact," said Harry, "he was fond of her at one time. But that's all over — or I guess it is. I never see her up here any more."

Lillian replaced the photograph. Her eyes lingered on it. "Do you think she's beautiful?"

"She's quite good looking, yes."

Lillian smiled softly. "But not beautiful," she said.

She changed her mind then: she would have a cocktail, after all. Harry might go and bring her just a little one? Oh, any kind. A champagne cocktail would be nice.

"Anything you like," Harry said. "Don't you want to have it in the bar, though?"

"No, out here. I like this big room. Or on the terrace, maybe," she said as an afterthought. Those fan backed chairs were picturesque. Any chair was more becoming than a stool.

Harry went. Lillian went hunting through the big room for her handbag, which she had put down some where as she passed. She found it, with her gloves, in a chair made of silver pipes and upholstery, and she took it to the corner made of mirrors. She saw herself coming: a girl in gray, whose hair was red in a drooped gray halo, whose outlines were as definite as if the room behind her were a page and she a colored paper-doll. "Cut on the dotted line." ... She loved this gray ensemble. It was a dress and jacket, and the jacket had wide bracelets of gray fox around the sleeves. It couldn't have been newer. On Thursday it had lain in a window on Fifty- seventh Street, and on Friday it had hung in a fitters' workroom with pins in its seams, and yesterday after noon, after six, they had delivered it. Just in time. Just in the nick of time, she realized now.

Half kneeling and half sitting on the divan built against the mirrors, she deleted her mouth with her handkerchief and revised it with her lipstick, and otherwise perfected her bright image. It took a little while. She had not quite finished when Harry returned with her drink.

"Will you hold it a second?"

Harry stood holding it. "Gaerste just phoned," he said. "He's on his way over. He told Henning to tell us to be sure and wait."

"Is that so?" Lillian said.

She still faced the mirror. She leaned a little closer to it, and with her forefinger removed an extra grain or two of powder. She smoothed her eyebrows with a finger tip, and touched the flat wings of her hair. She was satisfied then. Her eyes met her reflected eyes with shining understanding. So he was coming, was he? Let him come.

CHAPTER NINETEEN

On The passenger lists of the fast, expensive transatlantic liners, he was, "Gaerste, Mr. C. G., and manservant;" and this pleased him, always. He always looked to see it. He always turned the pages of a list to see how many other names were advertised as affluent in that same way. He took it for granted that every man traveled with a valet who had a valet, and that every man had one who could afford one. It was gratifying to note that there were never very many. There might be richer men on board than he — but never many.

He went often to Europe. He went because people were going, or because his tailor was in London, or because New York was hot, or cold; or because it was time he went again. Invariably he sailed on less than twenty-four hours ' notice. They could always find the right accommodations for him. Over telephones they said, "Booked solid, Mr. Gaerste — but we'll see what we can do. One of those A-deck suites? I'll call you back."

He liked the voyage itself. Though he affected to regard it as a necessary evil, though he took the swiftest boats, he never wished the five days over.

In the small world of a ship he was conspicuous, briefly famous — he enjoyed a notoriety hard to gain in larger, busier worlds. He was the man who had the Prince of Wales 's suite on this crossing. He was the man with eleven trunks of clothes. He was the individual bidder who overbid the syndicates in the nightly auction pool on the ship's run. He was the contributor of hundred-dollar bills when plates were passed — nor did he fold the bills, nor did he thrust them underneath the layers of other people's ones and fives.

The brokerage offices on board sent messengers to find him and hand him new quotations every half-hour during the market day. The maîtres d'hôtel of the à la carte restaurants on upper decks called upon him of mornings for conferences regarding his luncheons and dinners. In these restaurants, which were open all night, or in the private dining-rooms of his suites, he gave parties that were the talk of the promenade deck the next day. People said, "Did you hear about the party that that Gaerste gave last night for the Dancer?" (Or the Movie Actress. Or the Channel Swimmer.)

People who met him, people who accepted his hospitality, reported that he ordered epicurean dinners and suppers, that his knowledge of wines commanded the wine steward's actual respect, and that his French was quick and good enough to justify and pardon his persistent use of it in addressing English-speaking waiters. People who met him also reported that he was nicer than you'd think. He was quiet, not very talkative, and really not in the least obnoxious. His ostentation ended with his gestures, and he did not brag in words at all. He was a punctilious host, and an interested one: above all, he was a grateful one. The pleasure was his when you came. When you went, when you said to him that you had had a beautiful time, he looked at you eagerly. "Did you? Do you mean it?" his eyes said.

Little was known about him. He was an American named Gaerste. No one knew just who he was, or where his money came from. No one had ever heard of him who had not crossed with him before — it was as if, like stewards and seamen, he existed only on board ship, mattered only between shore and shore. You forgot him at Cherbourg. You forgot him during the crossing, in the intervals of his campaign for your attention. There were two things he liked to do which no one noticed or remarked, which no one ever thought significant who chanced to see him. He liked to go alone to the top deck at night, and stand there, and watch the slow relentless march of the great smokestacks in a line — magnificent, triumphant, incomparably lonely — through the infinite wind and moan and shriek, against the infinite starlight.

If no one came, if no consummate fool behind the glow of a cigar-end said, "Nice night," and spoiled his high, fierce exaltation, he would stay there long. An hour. Two hours.

There was another solitary thing he did on shipboard, another place that he sought frequently. Emerging from his cabin in mid-morning, dressed by Henning, he circled the promenade deck once or twice, and on the third round paused, and leaned upon the forward rail that overlooks the bow. A first-class passenger could go no farther forward than that rail, unless he asked to do so; and Gaerste never asked. He was content to gaze upon the steerage from on high. He could remember here as well as anywhere — or better that he had been a steerage passenger when he was ten, that when he was ten he had first crossed this ocean to America, and that his father had worn a blue blouse like that blue blouse moving down there now, and that his mother had had a shawl over her head.

He could remember, leaning on his English sleeves, and looking down. When he was ten. Twenty-eight years ago.

He had made one of those rapid fortunes that are sometimes made by the sons of the ignorant and fearless. At fifteen he had started; he had stopped going to school. At eighteen he had owned an interest in a small and shabby motion picture theater in Lynn, Massachusetts, where his parents lived. At thirty he had owned and operated twenty theaters — new ones, palatial, some of them — in Boston and vicinity. When he was thirty three, his holdings had been worth five million dollars. He had sold out. It was enough. It would buy all the things he wanted.... He had known then, as he knew now, exactly what they were.

He had made room for them. He had disposed of his house in Cambridge and his cottage at Revere, and he had suggested to his wife that she divorce him. Her name was Rosa, and she had been a ticket-seller in one of his theaters. They had been married (temporarily: he had always realized that) for seven years. They had no children, and they were not sentimental. Rosa said, "Maybe I don't want to divorce you," but this was courtesy. Chiefly she said, "Well, supposing I do? I got to live."

She had only a vague conception of his wealth. She mentioned one hundred thousand dollars — not very hopefully. Gaerste gave her two hundred thousand, some government bonds, and both the cars. He would have kissed her good-bye when they parted forever, but Rosa primly refused. It appeared that in the interval of the divorce proceedings she had acquired a fiancé, a pugilist named Wildcat Weise, who wouldn't like it.

Gaerste moved to New York. He took five rooms in a choice hotel, and from this base he set forth daily, to see, to hear, to learn - eventually to buy. He heard of a coöperative apartment house, just then being built, that was to have two duplex penthouses on its large roof. He bought them both, and retained the architects to turn them into one. He spent an evening in his shirtsleeves reading decorators' magazines. There was a Frenchman named Claude Durieux who did this modern stuff. ... He cabled Durieux. Receiving no immediate cable in reply, he telephoned to Paris, using a waiter as interpreter. They talked three hundred and seven dollars' worth. Durieux accepted.

"Voilà, m'sieur," said the waiter when he rang off.

Gaerste had an idea. "Look here, what's your name?" he said.

"Jacques, m'sieur."

"Zhock, eh. And d'you mind telling me what you're making here? I have a reason for asking —"

Thus it came to pass that when he sailed for Europe shortly, on his first East-bound trip, he was already, "Gaerste, Mr. C. G., and manservant." Jacques was the manservant. He was really more tutor than valet — he packed and unpacked, and put new black pearl studs into new starched white shirts, and laid dinner-clothes out, and that was his valetry. For the rest, he was Gaerste's professor of French, his instructor in food and wines, his lecturer on tips and table manners, and his guide in Paris. He was a great success. There was a certain sort of education that Gaerste wanted, there was a definite and long-established list of things he meant to learn and Jacques knew most of them. If he had only also known what a gentleman should wear, and when, he would have been perfect.

Since he did not, they went to London and found Henning

Inevitably Jacques outlived his pedagogical usefulness —after a year or so Gaerste retired him and bought him a small roadhouse in Westchester, which he now ran with enormous annual profit to them both. But Henning was different. Henning knew everything, and was forever invaluable. To this day, his master was still his secret pupil.

Henning had created an outer man so dapper, so correct, so impeccably garbed and groomed, that people were deceived: they assumed that Gaerste was a handsome man, which he was not. He was no more that than he was an ugly one. He had a plain and pleasant face, rather too lateral to a measuring eye, and a stature altogether average. He was five feet nine — though he would not have said so.

Like all men of all sizes, he believed himself to be a little taller than he was, he felt a little taller, and no evidence could convince him that he was not five feet ten at least, and very nearly six feet with his shoes on.

Accordingly he stood very straight, head up and shoulders back. He took long steps in walking. He danced with tiny women, and tried to prefer them to all others. It was annoying that he rarely did.

He weighed what he should have weighed. With less money and less leisure, he would almost certainly have thickened after thirty — there was that tendency, inherited from chunky parents. It appeared, alarmingly, during his sojourns in Europe, when in spite of Henning's scoldings he ate too much, and drank much wine, and did not exercise. Sometimes he gained so many pounds that Henning rushed him home, imposing a strict diet on the boat. At home he rode horseback, he took fencing lessons, he boxed with polite professionals in a fashionable gymnasium on the forty-second floor of a downtown skyscraper, he played squash racquets in the court he had had built on his own terrace, he walked to the garage and back, and to the riding-school and back — and Henning, who gave him an hour's massage a day, wherever they were, now became savage, pitiless about it.

So he was thin, this hand-made Gaerste, thin and muscular; in a bathing suit he had an athlete's waistline, belted snugly below a chest that he kept filled with air. The suns of Long Island and Florida and the Riviera, and the supplementary sun-lamps of New York, browned him all year — and this was well, since it is more aesthetic to be burned than merely swarthy.

He had dark eyes with constant light behind them; black accents of brows; a broad flat forehead. His lips were long, so that his excellent teeth were hidden when he spoke, and only showed a little when he smiled. His hair was black and damp and glossy, and not — not ever so closely trimmed as to thwart its inclination to curl up at the ends, above his ears and at the back of his head. His hands were unfortunate. They were his father's hands, with a manicure.

He had studied English with Henning as he had studied French with Jacques, and he spoke carefully now, choosing his words and articulating them, avoiding all slang.

He listened more than he talked, and people who scarcely knew him told him secrets. Afterward they worried, remembering how fascinated he had seemed. They were not aware that it was themselves, not their disclosures, that absorbed him. He watched eyes and mouths and hands, he studied expressions and inflections. Everything was grist for the inner mill that was still grinding, that would some day produce his finished personality.

He cultivated three kinds of people: those from whom he could learn; those to whom he could in turn communicate his learning; and those flamboyant persons, beautiful or notable, who were as Christmas-tree ornaments, as table decorations.... It was a question of someone's being impressed. Either people must impress him, or he must impress them, or their presence at his right hand must impress the world at large. He had a hungry mind and a hungry vanity. One or the other must be fed.

He was immensely extravagant where it showed, and he was proportionately generous where gratitude was certain. He loved to do things for the acquaintances, the guests, the beneficiaries, the mercenary ladies, whom he fondly called his friends. When he returned from travel, his trunks brought lavish presents for people who expected them and for people who did not. He enjoyed particularly the gasps and splutterings of the latter. He liked to surprise his theater-ticket broker with the gift of a wafer-thin Swiss watch, or his manicurist with an evening costume from Chanel. The cynical suspicions of such recipients were unkind. They did not understand him. No one did.

Inevitably, various of the mercenary ladies above-mentioned had tried to marry Gaerste in the past five years.

For equally various reasons, they had failed. His social inferiors among them had fared no better than the ladies who would have condescended, for his millions' sake. These last impressed him, but they patronized him — or he thought they did, or feared they might. It has been said that he cultivated people from whom he could learn. This was true of men and matrons. It was not true of young women.

Intelligent or otherwise, high-born or low-born, the mercenary ladies had all made one mistake. In their anxiety to conceal the fact that it was Gaerste's money that attracted them, they had refrained from mentioning his money. They had ignored his money. By their attitudes they had belittled its importance, and mocked his pride in it and his elation over it. "Pff !" they had said, in effect. " What's money?"

But Lillian Legendre was accidentally cleverer. She was more ingenuous. Sometimes it pays. One of the first things she said to Gaerste was that in her wildest dreams she had never imagined anything so marvelous as his penthouse. "Tell me something," she added.

Gaerste would tell her anything.

"Who are you, anyway?" she asked him, dimpling up at him. "J. P. Morgan? Or John D. Rockefeller?"

CHAPTER TWENTY

Sally was all packed. Her suitcases, the straw one and the patent-leather one, blond and brunette, waited beside the door. "I never did buy a new suitcase, did I," Sally remarked sadly. Now that she was leaving New York, perhaps she never would. Once back in Renwood, perhaps she would never need a new suitcase again, her whole life long. "I don't want to go back!" Sally thought dismally. "I don't want to ! Not just yet." But this was a mental wail, unvoiced. She had had twelve superlative days in New York. She could never repay Lillian, never thank her enough, as it was.

Besides, she did want to go back, in a way. It was not only that she hadn't been urged to stay any longer, it was that she ought to be getting back, for her own sake. There was Joe, and there was her business. Competition was probably raging.... After all, a girl had to think of her future; and Sally wasn't Lillian. She had no future in a town like this.

So meditating, Sally shut and locked her professional tool-kit and set it upon the suitcases near the door. She stood looking about her. "Now, let's see."

There was very little more to do. There was an elegant pink hat-box, a New York hat-box, to tie up and tag, and there was her handbag to load with all the small things from the top of the dressing-table. Then she would be ready, except for putting on her hat and coat, and pinning on her orchids. Sally had orchids of her own today. Sally, indeed, had had a corsage every day this whole week long. That was what you got for being Lillian's little girl-friend — you got two gardenias when she got four camellias, and three purple or green orchids when she got seven white ones. You also got a vanity case the day she got the bracelet. Sally had had a new vanity case since Friday.

This day of her return to Renwood was Sunday. It was morning. Sally had elected to take a day-train back, saying that she might as well see the scenery, while she was about it. "The Horseshoe Curve," said Sally. "And Philadelphia."

She wouldn't even mind twelve or thirteen hours of scenery, she said, especially not in the parlor car chair that Gaerste's chauffeur Richard, dispatched to the station yesterday for her ticket, had procured as a matter of course. In a pleased way Sally observed that she had come to New York on a sleeper and that she was returning in a parlor car. Her tone intimated that few sensations were left.

Since it was Sunday, and early, Lillian was still in bed. In honor of Sally's departure she was, however, awake, and sitting up. She had ordered breakfast, which was coming; and accordingly she had put over her shoulders and knotted upon one of them a double triangle of chiffon, called a breakfast jacket. Propped against pillows, she smoked, and watched Sally's activities lazily.

"Sit down and talk to me," she suggested. "You're all through."

"What time is it?"

"It isn't eight-thirty yet. Richard won't be here for an hour."

"What if he's late?" Sally asked, half anxiously, half hopefully. "I'll miss my train."

"He won't be late," said Lillian. "He's never late. If he was, C. G. wouldn't have him. Stop fussing, will you?"

Sally stopped fussing. She left the dressing table, and went and sat on the foot of Lillian's bed. The cigarettes were tossed to her. New York — and Lillian — had made a sudden smoker of Sally. When you weren't allowed to chew gum, you had to do something.

She lit a cigarette, coughed, and exhaled slight smoke on an abundant breath. It was a relief. It always was. She flipped the cigarette, jauntily if prematurely, to rid it of ashes, and rested the hand that held it on the foot board of the bed. She looked at Lillian. This morning Lillian seemed somehow more exotic than familiar. Already, Sally was aware that the mood of the past twelve days had changed. Already it was as if she were back in Renwood — and Lillian still here.

Resignation was in Sally's voice. "Well, what about you?" she said. "What are you going to do today? Or don't you know yet?"

"Depends. What kind of a day is it, anyway?" Lillian inquired. "Is that sky as blue as it looks from here?"

"Yeah. It's lovely out."

"Then we're probably driving down to Easthampton," Lillian said. "That's on Long Island. C. G.'s got a summer place down there he wants to show me. 'Hacienda on-the-Dunes,' it's called. It's right by the ocean. Twenty-seven rooms and fourteen baths."

"It hardly seems enough."

"And a swimming pool," Lillian added. " A private salt-water swimming-pool in a garden in back. Can you imagine that, with the whole ocean there to swim in?"

"No," said Sally.

"Of course," said Lillian, "the house has been shut up all winter. But he sent some servants down there yesterday — no, Friday — to work in it, and in case we came this afternoon, to get dinner for us. So we'll have dinner there, and then drive back."

Sally said, "Be sure you drive back."

"Oh, don't worry ! I know what I'm doing."

"I'm beginning to believe you," Sally said, which was high praise from her.

"So that's today," Lillian summed up. "Tomorrow oh, I didn't tell you !" She laughed. "Tomorrow we're going shopping and buy me a birthday present — and C. G.'s going to get up a birthday dinner-party for me !"

"For when is this, please ?"

"For tomorrow evening, or some evening this week."

"I see," said Sally. She nodded owlishly several times. "For twenty-one years that I know of, your birthday's been in September. And now it's in May, is it? It's tomorrow. Well. Many happy returns."

"Cra-azy!" said Lillian, laughing the more.

"One of us is crazy," Sally stated definitely. "And what are you going to do when September comes?" she wanted to know.

"Oh, then I'll have it all over again! C. G. won't mind. He just loves birthdays — and giving presents."

"He's found his mate, all right," Sally said. "That was no lie he told you."

Lillian was inordinately enjoying these acid comments.

"You're such a fool," she informed Sally fondly, and added, "I'm going to miss you, do you know it?"

Sally said she was glad to hear it.

"There's the breakfast. Answer the door, will you, Sal?"

"Yes, you're going to miss me," Sally thought, obeying.

The breakfast table was rolled in and placed beside Lillian, and a chair for Sally was drawn up to it. Lillian signed the check with her usual flourish, and signalled to Sally that there was money for the tip on her dressing table. While the waiter busied himself as best he could, a pantomime went on. Sally at the dressing-table held up a quarter, though she knew better. Lillian shook her head violently and pointed for more. Sally held up two quarters. Still it was not enough. Sally held up a hair-brush, a hat and Lillian's new diamond bracelet.

The waiter departed ultimately with a dollar.

Lillian smiled again. "You're feeling high this morning, aren't you?"

"Oh, sure. I'm just as merry as a little cricket."

Lillian looked more thoughtful. Sipping grapefruit juice, she watched Sally digging at an orange. Sally, conscious of this scrutiny, kept her eyes down.

Lillian said, "Look, you don't mind my not going down to the station with you, do you, Sal?"

"Uh-uh."

"I would, only I'm dead for sleep. I thought I'd take another nap till C. G. phones."

"Why not?" said Sally.

"Richard will tend to your luggage, of course, and see that you don't get on the wrong train."

Here Sally lost her temper. "Oh, of co'se !" she drawled in mimicry; and emitted a hearty snort. " What do you mean, "of course?" she demanded heatedly.

"You little tramp! Say, anybody'd think you'd had chauffeurs and limousines waiting on you ever since you were born —   instead of since a week ago! My God, you're getting snootier by the minute!"

"Well, and why shouldn't I?" Lillian retorted imperturbably. Sally opened her mouth, and closed it. She could find no answer.

The balloon of her exasperation collapsed, and she laughed feebly. "You win. Why shouldn't you, if you can get away with it?"

"And I can," said Lillian.

"Anyway, you do."

Peace was restored.

"C. G. likes me to be snooty," Lillian said. "I found that out. He likes me to say what I like and what I don't like. For instance — remember that pigeon with white grapes the other night?"

"Can I ever forget it ?"

"There wasn't a thing the matter with that pigeon," Lillian confided, "—as far as I know. I never tasted one before. But I just thought I'd say it wasn't cooked enough, so C. G. could have fun."

"Well, he had it, all right," said Sally morosely. "He had a circus, there."

"In a quiet way, though."

"Such a hissing in French," said Sally, "I never heard. And all the waiters running to get all the head-waiters, and all the head-waiters tearing out to fire the chef or something — and never a dull moment, as I said to Harry at the time. "Well, never a dull moment, Harry,' I said."

Lillian was smiling reminiscently. "He's so snooty himself," she mused, "C. G. is. I love the way he does things. The way he gives orders — and the way he always knows just what he wants, and how he wants it. And everything's got to be just so. Even my clothes," Lillian supplemented. "He's terribly particular what I wear. Did you know he doesn't like my purple evening dress? He doesn't want me to wear it again. He says it kills my hair."

"Kills your hair?"

"'Subdues the glory of it,' he said."

Sally suppressed a squawk. The purple dress might come her way.

"He's so different from Bill," Lillian concluded pensively, "in everything."

Sally was reminded of a matter of grave import. "Oh, speaking of angels—" she began, and stopped. She chuckled. "'Angels' is good ! That's what we aren't speaking of anything else but!"

"Don't try to be funny. It's too early in the morning."

"Not for me, it isn't," Sally said. "But speaking of Bill, let me ask you this: supposing I see him when I get back, on the street or somewhere? What am I going to tell him?"

"Oh, you probably won't see him," said Lillian, but she said it a trifle uneasily.

"You bet I won't if I see him first!" said Sally. "I'll shinny up a tree. But supposing I don't see him first? He'll stop me and ask me how you are, and what you're up to, and when you're coming home — and what the hell am I supposed to say?"

"He won't, though," Lillian thought aloud. "Bill isn't like that. I mean — he wouldn't try to pump you about me. I'll say that for him."

"Yeah, but maybe he wouldn't think he was pumping me. He'd probably just think he was showing a natural interest. After all," Sally argued, "he's your husband, isn't he? As far as he knows? So why wouldn't he ask about you? Here he hasn't heard a word from you since you've been gone — except one postcard, and that was mostly the Chrysler Building or something."

"Well ? What about me? I haven't even had a post card from him."

"Wait, we're getting off the subject, "Sally said. "Let's stick to business, here. The point is — if I do see him, and if he does ask me how you are and when you're coming home — what will I say?"

"Say, 'Soon,'" said Lillian. She bent her mind to it. "Say I'll be home just as soon as I finish having some dresses fitted."

"Is that what you want me to say?"

"Something like that."

"All right," Sally sighed. "I'll do my best. It won't be the first time I've lied for you, God knows."

Lillian admitted this.

"It looks like it was going to be the last, though," Sally said.

"It looks like it," said Lillian contentedly.

Her plans were understood. She would go back to Renwood, but not immediately, not for a week or two at least — and not to stay. She would go back to talk divorce to Bill, and to get him to agree. She would go back for a single day, for a few hours.

She did not have to go back. She could summon Bill here to New York, they could have the cataclysmic interview here, and she need never go back to Renwood at all. This alternative tempted her, but she was afraid of it. It wasn't wise. For Lillian's own good reasons, Bill must not know that there was a Gaerste. In New York he might find out, somehow.

Sally had said a day or two ago, when they had discussed it, "Well, but what if he does find out? What's the harm? You just this minute said you thought he'd be perfectly willing to call it quits — he wouldn't make any fuss about giving you the divorce, or anything. If you think that, why shouldn't you tell him you want to marry another man? I mean, if it comes up — or even if it doesn't?"

"Because," said Lillian firmly.

"Because why? I don't see."

"Well, in the first place, he'd tell his father."

"Old man Legendre ? What's he got to do with it?"

"Everything," said Lillian. " I want some money."

Sally was bewildered. "Some money?" she echoed in credulously. "For heaven's sake, what for? Aren't you marrying a millionaire?"

Lillian said she was. "But I'm divorcing a millionaire's son. I think I ought to get something."

She was sure of it. She explained to Sally, who could do with a little instruction, that you never knew in a world like this — you never could tell what would happen. "C. G. might die, or something," she said for illustration. "Before the wedding. Then where would I be, if I didn't have any money? Right back where I started from!" She shook her head most positively. "No, thank you."

Sally saluted genius. "You think of everything!"

"Well, you have to," said Lillian.

Thinking of everything, she had resolved to depart for Renwood neither sooner nor later than she would have, if New York had been unproductive. In a way she was impatient to return, she burned to go and get it over with; but she knew that a manifestation of this impatience might look suspicious. One did not hurry home ahead of time to ask for a divorce, if one had nothing definite in view. On the other hand, one must not linger longer in New York than one's husband's father's fifteen hundred dollars could have lasted. ... Legendre, Senior's contributions for her trip had reached that total. An unsolicited second check, a sudden additional five hundred dollars, had arrived by mail from him three days ago.

This deferred her departure. It had been intended to do so — of that there could be no question; Legendre, Senior, had not sent it out of the goodness of his heart, as Sally had at once concluded that he had. "You see ?" Sally had said. "He's trying to be nice and generous!" To which Lillian had replied succinctly, "Generous like a fox." She wondered whether or not Bill even knew of this second donation; decided that he didn't, in all probability. This check without a letter, without a word of explanation, was a matter strictly between Legendre, Senior, and herself.

They understood each other, she thought with grim amusement. She saw the whole transaction clearly now. The original thousand dollars had been Legendre, Senior's payment, accepted by her, for the loan of his favorite son, for a week or two; and this additional five hundred was his bid for an extension. This she must also accept, postponing her return awhile, since in the normal course of things she would have grabbed the chance so gladly, and since Legendre, Senior, knew it well.

She was not displeased, on the whole. If the postponement fretted her, her father-in-law's attitude encouraged her even more. His willingness to pay a big price for a little absence on her part augured success, and huge success, for the project in her mind. They could do business, Lillian and this old man.

She was prepared. She had made out her case — now she knew almost word for word what she would say, when the time came. Indirectly, through Bill, she would inform Legendre, Senior, that separation and distance had given her perspective, had shown her everything in its true light. Through Bill she would say to his father that her life in Renwood was unbearable and her position hopeless; and she would not hesitate to add (and Bill would not deny) that he was in part to blame for this — that she had tried, but that he had not helped her, and that his failure to replace the associations and interests which she had renounced as unworthy of the bride of a Legendre had left her utterly friendless, wretchedly idle and alone. She would say that she was tired of being a social outcast, tired of being a laughing-stock — sick to death, as Bill must also be, of the farce their marriage was. Now she wanted only freedom and the means to move away, and live. "And never come back," she would say to Legendre, Senior, through his son. "Never."

She would not have to say, "What am I offered?"

This was her scheme when Sally departed for Renwood, and it remained her scheme for a day or two thereafter.

Then Sally's bread-and-butter letter, with its news, changed everything. ...

Sally's letter came on Wednesday morning. Lillian, hurrying out of the hotel at twenty-six minutes past ten, received it from a room-clerk, recognized the writing, and stuffed it into her handbag to read later. She had a ten-thirty appointment with a hairdresser named Nicolai, who was so great an artist and so temperamental that he would not wait a minute longer than ten-thirty-five for a new patron, or ten-forty for an old one. Lillian was a very new patron. "Darling," Gaerste had said, "I think Nicolai should dress your hair, don't you? Surely you've heard of Nicolai? He's quite the best in town. The famous beauties go to him, so I've been told."

A session with Nicolai was far too tense an experience to permit of the reading of letters, or even of the remembering of letters to read. Then there was another delay. You could not have a manicure simultaneously with Nicolai's wave, lest he be distracted and upset; hence Lillian spent the next half-hour, with both hands occupied, in a corner of the hushed and fragrant main salon outside,

Here, in a drawing-room atmosphere from which the stray manicuring-tables and the manicurists in their frocks of pastel silk detracted little, a Japanese maid served coffee in small transparent china cups to Lillian and the several other pampered ladies present. There were only six in all — it was rather early in the day for pampered ladies — but Lillian nevertheless found much to look at and absorb. She was particularly struck by the fact that of the five besides herself, four ladies were accompanied by dogs. Leashes were tied to the arms of the cushioned chairs that contained the ladies, and at or near the ends of the leashes, one very large dog and three very little ones, all very bored indeed, lay dozing.

Lillian thought of Rufus, but rejected him on second thought. Rufus was middle-sized, and always excited, never languid. It occurred to his mistress that Rufus was small-town at heart, like Sally. He was not the dog for her, and she began to plan a new dog: a Pekinese, perhaps; a gift from C. G. certainly. C. G. should name him something French that she would memorize, oh yes, and Cartier's should make his little collar.

Her manicure was finished at quarter of twelve. She hid it in the fingers of white doeskin gloves with gauntlet cuffs, she paid and paid and paid, as women did at Nicolai's, and after ordering invisible hairpins and a jar of cuticle-cream to be sent, and arranging some appointments for Saturday morning, she rode downstairs and sauntered forth into Fifth Avenue. She could walk to the hotel, since the day was fine and the distance short. She bore in mind the fact that at Perdita Burke's, down the Avenue, where famous beauties and others went for exercise and massage, a uniformed nurse with a tape measure had proved, only last Friday, that she measured fully half an inch too much around the hips.

Perdita Burke's would remedy this, of course, in record time; but meanwhile walking was a good idea. Lillian walked, and stopped but twice to enter shops en route, once to acquire an irresistible pair of mules from a window, and once to buy a bead bag for her mother at a sale.

Gaerste had telephoned twice, according to purple scrawled messages at the hotel; and when she had reached her room and removed her hat and gloves and furpiece, when she had kicked off her shoes, which were new and stiff and not her size, and when, in her stocking-feet, she had carried three dozen elongated roses from a cardboard coffin on the bed to the bathtub in the bathroom, and half filled the tub with water, and dropped the roses in — when she had done these things she returned to the bed and, reclining upon it, called C. G. back and said good-morning to him. Tenderly.

C. G. wanted to know where she had been. He always wanted to know. She told him, and he said, "Are you lovelier than ever, then?" and she said, "Oh, much! Wait till you see!" Becoming serious, she added that Nicolai had raved about her hair, which was true enough. She quoted his encomiums, C. G. listening avidly. He was proud and gratified. They both were.

They discussed plans for the day. They would lunch together in an hour from now — and what would Lillian like to do this afternoon? Drive somewhere? There were races on Long Island. There was polo. Lillian voted for the polo. " What shall I wear?" she asked, and the discussion grew important. "The black and white costume, I think," Gaerste decided ultimately. "The new one. That's quite stunning, and entirely suitable. Only, darling, please: without the necklace."

He was such a help. She felt so sure, under his guidance. She sat smiling when they had ceased talking. Smiling to herself. She thought, "A couple of years with him. It was a thought she often had these days. Sometimes it seemed to her that it would not even take that long.

Still smiling faintly, she stood up and went to get a cigarette and Sally's letter. She had a minute now, at last. She could see what Sally had to say for herself. ... Upon this casual reflection she opened the letter unhastily and unfolded the four sheets of blue-ruled composition paper, covered with green writing, that were within. She settled herself comfortably — no premonition warned her that she would not remain relaxed for long. She blew smoke, waved it aside with her hand, and read:

"Dear Snooty,

"Well here I am back and in case you should be wondering if it is the same old town or not I will say it is. How is N.Y.? Joe met me at the station and he is all right and not mad any more because I went, only now we are fighting about the vanity case which Joe says must of cost 40 or 50 dollars if it cost 5c and how about it where did I get it and I say I got it on account of being a friend of yours and Joe says oh yeah so we are fighting. You were right that is a long trip on the day train but I read and looked out the window etc. and ate in the diner twice once with a man who was in my Parlor Car named Ernie Malloy from Columbus, I had dinner with him only we went Dutch just the same, still he was quite witty and nice, he sells typewriters.

"Well I guess this is all the news about me and it is time I told you the news here which is about Bill, and will probably make you sore but I hope not at me for telling you as I am only telling you in case you might want to know about it and do something. I thought I would call you up Long Distance when I heard about it but then I thought the operator here might listen in especially if it happened to be Alice McGuire which would not be so good. So I thought in a letter would be better. Well it seems Bill has been running around with Guess Who since you have been gone, with Irene, what do you know about that and the whole town is all excited. Of course you cannot believe all you hear around here but believe me I am hearing plenty and it seems that it all started a couple of nights after you left, that must of been the night we went to see The Little Show with Spud and that fat man his cousin I forget his name oh Roy it was. Anyway it seems Miriam Mason had a party and invited both of them and they both came, I mean Irene and Bill and they say they sat out on the porch steps the whole time it was a warm summerish evening talking to each other and when the party was over with he took her home in your roadster or is it his, I always thought you said it was yours with your inishals on it. Well so that started it and they say they have been seeing each other here there & everywhere including at your sister-in-law's house Mrs. Reynolds which everybody thinks is very funny and quite Shocking.

"So this is all I know about it and all I have got to say is I hope you will not be sore at me for telling you as I just thought you would like to know, I would certainly like to know if it was Joe. But after all you have not got any kick coming you must admit. How is C. G. remember me kindly to him also Harry & Eddie etc. if you see them only I bet you will never bother seeing them again will you. Well I must close as Joe is coming to take me riding so he said, though we are fighting, and I will make him stop at the Post Office and I will mail this so you will get it soon and please do not be sore at me when you do. Well I must close.

As ever,

SALLY.

P. S. I had a fine time in N. Y. as I told you before and thanks for everything including your white coat which I will wear tonight as it is cool out and I suppose if Bill sees me he will have Heart Failure thinking it is you ha ha.

S.

CHAPTER TWENTY-ONE

She took the midnight train that night for Renwood.

It was not necessary now to wait — there was every reason why she should not wait. As a wronged wife, she could, would naturally, go rushing back. She went with a high heart. Echoes and traces of the fury of humiliated pride that Sally's tidings had at first evoked in her were in her still — but she could use them. She could use them well tomorrow. Mainly she was gleeful, seeing the power and the perfection of the weapon given to her hand. It had taken her only a minute, only a cold swift second thought, to see. Her eyes that had blazed had suddenly narrowed, like the eyes of a villainess in a film. All her reactions were rôles. Like the villainess, she had laughed aloud — harshly, triumphantly. She had spoken a line aloud.

"And that," she had said, "is going to cost them plenty!"

Gaerste put her on the train. She was a little worried about it. Somebody else from Renwood might be going back tonight, some male or female busybody who would tell the town tomorrow that a New York dude, wearing what Renwood knew as a Tuxedo, and carrying what Renwood called a cane, and topped, moreover, by a dude's tall hat — a joke to Renwood — had escorted Mrs.

Bill Legendre to her train.

Mrs. Legendre would rejoice in the circulation of this story, so long as it did not reach the Legendre family ahead of her. She said to herself that it would certainly have to travel fast to do that; and on the whole she did not worry very greatly. There was small likelihood of a Renwood witness, anyway.

This began to seem rather a pity. She was aware of the picture they made, she and Gaerste, alighting from his limousine, advancing through the station. Gaerste looked his best, his wealthiest and worldliest, in evening clothes. He wore his opera hat tilted a trifle, just a trifle, and a fresh gardenia adorned his gleaming left lapel. He carried his stick under his arm, a negligent hand upon its knob, except when he occasionally used it as a pointer. He used it now.

"We go over here," he said, and indicated with the stick the tables where a line of night conductors took train tickets.

They went over there. Lillian's very long lace gown was an elaborate white whisk-broom across the stone floor, moving beside Gaerste. Earlier in the evening she had said, "But I'll have to change, won't I? Can I go to the station, dressed like this?" It had appeared that she could. She wore more than the usual number of orchids, cascading from shoulder to waist, but it was noticeable that she wore no jewelry. She was between New York, where she could wear her diamond bracelet and the emeralds that her recent inspired birthday had brought forth, and Renwood, where tomorrow morning she would wear her wedding ring.

They were not much too early for the train. It was almost midnight. At this hour the mammoth terminal was hollow, bright with dirty light, and filled with a faint roaring like the echo of the daytime roar. Small sounds reverberated, lived forever, in its vastness. There were few people. Porters, officials, travelers intent upon themselves — there was no audience for Lillian. Standing alone while Gaerste presented her tickets at one of the tables, she thought how much had happened since she had last seen this station. This was the thing to think, and so she thought it, and she wondered what would happen between now and Friday morning, when she came again. But the wondering, like the thought, was cursory. She knew. She knew what would happen. She did not see how it could fail.

She was humming under her breath when Gaerste said, "All ready, darling."

They found the proper gate. Their porter went ahead of them, and Gaerste exhibited a drawing-room ticket stub to the gateman and they passed through like fellow travelers and descended the iron stairs. The dark train slumbered at the bottom. It was somehow strange to think that this same train, these very cars, would be in Renwood in the morning, would run between remembered little houses by the tracks and between the striped bars at familiar crossings. People she knew would see these very windows in the morning. Renwood was not so far off, after all.

"Car 87," Gaerste said. "Yours is 88."

The windows, opaque, seemed to watch them pass. They entered Lillian's car and followed their porter through the narrow aisle made of buttoned curtains to the other end. There were moving bulges behind some of the curtains, and on the edge of one lower berth a man in tan shirtsleeves was sitting, his chin upturned, untying a crimson tie. Lillian looked hard at him. She almost stopped to look, from a little distance. He would be the Renwood native, if there was one on this train — that was the way things always happened.

But he wasn't. She had never seen him before, and his discovering stare at her was a tribute to a radiant unknown.

Her drawing-room was ready for the night, the window sheeted, and both berths and the narrow couch made up. "The porter is expecting a large family, evidently," Gaerste said. It was warm in the drawing-room, despite the whirring fan on high. They lingered long enough to see to the disposition of the bags, and then went back through the car and out onto the platform again. Gaerste consulted his watch.

"Five minutes," he said.

He hated to let her go. He had said to her more than once, "I am afraid you won't come back." He had smiled with his lips to show her that he did not really mean this, that he was not really apprehensive, that he trusted and believed her; but his eyes with their peculiar shine had fixed on her eyes as he spoke, as if still seeking reassurance from them. What he said was partly true. He was afraid of Bill. Lillian had given him good reason. For her own glorification, and for the enhancement of the compliment to Gaerste that she wanted her divorce to seem to be, she had exaggerated Bill, who had become with her description far more splendid than he was, more lordly than he ever had been.

Gaerste in his mind saw the young scion of the oldest and the finest family in a very old, aristocratic town. He saw ancestral wealth, an ancient heritage. He pictured a baronial estate. He imagined background, prestige and social leadership — things he could not replace, that Lillian was giving up, for him. She had not always had them: he was able to guess that. But that she had not gained them by her marriage, Gaerste did not guess, and it is certain that he was not told.

He knew the value of the things that he believed she was renouncing —

no one knew better than himself what priceless things they were. He wondered whether Lillian knew, who surrendered them so readily, with such a sweet and touching willingness, for love of him. Sometimes he thought she did, in his inflated moments. At other times he thought she didn't know, didn't fully realize her sacrifice; and only his belief that he could make it up to her in other ways assuaged a guilty feeling, secret in him. He would make it up to her with lavish gifts, with travel; with a fuller and more cosmopolitan life, which she would love. The Legendres, he had learned with satisfaction, stayed at home and the Legendre money, for all its quality, could not in quantity compare with his.

This he had learned when he had first heard of Lillian's husband and of her husband's family. He was already infatuated with her then, having known her two days. He had asked many jealous questions. "They have money, I suppose?" was one. It was perhaps the sharpest one of all.

Lillian had made the perfect answer. "You wouldn't call it money," she had assured him, with a little smile. "But they do. They're considered rich, cut there."

A glittering life, for her dull-golden one. That he could give her. He thought it almost, though not quite, a fair exchange. It was fortunate for him, he felt, that Lillian loved glittering things — that she had lacked, and longed for, just such things as he could best provide. Sables and pearls. A personal maid. A car of her own, with a chauffeur. Clothes by the great couturiers. Now she should have these things, and anything else her heart desired. He told her so, repeatedly. He wished her to remember it, not to forget it, while she was gone — and he delighted in her frank delight besides. When he promised her things, her eyes grew big with amazement and admiration, and bright with pleasure. She was such a child, his Lillian.

When she should come back to him from Renwood in two days — in less: it was almost Thursday at this moment — his anxiety could cease. All danger would be over then. She would get her divorce in Nevada or Mexico, where he could be with her, and she would never see Renwood again. She would probably never see Bill again in her life ... Standing on the platform now, in the train's falsely quiescent shadow, Gaerste took her hand and kissed it, and he spoke his thought.

"I wish it were Friday morning," he said, boyishly.

"I wish so too."

His luminous eyes studied her, and she produced a little bothered frown. Think of me !" she said. "Think what I've got to go through between now and then."

"Poor darling. I know. I wish I could help you."

"I wish somebody could. It's going to be terribly hard to do."

They had had this conversation several times before. There was no hitch in it now. Gaerste's anxious reminder, "But you want to do it," and Lillian's, "Of course. You know I do. I just meant, hard from Bill's standpoint," —these two original lines were omitted now, being understood.

"I hate to hurt people," Lillian sighed instead.

"I know."

"Bill is really rather sweet, you see. And he's so mad about me."

"Naturally," Gaerste said to this.

He believed it, he had assumed it even without Lillian's aid, and he had been spared all contrary information. Today, for example, he had heard nothing of Sally's letter from Renwood, beyond the fact that a letter had arrived and that Sally was well. On the other hand, Gaerste had heard of a telephone call that nobody else had heard of, that explained his love's decision to depart this night on her cruel errand. He had been previously persuaded that she must go some day soon. She must face the music. Her only hope of freedom lay that way. And now that Bill had telephoned, bewailing his loneliness, and threatening to join her in New York if she stayed longer here, it was obvious enough that the time had come.

"I'm afraid he'll take it awfully hard," Lillian was saying.

Gaerste nodded somberly. "Of course he will. He will be heart-broken. You must expect that. But don't — don't be too sorry for him." He took both her hands and held them tightly. "Will you," he said.

"I'll try not to."

"Promise me. Promise me you won't be influenced by anything he says, or does. You must promise me that," said Gaerste in a strained low voice, "or I can't let you go."

She promised him.

"Tell me you love me."

She laughed softly then. She borrowed her hands from the clasp of his and seized his coat-lapels, making a playful pretense of shaking him. "Silly ! Of course I love you."

Her hands slid around to the back of his neck. "Why am I doing this?" she demanded. "Why am I going ? — if I don't love you?"

Gaerste did not know. "Darling," he said, for the answer satisfied him.

CHAPTER TWENTY-TWO

Bill met the train at Renwood. She had telegraphed him, after some deliberation: would a wronged wife telegraph, or would she just appear unheralded? She might do either, Lillian had decided; and in this case, nothing was to be gained by surprising Bill. He would be at the office. It wasn't as if her train arrived in the evening.

Her train arrived at noon. It was raining in Renwood, it had been raining in all the coal-dust-colored towns along the line, that might have been Renwood except for the names on the signs at their stations. She had had a happy morning, this new New Yorker, gazing through the rain-scratched glass, observing how alike these small Ohio towns were, and how dreary, and noticing how squat and low the huddled buildings looked under the vast unbroken rural sky. From the miles of countryside unreeled for her between the towns, her contemptuous eyes had picked the ugliness, ignored the rest. This was a country of mills and mines, of potteries and brickyards, of oil derricks strayed over from the neighboring Pennsylvania hills, black skeletons, lost and occasional here.

This was a landscape dotted with small farmhouses and monstrous barns, and striped by red brick highways, wet and bright in today's rain, and by the mustard clay of unpaved roads. Here were thin thickets, fallow fields, a miner's settlement, a beacon for the air mail built upon a hill, a march of power lines northward through a gash across the land. And now and then, in intermittent glimpses from the train, there was the river with its saffron water that the mills had dyed.

"The beautiful Ohio," Lillian thought sardonically.

She watched it pass. Her eyes that looked at it had seen the sea, only the other day. She watched this width of poison water pass, remembering that once, she had attended unfastidious picnics on its banks — picnics of beer and hot dogs, consumed with appetite; evenings of bonfires, and ukelele music, and sweaters when the fires burned low, and amorous young men. She had gone boating on this river, in little boats and big, in rented red canoes and in the gorgeous floating palace that the excursion steamer Playland had at that time seemed to be.

She had even, she remembered now, gone swimming in this river, years ago, before there was a pool at Avalon. Wading in gingerly for fear of broken glass or bits of tin, or small stones sharper than the other stones beneath her feet, she had immersed herself and swum and splashed about for hours — in that! It made her fragrant white flesh creep to think of it, or she believed it did. For proof she shuddered delicately, saying, "Ugh!"

Many such valedictory recollections came. So imminent was her escape from all the scene outside the windows —things that she would forget from this day forward, things already half forgotten, she remembered now, for one last time. When she was still long miles from Renwood, practically she was there. Her native state, that once had been a far-flung foreign land, was as Renwood's back yard, since she had traveled.

These mines might be Legendre mines that she spied from the windows. That coal mine now, under the wooded hill, might be one of the three or four that she and Bill — "Mr. W. H." to her then ! — had visited in his roadster, one afternoon not quite a year ago. That muddy lane might be the detour that had made them late to town. "Scandal," Bill had said. Her eyes smiled now. He had said something

A little lake reminded her of Gleason's pond, near Renwood, and of a boy whose name she had forgotten. An amusement park outside a town recalled the park called Avalon, and the night the power had given out when she and somebody — Chuck Hansen — were in a shaky swing high up the side of the Ferris wheel, where they had hung suspended for two hours. Farther along the way, a house in some woods looked like the clubhouse that a group of Renwood business men maintained in just such woods as these. A retreat from domesticity, that clubhouse was; it had no telephone; no members' wives had ever seen its large rustic interior, its walls of logs to which the fibrous brown bark clung, its field-stone fireplace with the stag's head jutting from the wall above, its leather chairs, its brass-railed bar, which Lillian remembered now.

And now a baseball diamond took her back three summers — four; she was seventeen, and beloved of one Lefty McCarty, star pitcher on the Renwood professional team. She was McCarty's girl, and very proud of it at games. She had even journeyed with the team to other towns, and been proud there; boisterously proud, so everyone would know. "Oh, goodness!" she thought now. And even more incredible was the recollection of the costume that had been her favorite for those baseball expeditions. Had she actually, only four years back, been such a nitwit as to wear coral pink — a coral-pink cloche, a coral-pink slip-on sweater — with her hair?

And now the rushing train crossed a brick highway, the alarm bell at the intersection clamored for an instant, and there was a flicker of the several small white crosses in the bank, that meant that motorists, one cross for each, had been killed here. This was a custom of the territory. At the very doorstep of the house beside the tracks at Renwood Falls where Lillian had lived and where her parents still lived, two such sinister markers commemorated the awful midnight, ten years ago or more, when a couple in a touring-car, blind to her father's lantern and deaf to the dinning bell, had crashed through the gates and into the light-flooded path of the Pittsburgh express.

Lillian remembered. She must have been eleven then. She remembered the night, and the dawn, and next day she remembered the morbid search that she and a dozen other barefooted children had made along the tracks, all that next day. She alone had had any luck, which had seemed only fair. She was the watchman's daughter; it was her accident, in a way. If anybody else had found the lady's lipstick, she would have claimed it, fought for it tooth and nail — she had been a scrappy little fighter, she remembered, in those days.

But she herself had found the lipstick. She could see it still, a glint of gold through spears of grass. She had pounced upon it, examined it, discovered that it came apart, and that there was a cylinder of scarlet salve inside. Then she had known what the thing was.

Immediately and in wild excitement she had used it, smearing her eleven-year-old mouth and shrieking, "Look!"

She smiled now. That was the beginning. She had used that first lipstick in earnest, and with precocious skill, before another year was gone.

The Renwood station platform had a cover over it, a sort of large and long inverted trough, between two veils of rain. Under this shelter, Bill and the baggage-master and an empty baggage truck were standing when the Limited pulled in. Renwood was, as usual, a signal stop. The train would barely pause, and Lillian was out of her drawing-room and in the vestibule, the door of which was open for her and the steps exposed, when she saw Bill. He was standing, it seemed to her, precisely where she had left him when she went away, in the same spot. He even wore the same gray coat and knickers. He looked more sunburned, though. He must have played a lot of golf.

These things she noted as the steps slid past him, slowing, and he said, "Hullo." She heard him say it, but she did not answer, and she did not smile. She let her eyes look coldly down to his for that few seconds. He might as well know now, at once, what her mood was, or was supposed to be.

She thought, "It's the truth. He had no business treating me like that — making a fool of me before Irene and the whole town!" Thus summoned, some of the wrath originally incited by the reading of Sally's letter stung her now again, in a suitable way. By the time the car steps stopped, a few yards farther up the platform, she was ready to alight. She was as indignant as she wished to be.

She alighted, and tipped the porter, ignoring Bill's approach. At her shoulder he said, "Hullo," again, and when she turned, he bent his head and kissed her fleetly on the forehead that her black straw hat revealed. "How are you?" he said.

He was trying to be natural, Lillian told herself, and her eyes grew colder still. Did he think he could get away with that? Well, he couldn't.

"What's the matter?" Bill asked.

"You know perfectly well what's the matter."

He neither affirmed nor disputed that. He said, "You might say hello, at least."

It was aggravating that his glance was straight and steady, and that she could not seem to stare it down. When he glanced away, it was because someone should do so — clearly it was because he felt that they looked silly, eying each other here. "Well, anyhow," he said "Let's shove along."

One suitcase waited at their feet. Lillian had anticipated Bill's query, which came now, as to the whereabouts of the rest of her bags. She replied, "I checked them through, so I wouldn't have to bother with them."

"Got the checks?"

"They're in the suitcase. And I don't want to open it now," Lillian said shortly. "Let's get home. I'll drive down again this afternoon."

The car was parked at the other side of the station. "We'll go through the waiting room," Bill suggested. "Then you won't get wet." Lillian led the way, observing the length and breadth of the platform as she crossed it. It was still deserted. She had, then, been the only Renwood person on the train. So far, so good.

Here was her roadster, close along the curb. She had time to think that it was littler than she remembered it, and humbler. It was just a common little car. Irene could have it. Irene could have it back again, and welcome, after today. Irene could take the "L.L.'s " off. Would they come off, Lillian wondered? Funny if they wouldn't.

She hoped they wouldn't. Though the paint came off, she hoped the marks were deep enough to stay, to be discernible in certain lights — to trouble Irene's spirit, as long as the car lasted. Longer, even.

Bill opened the near door, and she got in by herself, making a point of eluding his hand that would have helped her. Cooped with side-curtains against the rain, she waited while he took her suitcase back and stowed it in the rumble seat and closed it in. Listening absently to the accompanying bumping sounds, she peered about her, darting quick detective glances at all the small interior of her car — at the floor, at the leather-cushioned seat, at a hitherto unnoticed, surely new scratch on the dashboard.

She was suddenly certain that even last evening, Irene had ridden in her car; she almost expected to find some tangible evidence that had subconsciously produced this impression, so strong it was. She thought, "I can smell her perfume," — though she knew that she imagined that. Perfume did not linger in a car for long. Or did it? Could it, with the side-curtains? She inhaled again.

In any case, the accusation would make an ideal opening shot. She would use it; she would fire Irene's name now at Bill, and watch his face. .... Even as she chose the words he reappeared, he filled the little door, and she turned instant flaming eyes upon him.

"You might have aired my car out," she said. "It reeks of Irene's perfume."

She said it well. But the effect was disappointing. To be sure, Bill paused, half in the car, half on the running board; but his face told nothing — nothing save that he had heard. Nothing that would incriminate him. He merely looked at her, levelly, as before.

Then he drew himself inside, under the wheel, and shut the door. "Oh, I doubt that," he said.

"You're not going to try to deny that she's been in this car since I've been gone?"

"No," said Bill, "I'm not." He was perfectly calm. "But I doubt if it really reeks of her perfume," he said. "It's an open car." The starter rasped under his foot. "And don't believe Irene's is that kind of perfume."

"I suppose mine is!"

"I didn't say that."

"You as good as said it !" Lillian stormed. This counter-attack, if such it was, had taken her unawares. She continued furiously, "You needn't insult me to my face, along with everything else! You've insulted me enough behind my back!"

"That isn't true, Red."

"Oh, isn't it! I suppose it isn't insulting to me that you started running around with your ex-wife the minute my back was turned — the minute you got me out of town! That isn't an insult to me, oh, no! That's a compliment, I suppose? I suppose I ought to be glad you were in such good hands!"

Bill seemed on the point of retorting; then he seemed to change his mind. He said, "Shall we wait till we get home to talk about it? Maybe we'd better."

"I will not! I'll talk about it now! I don't care if the whole town hears me — and every gossiping hick in it! They might as well have another good laugh at my expense — why not? God knows they've had plenty already, thanks to you!"

This was the stuff, she thought fleetly. She continued: "And I don't blame them for laughing! I'd laugh myself, if I ever saw any wife get treated the way I've been treated — by you, and your sister, and your whole family, and all your lovely friends, and everybody connected with you! And you not doing anything about it, just sitting back and letting me take it — I should have known from that that you didn't c-care anything about me !" Her voice broke realistically." I should have known!

And ever since we've been married, that's the way it's been! Hasn't it? You know yourself it has! And then when finally I go away and try to have a little rest and change — after the rottenest, loneliest, most terrible six months anybody ever lived through! —then what happens? Why, then you decide that what I don't know won't hurt me, and you think you can pull the wool over my eyes, and you start —"

"Wait a minute," Bill interrupted quietly, and she waited, because what he said in this quarrel was more important than what she said — it was all-important. She listened, watchful, wary.

Bill said, "You're quite wrong there. I wasn't going to try to pull the wool over your eyes. I intended to tell you that I'd seen Irene, and when, and where, and all about it. You would have known — what there is to know. Somebody beat me to it, that's all."

"Somebody certainly did!"

"Your little friend Sally, in fact. Not that it matters who."

"If you want the truth," Lillian said quickly, "it was an anonymous letter. I don't know who wrote it, except that I know it wasn't Sally. It might have been anybody. Maybe Irene wrote it herself, I wouldn't be surprised!"

That was neat, she thought, but Bill ignored it. He spoke again, and again she listened hard.

"Another thing," he said. "I didn't — my seeing Irene was entirely accidental, to begin with. You talk as if I had it all doped out beforehand — as if I sent you away for that reason. Which is absurd, of course."

"You kept me away for that reason!" Lillian cried instantly. "Or if you didn't, your father did!"

It was as she had thought: Bill did not know about the second check. He was honestly puzzled, glancing at her.

"What do you mean?"

"He sent me more money! Just the other day! What would you say that was for — if it wasn't to keep me over there?"

She had him. "Cold," she thought. She enjoyed allowing him to hearken for a moment to his own disturbed, unwilling silence. Then she added: "Oh, don't worry; you've got your family with you. They're all behind you, backing you up — and how! Your father keeps me in New York, and your sister has you and Irene at her house together! You couldn't ask for better team-work than that."

"You're pretty insulting yourself," Bill said. "Is that so! Can I help it if facts are facts?"

This was the last speech made in the car. They swung into their own driveway now, skirted the wet green lawn, and arrived and stopped, with Bill's customary abruptness, at the side door. Here Lillian sat still; Bill could just go for an umbrella, her attitude said wordlessly, and Bill complied, also without a word. He was gone for several minutes. "In the hall closet, stupid," Lillian thought, and to amuse herself she thought, "Say, I can't wait all day out here — I've got a train to catch!"

Everything in the house was dusty and the rooms were dim, the window-shades pulled down to the sills that were covered with specks of Renwood soot. Lillian switched the living-room lights on as she entered, so as to see her way; she crossed to the windows and jerked at the shades and let go of them, letting them spring to the top. Their tassels were still agitated when Bill followed her in, having deposited two suitcases, hers and a large one of his own, in the hall. He was just now moving back from his father's house.

"You didn't move back till you had to, did you," Lillian commented. "How you love our little home! I bet you haven't been near the place since I've been gone."

She was about to add, "No nearer than the Garden Apartments!" But Bill's expression stopped her. He was surprisingly smiling a little.

"Yes, I have," he said, "once. At the unanimous request of the neighbors, I dropped around one evening and shut the piano off."

"Was it going?" Lillian asked in spite of herself.

"For days. It must have been rerolling when I left the house the last time. Anyway it played from Monday till Friday."

"Where was Hoxie?"

"Staying at her sister's."

Lillian had been amiable long enough. "Well, where is she now?" she demanded irascibly. "Why isn't she here?

You might have got her back when you got my wire, it seems to me."

Bill was sorry. He had tried, of course. "I phoned last night, but they said she'd gone to Youngstown. She'll be back some time this afternoon."

"I should hope so! This is a nice place to come home to!"

"Isn't it," Bill agreed.

Evidently he thought that opening some windows might help. He set about it. Lillian at the mantel mirror removed her hat meanwhile and pushed at Nicolai's wave with automatic fingers. She could see the whole room in the mantel mirror. It was a frightful room, of course. Atrocious. She knew it now. She thought of C. G.'s living room, that would so soon be hers, and she thought that Renwood must hear all about that living room some day — Louise Bartlett and everyone must hear about it. They must see pictures. C. G. could arrange it. Photographs in a big slippery magazine would be the thing. "The Penthouse Studio of Mr. and Mrs. Carl G. Gaerste, New York." Renwood would know who Mrs. Gaerste was: the littlest child would know. The rise of Lillian Andrews would be a tradition in this town, when she was gone.

In the mirror she saw Bill turn from the last window, and she turned, and across a clutter of low chairs and end-tables they faced each other. Lillian put her hands on her hips, involuntarily; this was, had always been, her fighting stance. She looked at Bill and waited, and when he did not speak at once, when he waited too, she whipped him with her voice:

"Well? And so what?"

"You were doing the talking, Red."

"I'll listen to you now — if you've got anything to say. If you've got any excuse for the way you've acted— "

"I haven't," Bill said.

Lillian caught her breath. "You admit that!"

"I can't deny it, can I?" Bill said simply. His eyes were unhappy, and they strayed beyond her now. "It was a lousy trick to play on you," he said. "You're quite right. There's no argument there."

"You knew it was at the time, didn't you?"

"I suppose I did. Yes," he amended.

"But you went right ahead! You went right on seeing her! You knew what you were doing to me, but you didn't care! Is that it?"

"I cared—" Bill hesitated. "I can't explain it very well, Red. It just happened. She and I have the same friends— " He checked himself; shook his head swiftly. "But that's no excuse," he said. "I know it as well as you do. Except for that first time, I could have avoided seeing her and being with her — and I ought to've — but I didn't. " He made a little surrendering gesture. "And that's that."

But he had not finished. "As for the rest of it," he went on, his forehead wrinkling, "— all that about the way you've been treated, and the rotten time you've had — I can't deny that, either. And probably it was my fault, as you say. I suppose it was — I suppose I could have done something about it, though I didn't know what at the time." He thought a minute. "And all in all, I guess I've made a sweet mess of it."

"I guess you have !"

Bill's eyelids flickered. "It's a mess, anyway," he said, more shortly. "Let's leave it at that."

He paused, and his eyes returned to hers and held them. He said, "All right. What do you want to do?"

Lillian thought, "You'd like to know, wouldn't you!" Aloud she jeered his question, as the best way to evade it. "That's a good one, that is!" she said to him. "I just love that. You two-time me, you throw Irene in my face — and then you ask me what I want to do! Since when have you cared so much about my wishes and feelings, please? It's what you want to do that'll be done — I'm sure of that! So you tell me!"

She subsided abruptly; flung away from the hearth where she had stood. She dropped down on a divan and put out her hand toward a cigarette box.

She was amazed to see that the hand was trembling. Her will had not dictated this, and now could not control it. "Here!" she said to herself severely. "I'm only acting. What's the matter with me?" The cigarette box was empty. She slapped it shut and tossed it back to the table, and heard it skim across and drop to the floor. Then Bill said, "Cigarette?" and there was a moment's truce between them while he gave her one and held a lighter for her.

"Thank you," Lillian said dryly.

Bill lit a cigarette for himself. He sat down on the arm of a chair, his long legs extended, his heels on their edges on a rug. He looked uncomfortable, and apparently he felt so, for he stood up again. He was scowling, thinking what to say, or how to say it.

Lillian helped. The moment had come, she knew. She said, "Look here. The whole truth of the matter is that you're in love with her. Why not admit it? You're in love with Irene."

"I guess I am," Bill said.

"You always were."

He nodded slowly.

Lillian said, "You never loved me. Never." And now her voice trembled, and this was real, as her hand's unsteadiness had been. She could not have stopped it. Jealousy of Irene had become a habit of hers, that now outlived the actual emotion. She said, "You always loved her best," and the old hatred of Irene welled up in her and almost choked the quickened last words, " —didn't you?"

Bill remained silent. "Didn't you!"

"I'm sorry, Red," he said.

She stared across at him. She felt nothing row, she was all flint and steel again. Now she must make him say one other thing, just one more thing, for quoting to his father. It would not be difficult.

She said, "And you want to marry her — again — don't you ? You want a divorce."

She waited. He was a gentleman, she thought impatiently. Even now he was trying to be polite. "Don't be polite!" she snapped. "Just answer me. You're in love with Irene, and you want to marry her, don't you?"

Still he hesitated, and it maddened her. "Oh, for God's sake!" she cried at him. "Speak up — for once in your life!"

"All right," he said. "You know the answer. Yes, I do."

It was felt in Renwood that Mrs. Hoxie's absence from her employers' house that day was a pity and a public loss. Mrs. Hoxie might have been there, she could and should have been there — what she was doing gadding in Youngstown anyway, no one could think; and as the sad result of this frivolous truancy of Mrs. Hoxie's, Renwood would never know just what was said by the William Legendres, in what subsequently proved to be their final quarrel. That not a great deal was said, that the quarrel was short as such quarrels go, Renwood did know, from its deponent Mrs. Horace Coulter. Mrs. Coulter had heard the voices — Lillian's wild voice and Bill's low one — but she had not heard them very long.

"Not more than ten or fifteen minutes," Mrs. Coulter said, "at the outside. Then all of a sudden, the first thing I knew, it was all over."

Mrs. Coulter, hearing the voices as long as they lasted, had been unable to distinguish any words. In justice to herself and condonation of this failure, Mrs. Coulter pointed out that her house was thirty-seven feet from the Legendres' house by actual measurement, and that the protrusion of the bay window in which she had been ensconced reduced this thirty-seven feet by two feet only. Mrs. Coulter defied anybody to distinguish words at such a distance, with the rain coming down like pitchforks in between. Save for the fact that her combatant neighbors, evidently needing air, had opened every window in their living-room to start with, Mrs. Coulter would not even have heard the voices. But if her auditory efforts had been less succeccessful than Renwood and she could have wished, Mrs. Coulter's brilliant work as an observer compensated, at least in some degree. She had missed nothing; and since with excellent eyesight she combined remarkable powers of deduction since she was, indeed, one of Renwood's most gifted adders of two and two — she had emerged from her bay window at the end of a cramped half hour with an account of the happenings next door that, if not complete in every detail, was as nearly complete as was possible, brick walls being what they were.

When, for example, the voices in the Legendres' living room had ceased, quite without warning, and upon their highest pitch of all, Mrs. Coulter had not for an instant entertained the palpably erroneous notion that the war was ended and peace declared. Rather, she had inferred that hostilities had reached a point where one Legendre refused any longer to speak to or to listen to the other. That this Legendre was Lillian, Mrs. Coulter concluded without speculation. Of course it was Lillian. Lillian was the angrier; she was the aggrieved and affronted one as Mrs. Coulter and all Renwood were joyously aware.

And if Lillian had refused to speak or to listen to Bill any longer, it followed that she had rushed from his presence and from the living-room. It was therefore Lillian's hand that now raised two window-shades on the second floor, at windows that Mrs. Coulter well knew belonged to the principal bedroom. "Um-hmm," Mrs. Coulter thought, nodding. "Ran upstairs to her own room and locked herself in there." So much for Lillian. Bill was somewhat less easy to locate. Was he, Mrs. Coulter wondered, still in the living-room, thinking things over? Or was he outside the locked door upstairs, apologizing through the panel? In other words — Mrs. Coulter's other words — was he a blithering idiot, or wasn't he?

Mrs. Coulter believed he wasn't. She believed that he was cured. She concluded that he was in the living-room.

He remained there only briefly. In a minute or two, or three, the side door of the house jumped open, and Bill came out, alone, into the rain. Mrs. Coulter, hiding now for safety's sake behind her fern stand and peeping, pixie-fashion, through the greenery, perceived that he was bareheaded as always, that he moved in a reckless, lunging way, and that he looked, as Mrs. Coulter put it, "sick and tired. Just sick and tired, is how he looked to me."

He got into the roadster, started it, and backed it down the driveway at a rate of speed that made Mrs. Coulter nervous for her nasturtium bed. Then she lost sight of him, though she could hear his brakes and his tires as he turned in the street beyond, and the roar of his motor taking him fast away. Mrs. Coulter always said that she didn't know what made her look up just then, at the second story windows; but something told her to, and she did.

"And there she was," said Mrs. Coulter, — "as big as life-watching him go."

Asked by Renwood how Lillian looked, whether she looked sick and tired too, or how, Mrs. Coulter answered frankly that she didn't know. "I couldn't tell," Mrs. Coulter said. "She wasn't leaning out. She was just standing at the window. All I could see was that white face of hers, and that red hair."

Thus Mrs. Coulter. Her testimony ended here, and from this point on, the history of Lillian Andrews Legendre's last appearance in Renwood was a symposium, to which the contributors were numerous. Countless, in fact. During the days ensuing, more and more people, now that they thought about it, recalled having seen Lillian on that day, at one stage or another of her famous triangular progress from the railroad station to her house, from her house to the Legendre offices on River Street, and from the Legendre offices back to the railroad station. ... By the end of the week, the Renwood citizens who had not seen her at all, and who acknowledged it, were few: a forlorn little band, composed for the most part of infants and invalids.

When all the eye-witnesses had reported, when all the returns were in, and tabulated, and arranged in chronological order, Renwood knew almost everything. It knew enough, at least. It knew why Lillian had gone to the Legendre offices; and though Legendre, Senior's private office was a sound-proof room, and though no employee of his would have dared to eavesdrop anyway, Renwood knew the outcome of the thirty-minute interview between Bill's father and Bill's second wife, that had taken place inside. After all, the outcome was the important thing. Renwood knew, Renwood had it direct from Ella Mae Ryan's sister Edith — Ella Mae Ryan was Legendre, Senior's private secretary — that, according to stubs in his personal checkbook, Legendre, Senior had handed over the sum of twenty-five thousand dollars, and no cents, to Lillian that day.

Renwoodians said that they supposed he knew what he was doing: in stern tones that belied the words they said so. The funny thing about the twenty-five thousand dollars, aside from the fact that it had been paid at all, was the way it had been paid. It was because this was so singular that Ella Mae Ryan, who should have known better, had discussed it with her sister Edith. There were two checks, it seemed. The first was for five thousand dollars. It bore the current date, and the name of Lillian Legendre. But the second check, for twenty thousand, was dated four months ahead, and it was payable to Lillian Andrews — to Lillian Andrews, mind you! Her maiden name, and no Legendre about it.

The problem that Ella Mae Ryan indiscreetly took up with her sister Edith was whether, now, Mr. Legendre had just accidentally written it thus on the stub;

or whether the stub and the absent check were mates — and if so, why? Ella Mae did not expect Edith to call in all Renwood for consultation; but Edith did, and all Renwood at once confirmed her analysis. It was perfectly simple. It was, said Renwood, as plain as the nose on your face. Four months was ample time in which to get a divorce in this state or in any one of a number of other states, for that matter; and when you got a divorce, you could get your maiden name back, if you wanted it back, either for your own or somebody else's reasons.

Renwood chuckled. It relented, and forgave Legendre, Senior, and agreed that he was a pretty shrewd old trader, after all.

Lillian caught the four-forty train for New York. Renwood's best authority on the subject of her exit was Mr. Jonas Weatherbee, the baggage-master at the station. Nobody else could hold a candle to him. "I seen her come," Mr. Weatherbee was wont to say, "and I seen her go. "

Stripped to its fundamentals, the tale Mr. Weatherbee told was this: that Lillian, alone, had arrived at the station in a taxicab; that she had had some minutes to wait, and that she had waited down the platform, strolling up and down and smoking several cigarettes; that just before the train came she had beckoned a truck-driver out of his truck and hired him as a porter, afterwards tipping him fifty cents, no less; that, passing Mr. Weatherbee on her way up the platform she had smiled at him and said, "Good-bye!" in a kind of singing voice; and that when the train was in, and stopped, she had not cared which car was hers. She hadn't cared, as long as she got on.

THE END

PUBLISHER'S AFTERWORD

In 1943, Katharine Brush published an autobiographical book entitled This Is On Me. *In it she discussed how she came to write* Red-Headed Woman *and also how and when she started to write about East Liverpool, Ohio, which she called 'Renwood'. From her lengthy account, we have extracted a few sections:*

I didn't write any Renwood stories until four years after I had moved away from East Liverpool - and even then I didn't intend to, as far as I knew. It just happened. All of a sudden the dam burst, and I wrote eight or ten in a row, during the fifth or sixth year afterwards. One of them was a full-length novel.

That novel was Red-Headed Woman. *Her previous novel,* Young Man of Manhattan *had not contained any reference to Ohio, and took place mainly in Manhattan, as the title suggests.*

Now the reason I know I can tell you all about *Red-Headed Woman* in no time at all is that it had almost exactly the same history as *Young Man of Manhattan*, from beginning to end. It started out to be a short story; it took fifteen months to write, as I've said: I again had three deadlines, and they were the same ones, except that the movie company in this case was Metro-Goldwyn-Mayer instead of Paramount; and eventually it was a successful *Post* [*Saturday Evening Post Magazine*] serial and a best-selling book. ... Metro made it with the late Jean Harlow in the title role – they made a smash-hit picture, thanks to her performance, and to superb script treatment by a glittering string of specialists, including Scott Fitzgerald at one point, and Anita Loos all the way through. I can give myself credit only for the fact that if I'd written the book expressly for Harlow (who hadn't had many big roles up to that time, so that again I was disappointed with the studio's choice, like a nitwit) it couldn't have fitted her better, nor she it. ... There was another basic ingredient: and this one might amuse you. Throughout the writing of the first half of the book, I didn't know what the last half was going to be, and couldn't decide. (And that's what comes of letting short stories grow into novels, by the way.) But then one evening in a Broadway night club I heard a girl at the next table quote another girl as having said: "Just look at all these diamond bracelets – and I've only been in New York a year!' So there it was, in sixteen words, and that's the way I wrote it.

But Ms. Brush added the central point of the film and the story for her:

It was when Miss Harlow turned the tables on the town that she was best.

A joke photo from MGM promoting the film of *Red-Headed Woman* shows Anita Loos, author of Gentlemen Prefer Blondes, about to crack Jean on the head with a bottle for altering the title of her book. Anita Loos wrote most of the film's screenplay.

After the release of the film of *Red-Headed Woman*, the book was reissued with this new jacket image of Jean Harlow with red hair. (Jean was a blonde, but became a red-head for the film.)